SIMPSON GREARS was born in Glasgow and studied at the universities of Strathclyde, Glasgow and Edinburgh before following an academic career in Scotland, England, Wales and the United States. His first work of crime fiction – a collection of short stories titled *The Foot of the Walk Murders* – was longlisted for the prestigious Dagger award of the Crime Writers Association. He lives in Perth, central Scotland.

THE
COUNTERFEIT
DETECTIVE

FOR
MARGARET
yet again

THE
COUNTERFEIT
DETECTIVE

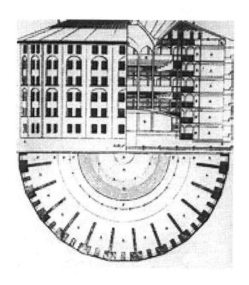

Simpson Grears

© Simpson Grears 2023

ISBN 978-1-7395960-8-8

Published by Rymour Books
45 Needless Road
Perth
PH20LE

A CIP record for this book is
available from the British Library
BIC Classification FF

cover and book design by Ian Spring
printed by Imprint Digital, Exeter, Devon

The right of Simpson Grears to be identified as the author
of this work has been asserted in accordance with sections
77 and 78 of the Copyright Designs and Patents Act 1988.

.

They say that in a dusty back room of some London sorting office there sits a functionary whose sole task is to open and answer the sackful of letters that are still arriving every day for Sherlock Holmes at his 221b Baker Street address. This bureaucrat is directed to send a standard answer which regretfully informs each inquirer that Sherlock Holmes has retired to the country.

Elizabeth Wilson, *The Counterfeit Detective*

Acknowledgements

Several people have read sections of this books. I would like to thank Alan Hellen, Stuart Campbell, Kirsti Wishart and Margaret Spring and to remember the late Keith Stewart.

Scholarly works consulted in the preparation of this book include Jonathan Schneer, *London 1900: the Imperial Metropolis* (Yale: 1999), Peter Ackroyd, *London: the Biography* (Vintage: 2001), Ian Gibson, *The Erotomaniac* (Faber and Faber: 2001), and the works of Gershon Legman including *The Horn Book: Studies in Erotic Folklore and Bibliography* (University Books: 1964) and his edited edition of Herbert Spencer Ashbee's *Index Liborum Prohibitoru* (Jack Brussel: 1962)

CONTENTS

Chapter One

IN DREAMS PERHAPS

'All books is trash, except one', observed Mr Drummer, winking his eye in an extraordinary manner. 'They teach naught but sweary, lewd conversation, ungodliness, and that worst of all vices—intemperance!'

George Reynolds, *The Mysteries of London*

Literature: a word of unknown provenance, generally attributed to 'litter' or waste.

Peter Ackroyd, *The Plato Papers*

You want to make your life a book? Consider. Books are as impermanent as people. Both are eaten by worms. Bindings loosen and break. Paper becomes yellow and brittle. Even vellum dries and cracks. Both lives and books are easily lost and forgotten. Sanctuary there is none. Books disappear into libraries and libraries sometimes burn…

Pittsburgh 1973

As usual, I read slowly and sonorously, hearing the ever-so-slightly laboured words reverberate around the old oak-panelled classroom—an effect that I had always found, delivered sparingly, suitably impressed the students.

'Suppose that you wake so aware of the fragility of your own existence that you could feel your sweat and stench soaking into the plaster of the walls. You walk the streets and each footfall burns a bright brand of heat into the cold stone of the street. The wind erodes a powder of skin from your face. The night moon draws a tide through your body until your feet sink into the soles of your boots and your head grows light and translucent in the twilight… '

I paused. I was reading from a first edition English translation of the novel. It was complete with a frayed and price-clipped dust jacket. The white sticker on the back, with the price in francs, reminded me that I had bought it from one of those little booths on the banks of the Seine on one of my occasional study trips to Europe.

I cleared my throat and scanned the rows of assembled students searching for some recognition, or, at least, interest. I continued.

' ... If you spoke, your words could rise to the sky and reverberate through the universe forever. However, you do not speak. Instead you silently exhale a bubble that fills your bedroom until the next morning when you will wake a little less and inhale the residue.'

I paused again and altered the tone of my voice to indicate that the author now shifted into direct address. 'You think that I am too inventive? An imagination over-extended into hyperbole, metaphor?'

I closed the book and laid it with a certain thud of finality on the desk. 'Ladies and Gentlemen,' I continued. 'You may recognize the opening of one of the most influential novels of the twentieth century, written by a famed existentialist writer from a small town in northern France.' I smiled as I looked around at the blank faces. 'If not', I added, 'it is on your reading list for next semester and can be purchased at the University bookshop.

'But... ' I continued, before the usual exodus to the refectory and pizza parlour, 'before we progress our discussion of the sublime in literature into a new century, you may wish to reflect on what we have covered this semester in the Enlightenment to Romanticism class. Remember, it is not clear whether the sublime actually exists! As we discovered, it was an invention of those doyens of the Enlightenment, of Kant, Burke and Hogarth, who delighted in creations of the mind but lusted after the exigencies of the body. They called something they didn't know the sublime and they sought its blend of ecstasy and terror in the mountain and the abyss. But where was it really to be found?' I paused. 'In dreams, perhaps.' I stopped there, content with the rhetorical flourish

I surveyed the classroom. A few students looked contemplative. A few had knotted brows. One girl with reddish blond hair at the rear beamed at me above the other heads of fidgety sophomores who were itching to start their winter break.

This was my favourite classroom of all the international classrooms at Pittsburgh University—the Scottish room, with its oak panels, gilt-framed portraits of Burns and Scott, heavy drapes and orderly benches. However, it would soon be deserted as this was the last class before the break.

I looked down at the desk and began to gather together my notes and books—a sign that the class was now at an end.

'Professor Nowell.' The blond-haired girl looked up at me as I gathered my papers from the lectern. I stood down from the raised dais. She was tall, almost as tall as myself, slim and attractive.

'Hi Audrey' I said, folding my arms around my collected belongings. 'I'm glad to see you're still following the sorry old tale of English literature through the ages,' I added.

She smiled broadly. 'Professor Nowell, I can't tell you how much I've enjoyed your lectures' she said, seeming genuinely enthusiastic. 'All that stuff about writers going to the mountains for inspiration… and how they seemed to love them and hate them at the same time!'

'Well, not quite', I said. 'Eighteenth-century scholars tried to classify and categorize everything they saw in the world. Wilderness and mountain areas were a challenge because they couldn't find any order or method in them…'

'And then you said that they grew attracted to them because the landscape reflected the chaos in their own minds.'

'Yes, in the Romantic period, the frightening sublimity of ravines, precipices, and storms, wild seas, then man-made artefacts like vaults and dungeons, all inspired a sort of terror because they were different and apart from the ordered world but, as we discussed, as the Gothic period developed, it wasn't just the strange and the supernatural that was scary, it was also, as you said, the chaos that was in our own minds, dreams, visions, the uncontrollable subconscious.'

'Yeah, just like the man on the wall wrote'. She was indicating one of the portraits on the oak panelled wall.

'The. Man. On. The. Wall.' I teased her a little. 'You'll have to be a bit more specific than that when you write your thesis.' I smiled. 'You mean Robert Louis Stevenson who wrote one of the novels we discussed: *The Strange Case of Dr Jekyll and Mr Hyde.*'

'Yes, that's it… and he was two people at once—a respectable doctor and a sort of monster.'

I accepted the presumption that she intended to refer to the eponymous protagonist of the novel and not the author. 'That's right. It was a turning point in literature and also the beginning, perhaps, of the science of psychology. It revealed that there is a dark, even evil, side to all of us. Stevenson also wrote another short story about it called *Markheim*, and there is another, more difficult, novel of about the same time, by James Hogg.' I examined her face. She seemed genuinely interested, unlike many of the students in the class.

Maybe I could lend it to you,' I added.

'That would be nice. I think it'd be really interesting! That even everyday boring old people have a sublime and scary side to them!'

I nodded and reflected for a moment. There was nothing of the sublime in my tenured post at Pittsburgh. It was *comfortable*. I had a comfortable room with a comfortable desk and a comfortable chair—albeit the room was temporarily shared with another professor. My students were comfortable with me and I had a comfortable house up in Squirrel Hill with a porch and two bay trees. In fact, I had been sinking into this congenial lifestyle for a while when, to my surprise, almost one year ago, I had found myself cohabiting with a Scandinavian postgraduate student called Brigid Thorensen who was writing a thesis entitled 'Eros and Thanatos in the longer verse of Byron, Keats and Swinburne'. She had no illusions about the worth of my own work on the Romantics. She said it was cold and passionless. Unfortunately, with regard to Brigid—in all but her work—I found the same.

'Professor Nowell… ' Audrey was gazing quite intently into my face, her dimpled chin upturned and her eyes slightly gleaming.

'Oh, I'm sorry', I said, 'I was somewhere else.'

'Dreaming of your vacation, I suppose.'

'No, not really. I really don't know if I'm going anywhere at all this Christmas.'

She knotted her eyebrows slightly, as if considering this admission, then she said: 'Me neither. In fact, I intend to spend quite a lot of time in the library here.' She hesitated. 'Perhaps you'll be in your office?'

'Perhaps… '

In truth I didn't know my plans for the break. The previous year, in order to resolve some annoying oppositions in my academic and my personal life, I had taken the Fall semester as a sabbatical and set out for Paris—thus the source of the volume I was holding, now closed, in my hand. I had been undertaking some research lately on the margins of my established work. In one study I had been trying to explain how in the nineteenth century, behavioural terminology—sodomy—had been translated into psychological terms—homosexuality, and how this was reflected in the work of some British and French writers: Oscar Wilde, Jean Genet.

Unfortunately, if truth were told, I had not found that topic nearly as fascinating as I had at first imagined and I had more or less consigned it to the category of 'worth one short paper in a minor journal'. I had to find something else to concentrate my efforts on. My life was becoming too dull, measured, like an incomplete Enlightenment project. My dreams were empty. I needed something.

I left the classroom and walked through the mock Gothic vaults of the Cathedral of Learning, that strange but impressive neo-Gothic forty-storey folly that was the keystone of Pittsburgh University. I got the elevator to the eleventh floor.

Due to the kitchen and storerooms requiring some renovation on my floor, there was a shortage of office space temporarily. As I had the biggest office, I had been asked to share for a time with a new assistant professor, Norman Levy. He was jokingly referred to as the invisible man because of his work on Ralph Ellison.

'Ah, Prof Nowell.' Levy looked up from where he was fiddling with some papers on his desk. 'Greetings to he whose name is whispered in the corridors of the Gothic rocket.'

I was rather surprised by this. 'Only for my good deeds, I hope,' I said.

'Well… ' his voice took on a different inclination. 'Not exactly.' He shrugged. 'I may as well be crude and to the point, as I believe is sometimes said of your lectures. Rumour has it you're fucking one of your students… '

'She is not my student,' I said, indignantly. 'She is a senior and she is merely sitting in on my classes to prepare for a potential masters thesis she has planned. And… ' I added, 'I am not fucking her!'

He perhaps felt my tone was too aggressive as he raised his hands.

'Hey, I'm just the messenger.' He smiled, 'Besides, I'm on your side.' He turned and took two books from the shelf. 'S'pose it's OK if you can get away with it. I wouldn't have a chance with my colour and inclination. I'd be burned, burned, burned.'

It was true. Norman Levy was black and homosexual. Since the Black Panthers had been formed and Eldridge Cleaver had published *Soul on Ice* about the black rape of white women, black politics had been contentious. James Baldwin was still writing, but he was marginalised. The University had a liberal tradition, but Levy knew only too well that, around the University and in general, it was wise to remain as invisible as possible for the most part.

'By the way,' he added, 'I found these books fallen down the back of the shelf when I was storing my things.'

The two books he gave me were both leather bound and, from their appearance, dating from the end of the last century. One I recognized immediately. It was my father's old copy of Sir Walter Scott's *The Antiquary*. The other, however, I had never seen before. It was a thin octavo volume in half calf with marbled boards. On the spine the title was merely *Fugitive Poems, &c* in gilt between raised bands. I opened it. There was no date but the publishers were indicated: 'Wm McDowall & Co, John Knox's House' and a label contained details of a book shop: 'Coulthard & Knowles; Book Dealers; West Port, Edinburgh.' The author was given as 'The City Voice'—a nom-de-plume, but someone, presumably some time ago, had helpfully written in sepia ink below the title 'by, John Ledbury' and below that again 'the counterfeit detective'.

Levy was looking over my shoulder. 'Nice little book. English literature—literature from England, I mean. That's your thing.' Then he looked me in the face and something came to his mind. 'Hey, you're actually English, are you not?'

'No,' I said, 'Scottish, actually.' I wasn't really paying him much attention as my mind was elsewhere, struggling to think where I might have come across this book and other things.

It was true. I had been born in Scotland, in Kirkcaldy, Fife, during the latter days of the war. My father shared my Christian name, Robert—he always claimed we were named after the poet, Robert Burns—and he came from a small village called Kingskettle. He was brought up by his adopted parents, an older couple whose life was simple, strict and God-fearing. He never really spoke about his birth parents; all I knew was that his mother had died in childbirth and he had never known his father. The only remembrance he had, he once told me, was an old silver sixpence and a collection of the works of Robert Burns inscribed with his name which, so he believed, had been left for him by his father.

My mother was American. Her name was Rebecca Lee, and she hailed from Abingdon, Virginia. Her family claimed a link with General Robert E Lee, but they were neither wealthy nor auspicious in any particular branch of life. They grew corn moderately competently on the rich, deep and easily-drained Virginian pamunkey soil. Her parents—my grandparents—and her three brothers and one sister were hard-working and comfortable enough but apparently never content. They regarded corn as an inferior crop and really wanted to be tobacco farmers. They talked about reseeding the land but never did. This was a lament my mother would repeat until her dying day. 'The money was there, but it was in the tobaccy' she would sigh.

My mother's early years were probably not as poverty-stricken as she sometimes pretended, but as the youngest of the Lee brood, especially when her elder sister upped and left home, she felt out of place on the farm. So, when America joined the war in Europe she decided to do something entirely on her own. She joined the Army Nurse Corps and was shipped to England to tend to wounded American servicemen.

During the war my father served as a gunner in the Royal Artillery, rising to the rank of lieutenant. In 1942, serving with the Eighth Army in Sicily, he had been invalided by a German shell that was to leave him with a slight limp for the rest of his days. Shipped to Brickbarns hospital in Worcester to recover, he met my mother. She seemed to have been attracted by his gentle Scottish accent and demeanour in a ward of more raucous American servicemen. So, when my father was well enough to leave the hospital they were married in a little baptist church in Malvern. My father became, therefore, the male equivalent of a war bride! And, in little more than a year, I was born.

By this time, however, they had moved too close to my father's home—the town of Kirkcaldy, in Fife, Scotland. Kirkcaldy had a long history—Adam Smith and Thomas Carlyle had lived there. But at this time, it was a pretty ordinary industrial town. My father worked at the linoleum factory and the whole town seemed to stink of the odour from the linoleum. There is no doubt that my mother hated it there—she would visibly shiver whenever she had to mention it in the future—and my mother was always one to get her way. So, as soon as she could, she moved us all back home to Abingdon, Virginia.

My father knew nothing about farming but he was good with machines. He started fixing lawnmowers and then began to sell them—used and new. Before long, Nowell's Lawnmower Emporium was pretty well regarded throughout Washington county and even further afield. My father did all the fixing and the ordering and paperwork, but he was no salesman so he partnered up with Gus Siddink, one of my mother's second cousins. My father had come to know Gus Siddink through their mutual love on mechanical things and contraptions. Gus was a locksmith by trade and could open most anything that was locked. My father used to joke that he should have been a safecracker. He was a jovial sort, the opposite to my father's quiet but slightly dour Presbyterian personality. And, unlike my father, he could sell things! He said he could sell snow in Alaska and got on with building up the business. So, together, the two of them did pretty well.

My mother was an exceptionally careful woman. Her domestic jurisprudence allowed no avenue for the extraneous and the frivolous. No pictures would adorn her wall nor music and dance be allowed in her house. Her reasons for this, strangely perhaps, were not based on any particular religious dogma or philosophy, but merely her own temper and personal preferences 'Books spread germs' she would say, and there was no room in her house for aught but one Bible and a Bible concordance, a Moody and Sankey hymn book, a dictionary and a domestic treatise called *How to Do Everything*. She made an allowance for my schoolbooks but her attitude to learning was itself quite contradictory. The acquisition of knowledge, in her view, was a necessary evil that could only be evaluated in its capacity to improve one's earnings or position in society. Art, literature, culture were, to her, extraneous and unnecessary in the pursuit of navigating the untrustworthy world without too much grief.

My mother was an unadventurous but fastidious cook. She would even peel mushrooms until there was only a little round white ball, seemingly determined to suck the flavour out of everything. And everything, more or less, was cooked in an ancient dutch oven that had been passed down from her mother. But the truth is that we fared well enough on plates of wholesome and slightly overcooked bland food.

My mother's parents had passed away before I started high school and she was left with a sister in Raleigh who visited once a year and her three brothers who ran the farm. The brothers said very little and I never knew them to hold a conversation that did not concern the farm or the demolition derbies and lawnmower races they frequented. My father, who had a great respect for all things mechanical, regarded these eccentricities with a sort of amused resignation. The eldest of my uncles, George, was a relatively short but large man whose party trick was literally to hang himself! At picnics or on any other plausible occasion when he could attract an audience, he would hang a fixed noose in the barn or somewhere similar and suspend himself from it by his big bull neck, lifting his knees to his chest and rotating until he thought the company had been suitably impressed.

Mostly my uncles didn't say much to my father or to me, but they seemed content enough that my mother had married anyone much. George, mostly, would call once a week for no ostensible purpose, it seemed, than to check if my mother was still there.

And so, for the formative years of my childhood, things went by smoothly enough. The family doctor, Elijah Marlowe, would call sometimes, when I had earache or chickenpox, or once when, much to my mother's dismay, I had caught cooties at school.

A few neighbours called round (although we seldom seemed to go to visit them). Our immediate neighbours were an elderly woman and her spinster daughter—known universally as Mistress and Miss Farthingale. They always seemed to be around their own yard, stiff and formal, like two peg dolls behind the picket fence. They ventured out to church on Sundays and to other community and social events and, almost in tandem, would comment on any event from their fund of Biblical homilies. They were somehow part of, but not within, the community. They would watch the adults meet in Luigi's for pancakes and maple syrup in the mornings and the youths shoot hoops in the park with a seeming dismay. 'The fashion of this world passeth away,' they would say.

On Sundays we would go to church—the Sinking Spring Presbyterian Church, one of the oldest in Abingdon. My mother and my father were keen churchgoers for entirely different reasons. My mother regarded it as an essential social task. Necessary to support and nurture the community, to check up on neighbours' births and deaths and gossip about anything that cropped up. To her, the churchgoing day was all about people, their entrances and exits and she sat almost oblivious to the actual service.

My father, on the other hand, regarded gossip, tittle-tattle and the comings and going of the community, unless it directly affected his business and livelihood, as properly the concern of women. But, reared in the stern Scottish Presbyterian tradition, he revelled in a strictly ordered service and a good sermon. He would often linger behind to discuss a theological point with the pastor—a tall stern man of indeterminate age with the redolent name of the Reverend Aaron Wigsby—seemingly reluctant to leave. The church, the churchyard and all its accoutrements were, to him, a duelling ground between God and the Devil and he accorded them his due respect. He was well versed in scripture, but would also occasionally, to the mystification of most of the churchgoers, come out with a Scots expression. 'Mind your mealpoke if you wish' he would say, 'but don't forget it will soon be time to shake hands with Auld Hornie!'

I attended the church only on the coatstrings of my parents but I have a vague memory of one day that I tried to be involved with its rather arcane ways. I had listened carefully to one of the Reverend Wigsby's sermons and, precociously, I decided to question him about it.

'Reverend Wigsby,' I asked him, 'Is there no one who is without sin?'

'No. We are all sinners. Sin is part of us all.'

'Does that mean we will all go to hell?'

He looked at me quite sternly.

'Only through our daily devotion to The Lord Jesus Christ shall we be redeemed and thereafter dwell in paradise at his side.'

That would have seemed to be an end to the conversation, but I persisted.

'I have heard that it is said that, through prayer, we can discern whether we have been chosen to the Elect and therefore are already redeemed.'

He seemed distracted and at this moment the Miss and Mistress Farthingale appeared and they had his attention for a short while.

I waited as I wanted another answer from him but when he had shaken hands and was free from the congregation, he dismissed me with a large stern hand almost imposed in my face.

'Boy,' he said, 'when you are grown more you will understand more. For now read your Bible and pray every day. Your father will instruct you.'

That evening I asked my father, as he was stirring the last ashes in the evening fire, is the Reverend Wigsby one of the Elect?'

My father looked at me in a strange way. I could not tell if he was pleased or alarmed.

'The Reverend Wigsby is a holy man and he may think he is saved, but *we* cannot tell. Only God will decide that on the Judgement Day.'

'But he says that we are sinners and will go to hell if we can't be saved.'

'We are all sinners, that is true. But we can try not to sin. Temptation leads many astray. Temptations of the flesh, of strong drink, of wealth, of power... '

'What do you mean by the flesh?' I asked innocently.

He looked at me a little queerly.

'I will get your mother to speak to you,' he said. 'Now get some supper and go to bed and don't forget to say your prayers.'

I went to bed and I suppose that was the end of my attempt to embrace my father's religion.

Schooldays, sometimes a trial for children not accustomed to mixing with other children in their own or extended family, were, in fact, generally pleasant and unproblematic for me. I was an excellent scholar, inbred to my mother's devotion to 'doing well' and my father's more quixotic anecdotal prompting, and I was generally top or thereabouts in every subject. Crucially, however, I was also good at sport. I was tall enough to be a utility player for the basketball team and I had a good throwing arm which got me into the ball team—a game, with its dirt-caked balls, resin-coated bats, bizarre rules and strange terminology—that I generally enjoyed (no-one could persuade me to try for the football team which seemed to me to consist of buffoons in helmets running into each other). Here, however, as in other aspects of my life, luck played a key part; for in my very first game and very first at bat for the Falcons, I took a big looping swing and hit a homer with the bases loaded. Mister Joe, our coach, whose baseball talk was almost as incomprehensible as his tactics, would remind me of it at the start of every game: "'member when you rocked that apple outta here with three little ducks on the pond!'

Because of this and my generally benign demeanour, I was respected by my fellow high school students. I say respected rather than popular because, even at that age—although I could laugh and jest and tease well enough in school company—I had a solitary streak, and I would as soon sit at home with a book, or walk through the meadows among the daisies, bluebells and buttercups to the woods with the flowery dogwoods and catalpa trees with their big heart-shaped leaves used to wraps pats of butter. I'd watch the red-winged blackbirds floating in the trees and walk in the spongy sphagnum moss to hidden paths among the trees carpeted with the four fingered fallen petals of the rhododendron, a much brighter violet in their death throes than they had been alive on the bloom.

Of course, I was also an avid reader, I never believed that great works of literature were solely created by reflection or written sitting at a desk. They were created from the world around us. Thus the connection between the real and the imagined, the cerebral and the visceral, was obvious to me from an early age.

So life passed me by quite contentedly in my own little backwater of Abingdon, the Commonwealth of Virginia, the United States of America, the World, the Universe. That is, until two things came along that changed everything for me—my mother died, and my father died.

To lose a parent while still a child, generates such a numbness and shock that often serves to make the immediate memories fade or remain as one seemingly totemic moment in the mind. To lose a parent as a mature adult often is the cause of reflection or reconciliation. Just short of my eighteenth birthday, I was neither an adult nor a child at the time of my mother's death. Nevertheless, I can say that I remember the aftermath of her demise and her funeral with complete clarity.

It was a middling to fine Fall day. The trees were blotched in browns and yellows, a diffuse but slightly warming sun shone through wispy clouds and, in the old squash tree just on the edge of the church grounds, a cardinal bird sat brilliantly but silently as if recording the whole proceedings. The overall impression of the scene was one of sadness but serenity. I had not anticipated in any way that my mother could possibly die. She had been sick for about ten weeks, I suppose, and Doctor Marlowe called about twice a week. But, with the naïvety of the young, I assumed that one of the various medicines that were prescribed would eventually make her well again. Then one day she just didn't wake up. I was already at school and I was stunned when my father came to collect me. So, here we were, at the Sinking Spring church, a few days later, prepared to consign her to the earth.

My father's face reflected a deep but composed sadness. He was well-scrubbed and neatly dressed. His collar freshly starched and, for once, his old grey church suit, somewhat shiny at the elbows, seemed to fit his body to perfection. Somehow, despite the circumstances, he was in his element. The parishioners, not impolitely, stared at him softly and silently.

Reverend Wigsby also excelled, given carte blanche to meld the service and the consignment as he wished (not for my father the conceit of pointless eulogies and testimonials).

From the graveside, we all shifted to the parish hall for coffee and cakes. The respectful silence merged into mumbled conservations and pleasantries, but, in general, everyone seemed pleased with the day's events. Even Miss and Mistress Farthingdale were quiet and subdued, only venturing forth to say to my father, in unison, 'It was such a NICE send-off, you know.' But the elder also said, almost under her breath, 'all things come to pass' and looked to the heavens.

A few days after my mother's funeral, it was my eighteenth birthday. I didn't expect, in the circumstances, any mention to be made of it at all. But, after our customary breakfast of coffee with porridge and pancakes, my father asked me to come with him to his workplace.

Nowell's Lawnmower Emporium was, mostly, a converted barn. Downstairs the entire floor space was given up to the collection of lawnmowers of all types and sizes. In one corner there was a small office with a window for the collection of checks and invoices. Then there was a timber staircase leading up to a balconied area where my father had his office. My father had never invited me there before and I had never thought of what might be there apart from the boring paraphernalia of the retail trade. However, what I discovered that day surprised me. The outer office was uninteresting—some shelves stacked with identical box files—but from there a glazed door led to a larger space. Here the floor was carpeted. My father's desk stood in the middle and beside it an old patched leather settee.. There was a window at the back, but the walls on either side were shelved from floor to ceiling and full of books. This was where my father came, it seemed, to avail himself of the pleasures of the literary world that my mother would only reluctantly allow into our home.

'The business will be yours one day', my father said, 'maybe soon', he shrugged, ' …and these too.' He indicated all the volumes on the shelf. Then he drew a set of keys from his pocket. 'You're old enough now,' he said, 'come here whenever you want.'

From that day, things changed. My father's personality shifted from the consummate calmness he had shown at my mother's funeral. Most of the work at the business he now delegated to Gus Siddink and he increasingly spent time alone in his bedroom. He became almost obsessed with some of his books—a Bible his parents had given him and his inscribed copy of Burns's poems and sometimes at nights I would hear strange sounds, like a low moaning and sometimes like a wailing and, sometimes, strangely, voices as if he were speaking to himself in different tongues. My father began to lose weight and he called in Doctor Marlowe to prescribe him sleeping pills.

Meantime, I was growing older and becoming a man. I did well at school, supplementing my official studies with visits to my father's library where I became acquainted with Scott and Dickens and Thackeray and Eliot. I was seeing a girl called Emily Goodlad, whose ancestors, generations back, had come from the Orkney Isles, I'd borrow my father's pick-up and take her to a drive-in movie or the mall. We even went to the county show where my uncles were engaged in smashing up their redundant trucks. My life was settling into a familiar pattern, but I was not, paradoxically, a particularly content or happy young man. Inside myself I knew that my life was coming to a crossroads, that I had decisions to make. I could remain in small-town America, marry, have children, continue to build my lawnmower empire, go to church on Sundays, a ball game come Saturdays…

But deep down, I don't think I ever really intended to take the conventional and predictable path.

Any choices I had to make, however, were precipitated by the events that soon followed.

One day—it was a muggy but stormy day and twister warnings were on the air—I had hardly been in bed for a few minutes and was reading a copy of Browning's poems from my father's library, when I heard an uncanny howling sound from my father's bedroom.

When I got there, my father's face seemed deathly white and his face unfocused and unnaturally blank. He was leaning over, grasping the cup in which he kept his sleeping draught, his shift pulled down over one shoulder, his brow sweaty and his eyes damp and glazed. In a hoarse whisper he said 'look not upon the wine when it giveth its colour in the cup'. And then his eyes focused a little as if he recognised me. 'Bad blood,' he said, almost spitting it into my face, 'Bad blood!'

I wiped his brow and settled him down. Then I prised the cup from between his fingers and laid him back in the bed. I took the cup to the kitchen and filled it again. When I returned his face was rigid, his eyes staring. I checked his pulse on the side of his neck. There was no doubt that he was dead. Then I left the cup by the bedside and, with my thumb, closed the lids of his eyes. All there was to do now was to call Doctor Marlowe.

The conclusion was that it was taking an over-abundance of the sleeping draught which may have induced the apoplexy that killed him, but there was no doubt in the Reverend Wigsby's mind that my father's decline and death was a determination of my mother's premature departure, and a few days later he gave a moving sermon on faithfulness, constancy, and fortitude until death with the usual cautions and caveats and evocations of hellfire and damnation that would have pleased my father. I looked on, reflectively. Unlike the day of my mother's funeral, the weather was wet and cold when my father was committed in the old churchyard. The Reverend Wigsby's face was so pale and emaciated that you might have thought he would slip himself into the same sorry sod as my father without a murmur. I did not weep, but I shuddered at the chilling thought of the inevitability of one's end.

From the night of my father's death, as I was not quite regarded as fully an adult, my mother's youngest brother, Johnny, had, annoyingly, been camped at my house. One night, quite late, I came home having dropped Emily at her house in the pick-up, to find Johnny quite agitated. 'Get in the truck,' he said, 'there's been a fire down at the emporium!'

When we arrived, the fire was at its height. Great flames flickered round the eaves of the barn as if Auld Hornie himself had taken possession of it. The firemen had given up any efforts at controlling it. 'It's gone,' they said. Since gasoline was stored in the building, sprinklers had been put in place, but it seemed that they had had little effect against the fury of whatever blast had caused this inferno. We stood as the roof collapsed causing a wave of stoor and dust laced with petroleum fumes. And that was the end of Nowell's Lawnmower Emporium.

In the morning of the dull day after, I returned and spent some hours searching through the dissecta membra of the body of the wreckage. While Gus Siddink retrieved the machines from among the charred and splintered remains of the building, I searched in the remains of my father's office. The collapse of the roof had snuffed out the most virulent of the flames and some things had survived. Strangely, the Scottish books seemed to have been the hardiest and fared best: I found Scott's *The Antiquary*, Stevenson's *Catriona* and the Hogg and Motherwell edition of Burns. There was also an edition of Tennyson's poems, *Middlemarch*, *Vanity Fair* and a few others. Rummaging a bit deeper, I found a little box, scorched but intact. In it were my father's war medals, The Defence Medal, the Africa Star, a couple of others and his gunner's cap badge, with an old cannon below a crown and the word 'ubique'. Also in it were a piece of a bomb that had fallen near his family home at the beginning of the war and some old coins—bun pennies, farthings, a silver sixpence, a crown and various others—that I remember he had showed me in the past. Memories, I suppose of the country he had left behind. I put all of them in a rucksack I had brought and carried them home.

Gus Siddink took charge of the clearance of the rest. Surprisingly perhaps, the fire, it seemed, had served only to make the robust cast-iron bodies of the lawnmowers more interesting, leaving a smoky black patina edged with a spectrum of violet or blue. They would later fetch a good few dollars at the fire sale.

After this, I appraised my situation. The insurance from the barn fire had only improved my lot, my father having exercised his native Scottish shrewdness and prudence in the provision of more than adequate cover. Although I was only eighteen, my inheritance was reasonable and I had a great deal of choice in how to proceed in life. I thought of my father's waxy white face in his coffin, of days at the movies or the soda fountain with Emily, of the ranks of lawnmowers for sale, of my mother's concordance and *How to Do Nearly Everything* lying by the telephone, of uncle George hanging himself in his barn. Then I made a decision which seemed spontaneous but, in truth, was probably in my mind since the day, a few months ago, that my father had gifted me the keys to his secret library. I would follow the paternal rather than the maternal path. Perhaps it was an old urge itching in my genes. A career in law was ruled out. I would study English literature at Harvard. I had the qualifications and I could afford the fees.

Abingdon had to be forsaken. Unfortunately, but prudently, I decided, my relationship with Emily also had to be discontinued. If I had a lust for anything in life, it was to see the Houghton Library, with its Shakespeare folios, its old Scottish manuscripts purchased by Professor Child...

'I have a class.' Norman Levy grabbed some stuff from his cluttered desk and woke me suddenly from my reverie. My mind had wandered again. Today, somehow, seemed a day for much reflection. Perhaps a turning point for me, like the discovery of the mountains or the invention of the subconscious.

I leafed through the little volume. It consisted of short poems and sonnets—typical of the average Victorian amateur poetaster. One such caught my eye:

Now that the rose in you doth timely bud,
To drive the Spring to Autumn's quick decay,
And plays the scent of you where I did softly lay,
Then all too soon your bloom bursts forth into the flood,
And my poor briar roots lamely in the mud,
For e'en in death you are the sun, the day,
And I, sad clod, and I am so much clay.

My field being largely prose rather than poetry, I could not claim any expertise in this type of work. But it certainly seemed a well-composed and professional piece of work, a cut above the work of many of the minor aspiring poets publishing countless books at this time.

Levy, having eventually sorted the material he needed for his lecture, paused at the door. 'What,' he asked, 'do you think it means by 'the counterfeit detective'?'

'I've no idea,' I replied.

'Well, if it isn't in this, it isn't anywhere.' He reached up and brought down from the shelf a heavy tome, volume one of Cartwright's *Dictionary of Victorian Literary Biography*. We looked up Ledbury, John and there was, indeed, an entry, but only of a few words: 'Minor English magazine editor. Said to have been nicknamed 'the Counterfeit Detective' because he was employed by Sir Arthur Conan Doyle to write letters to fans purportedly from Sherlock Holmes, although no evidence of this exists.'

This was tantalizingly brief, but my curiosity had been aroused. Perhaps, I thought, almost morbidly, here was a pointer to the abyss into which I had been chosen to gaze.

'By the way,' Levy said, 'this was pushed under the door.' He handed me an internal memo envelope..

I put the book in my briefcase along with the envelope—I expected it would read exactly the same as a similar one I had discovered in my pigeonhole that morning: 'It is essential that I meet with you before the vacation. Charles L Horton, Senior Vice Provost (Students)'—and left the University. I drove down through the Hill. I hadn't eaten much and I could have got a steak, but instead I stopped at Joe Costanzo's for a crown manhattan. I had to think. It was a pleasant enough November. It was a nice city and I was lucky enough to be here, I thought. I could have gone to Three Rivers Stadium to see Roberto Clemente float a homer into the bleachers. I could have gone home, gotten a beer or watched television, I could have sat on the porch and watched the slow lazy lightning bugs light and fade, smugly satisfied with my day's work. But it was winter and the lightning bugs had buried themselves in the dirt. The baseball season was over and, anyway, Clemente had perished in a plane crash the year before.

This was America at the end of 1973. Despite the Watergate scandal, Nixon was in the White House still. A great many happy or unhappy people had returned from the war. Many things may have been happening. Mostly, however, none of these things were what I really had in mind.

Brigid was sitting on an old rocking chair in the kitchen bolt upright, holding a book vertically in front of her face in a manner that made it hard to believe that she was reading it. I noticed that she had been drinking a brandy and had smoked one of the long menthol cigarettes that she sometimes indulged in, usually when some crisis, real or imagined, had come to her mind.

'Hi,' I said.

She didn't turn to acknowledge me.

I put my briefcase on the table and took out some papers and the book. She picked it up and fingered through it, absent-mindedly, then put it down.

'Is there any reason,' I asked, 'why you're not speaking to me?'

'You're fooling around with one of your students,' she said, 'Audrey Schapiro.'

'I am not fooling around with her', I said, 'and she is not one of my students, she is a senior and she is merely sitting in on my classes to prepare for a potential masters thesis she has planned.'

It occurred to me at the moment I delivered these words that perhaps I was too preemptive. I didn't know what it was about that day that made me forgetful and bereft of my accustomed calm and sangfroid. For some reason, although I didn't usually smoke, I leaned over and helped myself to one of her Virginia Slims out of the long striped pack, lighting it and exhaling slowly. However, Brigid ignored me and carried straight on as if the facts of the case were apparent to all.

'Not what I've heard. Her brother works for Josie next door's uncle down at the car wash. He told her uncle and he told Josie.' She looked at me with a sort of contempt and added, 'And just about fucking everybody else.'

If Brigid had been Italian or French, or even English, she might have created an unpleasant scene. But with her cooler Nordic disposition she simply gave me a condescending look, turned her back and walked out of the room.

I sat alone in the kitchen for a while and drank a beer, and then a scotch. Then I determined what to do. Today had not been a good day. My future, which seemed so secure only recently, now seemed so uncertain.

Sometimes in life a dramatic change meets you head on, other times perhaps it just creeps up on you. In truth I had been discontent for some time and it was even possible that somehow I had deliberately engineered this little crisis in my career, my relationship and my intellectual life. Maybe things had just been too easy for me, maybe something from the past, *my* past was calling me. I remembered an old saying of my father's—'grasp the thistle'. When I was quite young, I asked him what it meant and he said, 'If the thistle stings you, just grasp it harder, so that it will sting you less.'

Well, I thought, damn the Vice-Provost, damn Brigid. I would branch out into something new. I was not short of money, only ideas, and maybe, fortuitously, one had come along!

Upstairs, Brigid was lying silently on the bed. I went through the bedroom to the room we used as a dressing room and put together a small case of clothes and personal effects. Then I gathered some papers and documents from the drawer of my desk in the study and a little bag with a drawstring containing some of my father's memorabilia. I drove my car to the airport and parked it in the long-term car park. I was venturing forth on my journey in search of John Ledbury—the counterfeit detective!

I slept for a while in the executive lounge before boarding the first flight I could get. Before long I was gazing out of the window at the icy mountains of the southern coast of Greenland with that peculiar omnipotent feeling of distance from the real world. Then we pulled south on our arc across the Atlantic above soft, fluffy clouds and I felt a little sleepy. I've always wondered at the peculiar feeling of flying. Travelling so fast yet seeming so slow. Lost in time yet feeling yourself age, as if your teeth are poking themselves a bit further through the enamel. I took Ledbury's book out of my little travel bags and felt it in my fingers, but my eyes were heavy.

'Who am I, and what am I, and where have I come from?' Suddenly I awoke from my brief nap with some words going round in my head! I pulled myself into the conscious world. I still had the book in my hand and I felt compelled to look at it. It almost fell open in my hands to the last few pages and there was the last of the poems in the book, titled 'Riddle':

A tree that cannot flower,
A bird that cannot fly,
A pendulum that keeps no time,
A question with no why.

SIMPSON GREARS

Tell me Father Greybeard,
You that have travelled so long,
Who am I? And what am I?
And where have I come from?

It was not clear, unless I was somehow reading in my sleep, how these words had come into my head, nor what they meant. I read it again and part of a sort of dream seemed to come back to me, a dream of a dark and smoky place—but elusively, only on the margins of my consciousness.

I was puzzled. Why had Ledbury chosen to conclude his collection in this enigmatic way? Where had this little book come from and why did it seem to have fixed itself in my mind? Exactly why had I suddenly decided to take this journey and what, really, was I searching for?

There were many questions to be answered. I sat there, now fully awake and realised I was on a quest that I still knew little about and in flight towards a city that, in truth, I knew better from the novels of Dickens or Gissing than from personal experience—the great dark, foggy, throbbing metropolis of London.

Chapter Two

PANOPTICON

Watch your step. Keep your wits about you; you will need them. This city that I am bringing you is vast and intricate, and you have not been here before. You may imagine, from other stories you've read, that you know it well but those stories flattered you, welcoming you as a friend treating you as if you belonged. The truth is that you are an alien from another time and place altogether.

Michel Faber, *The Crimson Petal and the White*

The street conducts the flâneur into a vanished time. For him, every street is precipitous. It leads downwards... into a past that can be all the more spellbinding because it is not his own...

Walter Benjamin, *The Arcades Project*

It was a dank and foggy evening in the great throbbing imperial metropolis that was London. I turned my collar up against the spasmodic drizzle. On street corners hawkers were selling the last reports of the battles of Ventner's Spruit and Spion Kop. Despite the weather, the streets were busy enough with street cries, the clatter of hooves on granite setts and the rumbling of carts trucking all manner of things—timber, teas, spices, cotton, curios, furs and feathers—from the docks.

Walls were plastered with notices for Monkey Brand soap, Bovril Eno's Fruit Salts, Dr Browne's Chlorodyne and Mariani wine. Some stores were closing. A greengrocer was starting to pack his baskets of wilting vegetables that had seen the best of the summer and autumn—snow peas, blunt-rooted carrots and golden beetroot. A chandler was closing his louvred shutters, the blinds of a temperance hotel were drawn and only the slight gleam of dim single candles indicated any life within, but next door, a hosiery and shirt warehouse was brightly lit and a few customers were gathered. After a while, turning down a dirtier and darker alley lit by only a solitary gas mantle, I passed a pawnbrokers and a lodging house for travellers. I paused for a second, feeling the damp creep up the back of my legs and the noisome effluence of the sewers play with my nostrils. This great city had been illuminated by the genius of electricity for some years, but here even the few gas mantles seemed choked by the setting fog. I was certainly in the penumbra of the city. Still I moved on as the cobbles in the lane turned to mud and occasional horse dung. When I thought the alley could not get any narrower and darker, I eventually came to a public house with crudely whitewashed walls stained with soot and mud and windows with leaded glass panes that had sometimes cracked with the warping of the timber frames. Stickers advertised 'Brandies' and 'Intermediate Ales'. The pendulant sign above the door, cracked and creaking unsteadily featured a crudely painted globe representing the Earth but with the poles reversed. This was The World Turned Upside Down.

Entering, the premises turned out to be larger than they seemed from outside. A knot of women who were maybe whores were gathered in the corner drinking gin—buxom and in gaudy frocks muddied at the hems from the rainy streets. A man in a silk shirt and a crumpled hat was playing the pianola and one of the women began to sing. She seemed to have no teeth and her voice was slightly cracked but melodious enough and the song pathetic and pleasant:

> She's only a bird in a gilded cage,
> A beautiful sight to see,
> You may think she's happy and free from care,
> She's not, though she seems to be,
> 'Tis sad when you think of her wasted life,
> For youth cannot mate with age,
> And her beauty was sold,
> For an old man's gold,
> She's a bird in a gilded cage.

I approached the bar and the landlord pushed toward me a pewter tankard full of ale. 'Finest old toaster', he said, looking me up and down. 'Or perhaps you would prefer a bottle of claret or a stoup of gin.' He looked over towards the corner. 'The ladies would welcome a gentleman to visit them.'

I shook my head. 'No, I didn't think that was your business,' he said, shifting his gaze to the other side of the bar. 'In there,' he said, 'His Nibs is waiting for you.'

In the back room, a big-boned man was sitting at a table on which was a solitary gas lamp and the remains of a glass of claret. Behind him was a grate tinted with the glow of some ebbing cinders. He was wearing a top hat and had a full and well-groomed beard and whiskers. His demeanour was somehow regal and he could have been Prince Edward himself. He leaned with his elbows and clasped his hands together. His fingernails were unusually long and clean, but the cuffs of his jacket were very slightly frayed and marked with some dust or chalk.

He beckoned for me to sit opposite him.

'All sorts come to see me,' he said. 'Sweaters or even merchants who want to join the docks. We've lost a few Lascars and stevedores from sucking the monkey… ' He must have noticed I looked puzzled. ' …Extracting brandy from the casks with a straw, that is.' He smiled as if indulging his pupil. ' …Or the robbery of tea or tobacco.' He paused for a moment to take a coal from the fire with some tongs and light a long Calabash pipe with a meerschaum bowl.

'I see, however,' he continued, 'that you are a gentleman of sorts from your well-polished boots. What is it that you want of me?'

I said nothing. In truth, I did not know how to answer. However, he continued as if anything I had to say was unimportant.

'Perhaps then I can offer you something more exotic—the teeth of the hippopotami perhaps, or Jordan almonds, or Dr Powell's balsam of aniseed, or cowhair or cooked tongue,' He smiled a little. 'There is very little I cannot provide; I am the very professor of provisions.' He grinned now, exposing his teeth which were very like those of a wolf. Two figures in the shadows behind me chuckled and, for the first time, I realized they must be of his company.

I looked around me but said nothing.

'My interests stretch out to the far corners of the empire,' he continued, 'to the remotest regions of the civilised world. To those places where good Christian gentlemen ply their trade in the interests of Queen and country. Is that not a wondrous thing?'

'It is good that the Empire spreads Christianity and civilisation,' I said. 'But I fear that those are not the only interests of the gentlemen you mention.'

'Come now, would you not wish to profit from the largesse of the world, in the cause of your country, of course.'

'I hope,' I said, 'that the Empire will serve all men well enough that they may benefit from their industry and allegiance to a country in which all men are equal in the eye of the law and of God.'

'Is there nothing, then, that I can offer you?'

I shook my head.

'Well, then,' he said, 'I can only presume that you must be in the pursuit of a much rarer beast, Mr Ledbury, or should I say *Mr Holmes!*'

For the first time, I seemed to sense that there were also men in the shadows behind him. They must have been standing stock still. They now advanced a little towards me and, suddenly, I felt in peril of my life. I grabbed the legs of the table and toppled it over towards them. The lamp broke and there was darkness, but I could see the light from the main part of the bar through the entrance. I bolted past the piano and the singing lady and forced my way through the throng and soon I was out in the foggy night air.

I ran quickly, feeling the damp coldness of the night after the smoke-reeked birr of the tavern. My feet felt queerly on the street, but by leaning forward I soon built up a momentum that surprised me. The streets grew darker. I knew I was escaping from whatever lay behind, but I had no idea or inclination as to where I was heading.

After a little while, I stopped and gasped for breath in the dank smoky air. It was, I suppose, only a few minutes after I had left The World Turned Upside Down, and now I found myself descending the narrow cobbled streets that led from its vicinity, uncertain of my direction or destination. I periodically peered behind me to ensure that I was not being followed. Each footfall seemed to suck a little more heat from my already numb tight-booted feet.

After a little time, I turned into an arched niche at the end of what seemed to be a dead end. A fulsome stench rose from the guttering that ran along the oppressive stone walls on either side of me and through the rusty iron slots some feet below ran streams of ordure and decay suspended in bubbling streams. There was only blackness above me and the passageway sloped downwards and narrowed. There were no regular cobbles or bricks here but only a crazy pattern of irregular stones. There was a little light that let me see my way, but, as I moved on, I had the peculiar realisation that this light was somehow different—devoid of colour or expression. It seemed that the wider world outside had sucked all the colour or complexion from this dreary conduit into the earth.

I continued downwards until I came to a series of broad steps set in a portentous archway between two large decayed doric colonnades. The steps turned a corner at about fifty feet. And I imagined I could hear the distant sound of clamouring voices and busyness. There was a little light and a waft of warm air which made me believe there was a railway above. I followed the steps and with each step downwards I seemed to settle deeper into oblivion. It was not that I was not afraid—but fear had settled into my body and bones like a fever. My nerves were so far stretched to the extremity of their tolerance that their sensitivity had deadened to an utter consuming weariness that I had never felt before.

As I progressed the fog seemed to thicken and the dampening darkness enveloped me. However, I began to detect, perhaps fifty paces ahead, the gleam of a light and, suddenly, I thought I heard a sound, like a slight cough. The outline of the gleam soon became clear to me. It was a lantern held by a man—a small man with lambchop sideboards. He was wearing a tight-fitting greyish tunic and held, in one hand, the lantern and, in the other, a bunch of large lumpish keys. He looked me up and down for a moment then turned and indicated a way ahead..

'Come along', he said, seemingly not surprised to see me.

I dumbly followed as he led me further into the fog. I followed on, not least because I could not discern any other way to go. Then, not very far on, I detected a shape appear from the mist. It was a large iron-banded oak door.

Hanging the lantern on a hook on the door, the man selected three of the keys and, inserting them into three separate keyholes in turn, unlocked the door which opened creakily.

'Follow behind me,' he said, 'I'll hold the light up high so you can see your way.'

I followed him as instructed and realized he was leading the way up a steep spiral staircase equipped with a brass banister that gleamed from the light of the lantern in a sinuous curve.

Eventually, we reached a platform at the top totally enclosed in, it seemed, a small circular chamber. He hung the lantern on a hook suspended from a chain. Ahead of us were five shuttered panels that consisted of the whole circumference of the room. Swivelling a catch on each he swung the shutters upwards letting a grey cold light, more twilight than daylight, flood into the chamber. In the distance I could see what seemed like identical boxes, open but with vertical bars in the direction facing us. In each, also facing us, was an almost identical figure, a man, it seemed, bare-footed but wearing coarse trews and a jacket of sackcloth. I could not discern any individual features and all stood stock still against the bars that contained them. This scene was repeated as I turned around the chamber, and I realised that, in fact, these cells, I guessed that there were about forty in all, formed a continuous circle around us and by turning my head, and then my whole body I could look directly into each of them.

I turned to the guide. He had taken a little clay pipe from his pocket and lit it with a Lucifer.

'Who are these people?' I asked.

'Oh, they are divers peoples,' he answered, 'but not worth your concern. Homicidals, Fraticidals, Aliens, Arabs, Costermongers who sold rotten fruit, Paupers, Buggerers of children, Jews, Usurers, Melancholics, Sodomites, Servants who thieved from their masters, Street urchins, Cut-throats, Counterfeiters, Chapmen, Resurrectionists, Poachers and Petermen, Gypsies. In short, a collection in motley of those who form the underbelly of our society—the great unwashed, unshriven hordes who reside beneath the cognisance of fine gentlemen like you and I.' He seemed to wink at me.

'But surely,' I argued, 'they are men like you and I. Why are they caged like this? Jesus said suffer all to come to me whether ye be sinners or no. Is it not the duty of gentlemen and gentlewomen to show mercy and compassion to such as these?'

He shook his head. 'You think that these are the only sinners we should take concern of? No, indeed. We would make room for the Fraudsters and Lechers if there were not too great a number of them. Most of the citizens of every city would be consigned to the underworld—journeymen, clerks, priests and even gentlemen like yourself.'

'But what of the law of England, and justice, compassion and charity—those precepts on which our civilised society is based?'

'Law? The law has precious little purchase down here.' He waved me away and turned to fixing his tunic in a disinterested way. 'I'm sure that you are right, sir. But, for myself, I have little time for conceits such as that. The way I see it is that sheep have to be sheared so that gentlemen have their fine woollen cloaks, cattle subject themselves to our mercy so that we can dine on roast beef, and these forsaken souls have given themselves up to serve the machinery that enables our superior society above the ground to function.'

'Machinery? What machinery are you referring to?'

'Oh, of course, you haven't worked the mechanicals yet.' He waved his hand at two wooden wheels with brass handles, one large and one smaller, that rose from a plinth in front of me. 'Well, help yourself,' he shrugged, 'My shift is over.' He turned to leave. 'Don't think that we are complete here, or very special. You know, we're just one little cog turning amongst all the others.'

Before I could question him further, he had left, scuttling down the spiral staircase.

In the enclosure I felt a heavy sweat running across my forehead and behind my ears and a sickness rose in my gorge. But my inclination to escape the compartment was equally weighed alongside my compulsion to discover the purpose of the wheeled mechanism.

Tentatively, I reached down and laid my hand on the small-handled wheel. I hesitated a minute, dizzily. A film formed before my eyes and for a moment I expected to faint. But the wheel slid round easily in my hand and, surprised at the simplicity of its purpose, I recovered my composure. The wheel served to turn the viewing compartment around a full circle—allowing me to observe, through the slatted windows before and behind me, all of the cells in turn.

Encouraged by the success of my first experiment I turned to the larger handle. It was heavier and, although there was some give, it took both my hands to start it moving. At first there seemed to be no reaction—then I realised that the creatures in each of the cells were beginning to shift. Slowly I began to perceive what was happening. As the mechanism was turning the walls and ceilings of each cell began to move—on some sort of crank, I presumed. The effect was for each cell, in a way, to collapse into its neighbour, proceeding round the circle like a pack of playing cards tipped over. So that, as the ceiling of one cell lowered, constricting the height, one wall moved out, constricting the width of the next and so on—so that, gradually, all the cells were becoming distortions of their original square proportions.

This was the cause of the frantic activity of the inhabitants of each cell. For, I soon realised, situated in each was a crankshaft similar to that in front of me. In each case, by turning as fast as they could, it seemed, they could reverse the distortion of the cells. Thus, working flat out, each could just maintain an equilibrium and not be crushed by the mechanism.

For a minute I almost laughed at the absurdity of the scene—

with each of its inhuman matchstick figures contorting itself to the whim of my manipulation—as a child might gape at ants stuck to a stick of sugar. I wondered at the strange term the man in the tunic had used—were the 'mechanicals' the machinery of the cells or their unwilling inhabitants?

I released the handles but by now the movement had such a momentum that it carried on alone. Releasing my grip I became giddy and grabbed onto the grid in front of me. I looked over my right shoulder for the handrail of the spiral staircase I had ascended, but it was not there. I looked up and detected the twisted shape of the wrought iron some yards above me. Clearly, what had happened was that the revolution of the capsule had either forced the structure upwards or carried me downwards—like a corer in an apple. Simultaneously, from below on either side of me, twisting closer, were two curved polished metal plates. These functioned like mirrors and in them were reflected the cells and their occupants, but now multiplied.

In a panic and in a deadly fear of being sucked further down into whatever inferno awaited me, I braced my feet against the lower wheel and grasped for the handrail, pulling my whole body upwards until the metal bit into my chin. For a few seconds my feet flailed in the air and my arms and fingers ached for release. I closed my eyes anticipating a fall into whatever horrors lay below.

But then, suddenly, I felt my feet on firm ground. Strangely, however, I did not now seem to be on a staircase but on flat ground. As I opened my eyes and they grew accustomed to the light, I realised that I was now at the end of a passageway surrounded by stone walls and cobbled similarly to the street I had first descended.

But as soon as I began to locate myself, the fog thickened and it seemed to grow darker again. All I could discern was that the best of the fading light seemed to come from around a corner to the left. I hastened to reach it before I was lost in oblivious darkness.

As I turned the corner I saw what at first looked like a ragged bundle of an urchin collapsed on the pavement! My inclination was to ignore it but my eyes were drawn towards it. Suddenly, with a horrifying shock of recognition that sent a sudden pulse to my brain, I realised that it was my Dorothea—but what seemed like an older much-travailed Dorothea with filthy lines etched on her face and an empty black slit where once was her pretty lips and mouth. She was dressed in only a ragged chemise and her feet were bare and toes bent inwards and ingrained with dirt and grit like a scivvy's. Impulsively. I leaned towards her, but then she turned her head only slightly towards me and her eyes, deep, yellowish and dead, stopped me.

More shocking, however, than her own condition, I now realized, was the bundle that she held cradled in her arms. As my eyes accustomed to the shadows it grew more plain. I saw that it was an infant suckling at her breast—fat and naked. It seemed to be a boy as it had a little stiff pego. It started to pee and turned its head from the breast, the pap fell loosely and a little milk squirted on to the baby's face which it licked greedily with a worm-like tongue around thin stretched lips. At this, Dorothea issued a deep sob and her eyelids closed.

Filled with an unutterably deep impulse to tenderness, I stretched down to touch her shoulder, but as I did so the scene seemed to recede from me and I was no longer where I had just been but instead facing a blackness that, from the sound of dripping and a dampness in the air seemed to be a leaking wall. Suddenly, I felt a hand on my shoulder and I spun round in a panic.

'Don't pay no attention to her, sir.' It was an older woman, fat and haggard, with lumps of misshapen flesh falling from her rouged face. The features were indistinct—but it could have been Mrs Merrilees or any respectable women somehow gone to seed. The clothes she wore were of a gentlewoman, but dirty and ill-fitting and in a macaroni mix.

'She has the manners of a Billingsgate fish-hag, that one. A clever cheese like yourself don't want nothing to do with her and her sort.'

Encountering my landlady, or at least a countenance of her, suddenly drew me to a partial recovery of my senses. Surely, I thought, these horrible sights cannot be real. I must be in my own bed, in a reverie.

The woman stretched a hand towards me and I instinctively shrunk back, but at that moment the whole scene in front of me suddenly dissolved into nothingness. I closed my eyes and then opened them again to find myself, sitting bolt upright, my heart pounding, in my bed in my rented room.

As I came to my senses, everything became more clear. I was in my nightshift, in my cot. My little oil lamp was lit at the desk at my side and I was holding in my hand the letter that I recently received from he who called himself Jeremy.

Panting and shaking, I focused my eyes on the lamp and then on the letter, dragging my mind back to reality from the horrors of my dream. The letter was as I had first read it, with its spidery hand in black ink. 'My dear Mr. Sherlock Holmes', it read:

I am reliably informed that you are the nonpareil of personal detectives.

I sincerely do hope that you will enjoy greater success than your counterparts at Scotland Yard. Their amateur and fumbling efforts have not improved since their abject failure with regard to the Whitechapel case. They have, of course, been subject to the ridicule of the press and have earned the contempt of the common folk. They are lost in the circle of which I am the centre.

Therefore, in respect of your superior facilities, I am writing to inform you that you will soon hear of the unfortunate fate of the Kilburn girl.

Thereupon and subsequent to further manifestations of signs of my intention, you will have the opportunity to pit your wits against mine.

Jeremy

But as I read the words, they seemed to dissolve in front of my eyes, as if the ink was seeping into the paper! Then, I suddenly perceived, the edges of the letter were aflame. I dropped it onto the bedclothes and they too began to burn. I reached for the water jug by my bed to extinguish it, but instead my hand bumped into the oil lamp. It fell to the ground and, within seconds, a roaring inferno seemed to envelop the room. I was trapped. Just as I was about to cry out in despair I heard a voice within me—though I could not be sure it was my own. 'God save me from this dream of death', it said.

I awoke! I was lying in my own bed, the bedclothes tangled around me. I was drenched in sweat. There were no flames. There was no letter—I had given it to Superintendent Ord two days previously. I rose and rushed to the window. It was partly frosted on this dull November morn, but after rising and pulling the curtain aside I could see the same damp pavements, yellow fog and dun-coloured horses beginning their rounds that told me I was still in this city, this London, in its waking glory.

Chapter Three

MOTH CIRCLES FLAME

Black winter happit Embro sair,
The haar deil-loupit doun the wynds,
Aa Scotland bleak wi grugous hayr,
An boggarts thrang in ilka mind.

Sydney Goodsir Smith

The loves we share with the city are often secret loves.

Albert Camus

The wind tousled my hair and slightly stung my morning eyes as I ascended the radical road below Salisbury Crags and gazed down on the city of Edinburgh in its waking glory. I was on the old volcanic plug known as Arthur's Seat almost in the centre of the expanded city. Above me the clouds were grey and gathering angrily. Below lay all the landmarks of the old city: Castlehill and the castle, the spine of the old town meandering down to Holyrood Palace, to the north the turret of the governor's house of the old Calton Jail and the monuments of Calton Hill. It was silent apart from the wind and I seemed alone on the hill, but on the main arteries going to and from the city centre, I could see and feel the busy whirr of cars and commuters streaming to work in the city's banks, offices and shops.

This was my third day in the United Kingdom since I had flown from Pittsburgh. I had often told my students who were preparing dissertations or theses that discovering nothing was an important part of research as it successfully narrowed down the avenues of exploration. However, I was rather disappointed that that was what I had discovered—precisely nothing. My first day in London had been pleasant enough. I liked the vicinity of the British Museum and Library. The tourists eager to see the Elgin Marbles and other treasures, the chestnut sellers with their mufflers and fingerless gloves in the street, the steamy heat and roasting smells providing little beacons in the tart cold of the winter, the little shops that sold books, maps and prints, antiquities and coins. I had a lunch of what the English call steak pudding in the busy and ornate Museum Tavern where Karl Marx once sat and drank and ate. The food was warm and filling and the beer had a full English nuttiness. It felt good. I could have stayed there for days taking in the atmosphere. I could have spent hours happily searching in the library for new avenues or byways in Romantic literature. However, I had set myself a specific task.

In the library itself, however, I had gained very little from a whole day's work. Yes, they had a copy of the Ledbury poems, identical to my own apart from the inscription. However, there were no other works attributed to John Ledbury. Enquiries in the manuscript department also drew a blank. I spent some time searching in the large heavy catalogues of pasted slips. I checked under 'counterfeit detective', I searched for poetry books or anthologies published in the same year, I looked for books from the same publisher. These included diverse items such as a collection of vignettes of Edinburgh with collotype illustrations, a book of woodcuts of old closes by Bruce Home and a history of John Knox's house, but no other poetry or anything relating to my quest. To reassure myself I checked again the book that Levy had referred me to, Cartwright's *Dictionary of Victorian Literary Biography*. But in this edition the entry on Ledbury merely stated 'Minor English poet'.

Frustrated, I determined that my next best step was to fly to Scotland where, of course, the book had been published. Because it was more convenient, firstly, I got a flight to Glasgow and searched in the Mitchell Library, the largest library in the country outside of the libraries of record, but found nothing new. Then I came to Edinburgh and tried the National Library of Scotland. The result was the same: each had an unannotated copy of the book, but nothing else relating to Ledbury in either the printed books or manuscript departments. I knew that research could lead to many fruitless conclusions but I was not prepared to run into a completely dead-end. Surely, I thought, with an emerging feeling of panic, there had to be something!

I had spent an uneasy night in an Edinburgh hotel and risen this morning to the stodgy Scottish breakfast of sausage, bacon, eggs and black pudding. To clear my head, I had walked up the hill. Now I was going to take the last opportunity I could think of to follow my quest—Coulthard, Knowles & Co, booksellers which, amazingly, still existed and traded in the West Port, now named Coulthard's Edinburgh Bookshop.

Wandering a little while I waited until the time that I knew antiquarian book shops usually opened—which wasn't particularly early, even for the British—I walked up and round the steep red rhyolite of Salisbury Crags, around and down into a sort of valley where the rocks gathered in a formation known as Samson's ribs— old rock with dolerite sills that the famous geologist James Hutton had studied in order to determine the age of the world.

The rock was hard and cold; the grass greyish-green and alternatively wet and springy or flattened and mud-caked. People had lived here once, secure on this hill with its viewpoints to detect intruders, they had farmed the hillside and built a church—St Anthony's Chapel—the ruins of which still remained. Although this was my second time in the city, I was familiar with quite a lot of it due to my father's library which included topography as well as literature. One strange thing I had read was that, over a hundred years ago, someone had looked behind a stone on the hill and found a cache of little carved wooden coffins with little carved people in them, like peg dolls. Nobody knew who had made them or what they were for but some think they were for witchcraft, others that they represented the victims of a serial killer. I was thinking of this and walking downwards when, almost by surprise, I found myself suddenly caught in a patch of morning mist, not like a summer mist, but a cold, slightly damp, clinging grey mass. For some reason I felt lost, then I remembered something, a passage from a book, an old book, I'd read about this place. I stared into the white space, expecting to see something, but there was nothing there but whiteness. Panicking a little, I decided to retreat the way I had come, gaining some height, and in minutes the mist was gone.

I descended a steep path down to the Pollock Hall, then cut down through the University and George Square. The walls were redolent with history recorded in plaques to city notables or events: the authoress of *The Flowers of the Forest*, the birthplace of the *Edinburgh Review*, the houses of Sir Walter Scott and Lord Braxfield, the hanging judge. Then I cut down by Heriot's Hospital, now a school, and right to take a lane and steps by the old Flodden Wall, a surviving part of the wall that once demarcated the limits of the city and kept out intruders. It was pitted and uneven, but it was still there. Then I turned into the West Port, a winding street named after the most westerly gate and entrance to the old walled city.

The bookshop had a double fronted aspect with the entrance between the two windows. There were a variety of items on display: books, maps, sheets of music, a viola, a case of some stuffed birds, a diorama of a white stoat. My eye was immediately caught, however, by one item—a small hardback book amongst others on a little shelf in the right hand window.

When I entered the shop a little bell tinkled. There was a desk immediately right of the entrance and there sat a young woman. She was sitting in front of a single element electric fire, presumably as some protection against the chill of the day. She wore a chunky mohair jumper. A voluminous neck tie buffered her chin and the cuffs covered most of her hands, but her fingers featured longish nails painted a deep red. Her hands held a steaming cup of black coffee and beside her was an ashtray with a tartan emblem and the logo of the Scottish brewers Wm McEwan and a half-smoked cigarette. A book was in front of her, open and face down on the table. It was a Penguin edition of *Madame Bovary*. Her hair was straight, shoulder-length and auburn and her eyes were partly hidden behind large round spectacles but when she looked at me and smiled, I could see she was pretty.

I indicated the book in the window and she retrieved it for me. It was a early edition of a book by James Hogg which was titled *The Suicide's Grave*. A hardback in half leather with marbled boards, dated 1895.

She checked the pencilled price in the front cover and then looked at me. 'It's twenty-five pounds, I'm afraid,' she said. 'We haven't had it in long. It's a nice book...' She handed it to me.

'Yes,' I said, 'you might know it. It's better known as *The Private Memoirs and Confessions Of A Justified Sinner.*'

She thought for a moment. 'I think I've heard of it,' she said. 'It was mentioned in our Scottish literature course when we did Scott and Stevenson and Galt. But I haven't read it. I don't have time at the moment. I've too much reading of my own to do.' She smiled.

'You're a student of literature?' I enquired.

'Yes,' she replied, 'I'm doing a PhD at the University.'

'I teach literature,' I said. I took out my wallet and gave her my card. Then I counted out five five pound notes and gave them to her also. She seemed pleased to receive both.

She put the card in a little address book on the desk. 'You're an American professor!' she said and smiled quite broadly. She had nice white teeth and her lipstick was subtle, not gauche, red.

'I am, I'm afraid.' I smiled back. 'Just over here to do some work.' She tore off a till receipt and put the book into a paper bag. 'But tell me about your research. I'd be interested.'

'Ach, it's nothing much. It's about the fallen woman in Victorian literature. I've just started really. I've been reading Dickens and

Gaskell and Eliot and Hardy. But then I started reading some French stuff. I did French too.'

'And are there many fallen women in French literature?'

'A great many!' She grinned. 'But they're not as puritanical about it as the British. They classified all the different types of prostitutes—the poorest they described as 'carrying a basket'.'

I looked puzzled.

'To stand in,' she said, 'when they were working in muddy and shitty places.'

She put out her cigarette and took a sip of her coffee. 'But I must be boring you, it's not everybody's cup of tea…'

'You're not boring me at all,' I assured her. 'I could talk about English literature all day. It's what I do.'

'I know,' she said, 'but you must be on holiday. It's nearly Christmas. The university term's over.'

'Well, I'm not on holiday, actually. Not yet anyway. I'm doing some research into a book.' I took the Ledbury book out of my pocket and showed her it and the bookshop sticker.

'It's a long time before my time!' She laughed. But maybe Mr Coulthard will know something about it.'

'Coulthard? Is the shop still in the family then?'

She smiled. 'Well, you could say that. Mr Coulthard set up the shop. A long time ago. He's well into his nineties now.'

I was astonished. 'And he still comes here?'

'Near enough every day. Three o'clock. On the button!'

I had a walk around the Grassmarket and stopped for a drink in The White Hart Inn, named after a fantastic vision of a deer and a holy cross—rood—that had appeared in Holyrood Park to

King David. I had a pint of McEwan's eighty shilling ale, dark and sweet. This was where Robert Burns used to stay—his portrait was above where I was sitting. It was the very dark heart of old Edinburgh. Further up the road was the gallows where felons were dispatched to eternity and a little further up the site of the stakes where witches were burned. Walter Scott had set the opening of his *Heart of Midlothian* here, and here the resurrectionists had plied their trade—supplying freshly buried corpses for the anatomists.

The pub smelled of stale beer and burnt toast from the kitchen. I sat at a wobbly three-legged table. There were various caricatures of old Edinburgh citizens on the walls of the pub. Two stood out—William Burke and William Hare. Burke and Hare had lodged in the West Port and had circumvented the task of digging up graves by murdering innocent people to sell to the anatomists. Sixteen people, it was reckoned. Sixteen peg dolls in sixteen coffins. I shivered, Perhaps this city was just too old for me.

So there I sat, amongst the heavy burden of literature and history until it was nearly three o'clock.

As I turned the bend by another pub called the Fiddler's Arms and walked up the street, I looked up towards the shop and saw an old man in a gaberdine coat and a tweed cap with a stick entering the shop. Could this be Coulthard?

When I opened the door I saw Amelia standing, gazing at a small staircase at the back of the shop.

'Oh.' She seemed surprised, maybe disconcerted. 'I gave him your card and told him what you wanted. He just went straight down to his office… '

I descended the few steps. I first saw his face in a mirror against the rear wall as he had his back turned to me. Coulthard looked old, almost impossibly old. His face was lined with deep creases that seemed like dark crevices in some ancient landscape. His eyes were dark but dull in sunken sockets and seemed a little too close together. Only his mouth seemed more bright and lively, his lips quite small and pursed, almost ladylike.

'Mr Coulthard?' I said.

He turned round, clearly startled at the mention of his name. As he did so, a book and a sheaf of papers fell from his hands. I stepped forward and picked them from the ground bundling the loose papers together. He leaned forward and almost snatched them from me with a surprising agility. His fingers were long and bony, his fingernails broken and dirty. He opened his mouth as if to say something but nothing came and he bent down to put the items in the bottom drawer of the desk.

'Amelia. Your assistant,' I said. 'She said you might be able to help me with some research I'm doing, into a minor poet called John Ledbury.'

He looked me up and down in a strange way

'Yes,' he said. 'She gave me your card, Professor...' His lips quivered and he looked frightened. '...Nowell.' He seemed to have some difficulty saying my name and almost spat it out as if it were the name of the Devil himself. 'John Ledbury... '

'I'm interested in a book he published.' I took out the volume from my inside jacket pocket. 'It has a sticker from your shop.'

He looked at me but didn't seem to want to look at the book, instead he seemed distracted by my business card which lay on his desk.

He shook his head. 'That was a long, long time ago,' he said. 'We have no records of that time. None at all.' He continued to shake his head and didn't seem able to stop.

'Well, maybe you have come across his name or some other works by him?' I asked.

He stopped the almost involuntary movements of his head but his whole body seemed to start shaking a little

'I know nothing about it,' he said. 'I really can't help at all.'

He looked upstairs. 'If you ask my assistant,' he said in a trembling voice, 'she will give you a printed guide to Edinburgh booksellers.' He pointed with a bony finger which I took as a clear indication that he wished me to leave. 'Perhaps Blackwood's or Thin's can help,' he said. 'She can direct you there.' He looked down at the floor as if he couldn't bear to face me. I was clearly dismissed and I had no choice but to leave.

After I had exchanged a few pleasantries with Amelia, wishing her well with her thesis, I left. I was puzzled as to why the old man seemed so afraid. I thought about it as I walked down the road and flung the directory in the waste bin.

I had no need of Blackwoods or Thin's. I had only glimpsed the papers that Coulthard had dropped briefly, but long enough to see that they constituted a holograph manuscript and that the top page read in large looping handwriting 'Poems, &c, John Ledbury'!

I wandered around the streets for a while, confused, trying to formulate a course of action. Coulthard was not going to talk to me unless under duress. He had markedly flinched even when I came near him! What could I do? I could abandon my quest, go home, meet the Vice-Provost and learn what he had to say. But there were various reasons why that could not happen, and why would I come so far on a seemingly insane quest and then abandon it. It wouldn't make sense. No, in some way, I had to get hold of that manuscript and that book. And so, after a little while, I came upon a half-baked plan that, even then, I realised, could go badly wrong.

I had a coffee in a cafe in Forrest Road and then went into a fish and chip shop in the Grassmarket and bought an *Evening News* and some British cigarettes. As six approached I stood surreptitiously at a corner about one hundred yards from Coulthard's, smoking and pretending to study the pages of the paper. It was a chilly evening, already dark in Edinburgh, and I fastened the buttons of my overcoat to protect me from the gusting wind. I shifted my position a couple of times, but the burgeoning Edinburgh winter wind was persistent and annoying. Fortunately, however, two minutes after six, the lights in the shop were dimmed. Amelia came out, wearing her woolly jumper and a hooded anorak and carrying a knapsack. She locked the door of the shop and then the grille at the front, turned right and walked down the road. I followed at a distance. However, she didn't go very far. Only a few hundred yards down the road she turned and entered a small public house on the corner called the Western Bar.

The facade was unprepossessing, but there was a sort of theme. The 'WESTERN' was surrounded by a logo of two horseshoes. Underneath it said in plain large painted letters 'GO-GO'

I hesitated, looked up and down the street and then entered the pub.

The Western Bar was a pretty plain sort of place. There were a few basic tables around the fringes but nearly everyone was standing and everyone in the pub was male—small knots of men of all ages, standing and holding pints of beer. I squeezed in at the end of the bar and ordered a pint of lager. The barman poured a frothy beer in a straight-sided pint glass and gave me my change. He nodded towards a small stage at the extreme end of the bar.

'The dancer will be on in a minute,' he said.

I wriggled my way into a reasonable space at the back of the bar and, indeed, after a couple of minutes some lights came on at the little stage and a multi-faceted disco-style globe on the ceiling began to rotate. The music began—a contemporary hit song: 'Stuck in the Middle With You', by Stealer's Wheel.

And then a girl stepped up on to the stage. She was dressed in a leather cowboy jacket with strips of brown leather hanging down from it and a short leather skirt fastened at the top left with a buckle. Her feet were bare and her toenails were painted the same deep dark red as her fingernails. Her lips too, were rouged and went well with her red hair and her deep dark eyes. She looked quite different from when I had last seen her, but it was Amelia.

She began to dance, slowly at first, in phase with the music, each beat seeming to summon a slight jerk of the body, mesmerising but not too abrupt to disrupt the continuity. In between the beats, she unfastened the toggles on her jacket, then with one hand, removed it from her shoulder and, a moment later, with the other hand, flicked it off and threw it on the floor. Now you could see her breasts, still cocooned in a tight black bra, gyrate as she began to spin round more quickly in time with the music, building up a pace to the accompaniment of the beat until, next, she unfastened her little skirt and, with a flip of her wrist, it was gone too. Now she was dancing in just a bra and panties, leaning forwards with the tempo of the music to show her full cleavage. Then before it was obvious, she put her hand behind her and in a second her panties were gone. Only, however, to reveal a slight spangly g-string.

Now she began to dance more slowly and sinuously, her arms raised in the air seemed to create a wave effect that moved downwards to be replicated in her leg, and then again the same on the other side. Then she reached behind her back and unfastened her bra. She continued dancing for a while while it hung loose. Then she turned her back to the crowd and removed the strap from one shoulder, and then the next, and then dancing slowly, facing forward to the crowd until her bra slipped down and she only barely covered her breasts with one hand, the thumb and the forefinger on her nipples.

Then, on the beat of the song, she pulled her hand slowly away, exposing her full breasts and then danced for a while, directly looking into the faces of the onlookers and smiling until the act was over and she slipped off into a back room.

The faces of the onlookers had remained largely expressionless throughout. Now some chatter and drinking recommenced.

I found a space on a stool in the corner of the bar near the window and hid myself behind my crumpled newspaper, playing incognito again. Eventually, Amelia came out and left the bar, waving to the barman and exchanging a couple of words with the man at the door. I left behind her, crossed the road and walked speedily and directly down the other side of the road, hoping she wouldn't see me. When I was far enough ahead I crossed the road diagonally so that I would cross paths with her.

'Amelia!' I said, 'what a pleasant surprise to see you.' She stopped and looked directly at me.

'Dr Nowell', she said, 'Are you still out?' Her face wrinkled a little in either a frown or a smile. 'I hope you haven't forgotten your book.'

I patted the inside pocket of my overcoat. 'No, just been taking in a bit of the city.'

'I see,' she said and paused and then she asked 'and did you enjoy my dance?'

I must have looked embarrassed as she laughed a little. 'Are your American students really so unobservant,' she said.

I hesitated a moment. 'Do you think', I said, 'that we could go somewhere for a drink, or a coffee? For a chat.' I smiled, 'I'm keen to hear more about your work.'

She gave me an appraising look and looked up and down the street, pausing for a moment, reflectively.

She turned to the right. 'I live just down this street here', she said. 'Come up and I'll make you a coffee.'

We went into a close a block down. Amelia lived on the top floor, so we ascended a winding staircase; stone steps worn in the middle from a century and more of human traffic. She opened the door which had a total of three locks on it and, when we had entered, turned the key in the mortice lock, leaving the bundle of keys in the door.

It was a small flat, what is sometimes called a room and kitchen, in a Scottish tenement. That is, two rooms separated by a corridor with a bed alcove in each. My father had told me he had lived in a similar flat in Kirkcaldy. One room had the effects of a kitchen with a hob and a Belfast sink. Off the corridor, what had maybe been a cupboard had been reconstructed as a small toilet and shower room. It was sparsely but adequately furnished. Amelia took off her jumper and draped it over a small settee. She was wearing a red blouse that went with the colour of her hair loosely over a T-shirt. She struck a Bluebell match which lit with a slightly sulphurous odour and used it to light a gas fire and the gas hob. She filled a kettle and put it on the hob. She took a cigarette from a packet and lit it on the naked flame. She offered me one but I declined.

I looked out of the window, the flat had a magnificent view of the castle. The grey bulk was silhouetted against a sky of deep dark blue that was typical of the Edinburgh winter. There was the sharp curve of a scimitar moon and the yellow neon streetlamps, their lights haloed a little in a slight haar, gave the view a ghostly look. It had a sort of sparse beauty.

Amelia gave me a steaming mug of coffee and from a shelf took two glasses and a bottle of scotch. 'Aberlour malt whisky. Is that OK?' she said. 'Aberlour, it's the little village I'm from. Up north. My names's Gammack, it's a local name. The whisky is made from water from a spring the monks discovered in the thirteenth century.'

She poured a dram in either glass. Before I could drink it she took the glass from me and held it under the tap. 'Just a drop of water', she said, 'to bring out the flavour. Not ice, like you Americans put into your scotch.'

I smiled, tried the nose of the whisky and felt the taste on my tongue. 'Do you live here alone?' I asked.

'Most students share,' she said, 'but I prefer to be on my own. I must be the solitary type.' She smiled. 'It's a bit more expensive,' she added.

'So that's why you have two jobs.'

'Yes,' she said and looked me in the face almost defiantly. 'I need the money. I can dance, and I have a nice figure... '

I wasn't sure if this was a statement or a question. I said nothing but looked her in the eyes.

She seemed disconcerted. She looked down, away from me. 'And I like it,' she said, then almost sotto voce, 'I like the men... the men looking at me... '

I ran my fingers through her hair and gently down her neck and kissed her on her sweet wet mouth.

She raised her arms above her head compliantly and I peeled off her blouse and t-shirt. She wasn't wearing a bra. I felt the weight of her full breasts in my hands, touching the tips of her erect nipples just and no more with my thumbs, then with the tip of my tongue.

Then I took them in my mouth, rolled my tongue round them and tugged them a little between my teeth. Amelia gasped and then moaned a little.

As I walked back along the street in the chilly but clear night, I could hear in the distance some sounds of revellers making their way home after the pubs had shut. I felt in my pocket. The keys to Coulthard's bookshop were there. I felt guilty. Amelia was a nice enough girl. I didn't want her to get the blame, but I had taken the keys from the keyhole in the door as she lay sleeping. My initial plan had been to go back and put the keys through her letterbox, but now I wasn't sure if it would be auspicious to return them. Alternatively, I thought, I could leave the bookshop grille unlocked and the keys in the door. It would be careless but not culpable and unlikely to be discovered until the next morning.

I stopped at the corner to scan the street, but there didn't seem to be anyone about. So I walked up to the shop door and without hesitating put the key in the keyhole, opened the door and walked in. As soon as I entered, I realised that something was not quite right. Amelia had also locked the grille at the entrance when she left but it was unlocked now. However, It was too late to abandon my plan.

I had tried to memorise the layout of the shop but I still found myself kicking some piles of books on the floor. I edged round and felt my way to the staircase and fingered the banister. Slowly I felt my way down the stairs in the dark, but, as I turned the corner, I was surprised to see that there was some light, as if from a desk lamp. I hesitated, but I couldn't go back. I took the last step and turned right.

Seated at the desk in front of the glazed bookcase was Coulthard holding a book in his hands and staring straight at me. Some times in life things suddenly surprise, even shock you. I moved forward and took the book from his stiff hands. The binding was in shreds, but the front card had written on it (in the same pen and hand as the inscription on the poems) 'John Ledbury; notebook'.

Suddenly I froze. There was a sound. Then I saw a flickering shadow. It was only a moth fluttering in the shade of the light.

There was no doubt that Coulthard was dead. His hands, in his fingerless gloves, were cold. He looked peaceful enough. There was no sign that anything had caused his death other than old age, passing away at his desk, among the books that had shaped his life. I took a handkerchief from my pocket and, with my thumb and forefinger, closed his eyes. Something about him reminded me of my father on his deathbed.

The small hotel I had booked into in Manor Place at the West End was dark apart from a hall light when I returned. I had a latch key. In my room I switched on the bedside light. There was no mini-bar, but a small electric kettle and cups allowed me to make myself a black coffee. I sucked in the caffeine and, for a moment, my hands beginning to shake, I had to steady myself and breathe deeply. In a matter of a few days, I had transported myself into a world unfamiliar to me. Once my mind had settled and I felt some warmth seep into me—the British, I had discovered, were economical in their heating of hotel bedrooms even in winter—I lay in bed and, with an eagerness tempered by trepidation, opened the diaries of John Ledbury.

I had experience of reading manuscripts of this period and soon became accustomed to the small, but neat and regular, handwriting. The first section, evoking a sort of Dickensian London, at first puzzled me. Also a reference to a 'Mr Holmes' led me to believe that it was some kind of fiction—perhaps inspired by Ledbury's work for Conan Doyle. The gist then became stranger and I was nonplussed until I read on and realised that what was being recounted was a dream or a vision!

I put down the book and rubbed my tiring eyes. It had been a long day and much had happened, not much of which I had planned. I wanted to carry on reading the diaries, but my academic instincts held me up. I needed to read the text more deeply, refuse to suspend my disbelief, evaluate each section of the text before I moved on so that I would genuinely follow the sequence of the narrative as an informed, not a casual, reader. I found a notebook in my favourite old briefcase that I had brought with me and a pen and I turned to the first page to start again. But then, in my tiredness, I felt the dead weight of sleep...

I shook myself awake and reached, without opening my eyes, for the little bedside lamp which always sat beside me at my home in Pittsburgh. But instead of its comforting grasp my hand brushed against something of glass and metal, and it fell to the floor, breaking with a crash. Panicking, I jumped out of bed, the thick covers almost trapping my legs until I was stumbling, kicking myself free across to the washhand basin on the opposite wall. I forced my eyes to open wider in the gloom and braced my hands against the mirror, but there was no strip light, the accessories from my travel bag were gone, the mirror was cracked and the frame all awry.

And then I saw reflected a reddish glow and turned to see flames licking around my bed from an oil lamp I had overturned. As I gazed, gripped in motionless terror, the bed itself seemed to float away from me and, simultaneously, I saw myself lying, arched and contorted as if in the throes of death itself.

Inside myself I said 'God deliver me from this dream of death.' I tried to feel my hands, my legs, my eyelids which were numb, imprisoning me. Somehow, straining every nerve, I pushed and pushed, and, just as I thought I had sunk too far into the dreadful reverie, I broke through the barrier of sleep, and awoke, sweating, and clutching the light sodden quilt of the hotel bed, slowly ebbing back into consciousness until my breath was regular and I was delivered safely to the waking world. It was still dark and the quietness told me that it was not yet morning.

I had fallen asleep still reading the first part of the Ledbury diaries! Obviously, in my heightened emotional sense I had replicated the dream in part that Ledbury had recounted. Once again, as on the plane, it seemed that reading the words of John Ledbury had seeped from my conscious through to my subconscious mind.

And a little time later, having felt my way back into the comforts of the modern world, I doused my face with water, made myself a black coffee with two sugars and switched on the bedside radio at its lowest volume to ensure I wasn't alone, and I sat up in my bedclothes and began to read the rest of the manuscript of the Counterfeit Detective. It began 'Arthur Conan Doyle had left to serve his country in the African war and Sherlock Holmes had been assumed dead for seven years, lost in the Reichenbach Falls… '

Chapter Four

THE EROTOMANIAC

O, dreadful is the check—intense the agony—
When the ear begins to hear and the eye begins to see;
When the pulse begins to throb, the brain to think again;
The soul to feel the flesh, and the flesh to feel the chain.

Emily Brontë

Through the corpse of the victim, the murderer establishes a kind of connection with the investigators.

Donato Carrisi, *The Whisperer*

Arthur Conan Doyle had left to serve his country in the African war and Sherlock Holmes had been assumed dead for seven years, lost in the Reichenbach Falls, and yet the letters still arrived in a steady flow, mostly querying the circumstances of Holmes's death, some asking for his help, others just expressing their appreciation of the stories. My job, on behalf of the publishers, was to study them for any indication of the public reaction to the stories that would be useful to them and, usually, to write short letters in reply, in the name of Holmes, assuring the readers that he was not, in fact, deceased and would return soon. That time, I understood, would be as soon as his agent could persuade Doyle to write another Holmes story.

Some letters were odder than others, such as the letter from Jeremy. It had always occurred to me that I might actually receive letters from real-life criminals, or even a veritable Moriarty! The reference to the Kilburn girl had provided that moment. Only a day previously I had read in the *Evening Standard* that the Metropolitan Police were seeking any information on the disappearance of a young lady in Kilburn one week earlier.

At first my approach to the local police office had seemed to meet with little interest, but somehow, it had filtered upwards to someone of importance. An officer had called the previous day to collect all the letters and notes I had still in my possession. Today, having made a careful toilet and sipped some weak tea to recover from my dream—I had refused my usual practice of breakfasting with Bill Bartholomew, Mrs Merrilees's other lodger—I was awaiting a call from Chief Superintendant Robert Ord, of the Metropolitan Police, who was to question me.

I suppose that I was excited and curious, but the situation had also created for me a dilemma or, to be honest, a greater dilemma than I had already been facing. The income I made from the Holmes correspondence had been little enough, but without it I would only have the pittance I made from fillers for a few magazines, and that would scarcely pay my rent. I had promised Dorothea that I would come to the big city to work, to succeed—to achieve more than I ever could in the little parish of Godalming—but that had not yet happened.

I was not quite desperate, but, three days earlier I had answered a small advertisement in the *Times*. 'Capable writer required,' it had said. 'Able to write on instruction for gentlemen in divers styles.'

A response to my application had come almost immediately and, since the address was nearby, I had walked round to 46 Bedford Place which was an imposing terrace from the early part of the last century. A butler had answered the doorbell.

'Mr Ledbury?' he enquired.

'Yes.'

'The family rooms are downstairs. Please follow me upstairs to the library. Mr Ashbee will join you shortly.'

The furnishings downstairs were elaborate but a little fusty and weary in tone. The library, however, was superb. Well lit with large case windows to one wall, three walls consisting of magnificent glazed bookcases, polished mahogany and gleaming brass. The books therein mostly looked old and expensive, bound in full leather, morocco, calf or vellum. Each wall had its own set of library steps. Towards the centre of the room was a large walnut librarian's desk. On it, almost out of place among these antiquities, was a new Remington Type-Writer. To one side was some writing paper and a quill, to the other a wooden tidy or tray with the inscription 'cataloguing'. A few more modern books lay in it. I noticed the top one was a slight new book or pamphlet with the titles on the paper slip cover: 'The Horn Book: a Girl's Guide to the Knowledge of Good and Evil; 1900.'

Ashbee was some time in greeting me—I realised later that this was probably deliberate—so that I had a chance to peruse the books in his library. One whole section was devoted to editions, of all sorts and in all languages, of *Don Quixote* and biographies or commentaries on the work of Cervantes.

Most of the rest of the library, however, was devoted to a great many books from different origins—Abbé Boileau. *Histoire des Flagellans,* de Sade, *Journées de Sodome,* Millot, *Escole des Filles,* Bienville, *La Nymphomanie,* Fabritii, *Origine delle volgari proverbi,* Tottell, *The Court of Venus, or Boke of Balettes,* Berkley, *Correspondence,* Burton, *The Perfumed Garden,* The Empress of Asturia, *Modern Sappho*—the contents of which I was not familiar with but the nature of which I was quite sure of. They were salacious!

I was still looking when I heard a soft footfall behind me. Henry Spencer Ashbee was a man perhaps in his early sixties and a little turned to fat, but he was broad-shouldered with a steady upright stance. He was full bearded and his face was a little jowly and his eyelids droopy, but his large-featured face and his manner invoked authority.

'Mr Ledbury.' He shook hands briskly and formally. 'I see that you have had a chance to look at my library.'

'It is very impressive,' I said.

'There are items here which are very rare and sought after. There is the first edition of *El ingenioso hidalgo don Quijote de la Mancha* of 1605 with an inscription by the author. There is a copy of Poggio's *Facetarum liber* of 1470, the only copy to survive the Inquisition... ' He spread his arm as if inviting me to savour these literary treasures.

'It is a very fine collection,' I said.

'It is the culmination of a life's work. Or not quite the culmination,' I should say, 'there are still sundry volumes I would like to possess.' He beckoned me to take a chair at a large desk on which sat a few piles of volumes of books.

'But they are extremely difficult to obtain,' he added.

There was a brief silence. 'I believe that you have work for a writer?' I enquired.

'Business is sufficient, but, as I said, these materials are very rare and seeking them out is very expensive. So I supplement and support my activities by some writing when I am at home in London.'

I must have looked a little quizzical at this point as he took a moment to look at me more closely. 'I can see that you are a shrewd young man and I suspect you are asking yourself why an ageing man like myself is working so hard in pursuit of what you may think of as a little peccadillo.'

'I think your collection is admirable,' I said. 'I too, love books, but it must be a considerable expense of time and effort for you to maintain this... and you have a business and a family.'

'It is a fact that I am getting old and that my health is not at its best. But I have made arrangements for my collection, you see. The British Museum has agreed to take them for its library. My business and my family will continue with their ways when I am gone, but I also want to leave something for the nation.'

At this point, I saw something strange, almost contradictory in him, as if there were two men in the same body. The overall impression was of someone weary, with a burden still to bear although beset by age and ill health, but also there was a bright gleam deep in his eyes, of someone still in love with his unfinished project.

'So, you will see,' he continued, 'between my collecting, keeping my diaries and business and other adventures, I cannot satisfy the demand for the product that enables me to do what I do.

'I write material for gentlemen. Material that they require but of which there is not currently enough in print—although there is already, in fact, a great deal more than most people know of! It is well paid work, but requires a certain imagination and aptitude.' He emphasised the last word.

'I could explain further. However, it is simpler if I show you a short sample of a piece I am currently completing for a very eminent client indeed. I will show you two pages but there is a great deal more of the same.'

I took the pages in my hand and read them. They were clearly typed and well spaced and remarkably easy to read:

Niches in the dark cavernous walls contained church candles but the main source of light in the cellar was a blazing coal fire in the centre of the wall farthest from the door. In front of it the girl was fastened to the whipping stool, her feet fixed in stirrups that held her legs apart so that the little golden hairs and pink slit of her quim were visible. She was completely naked. Her hands were tied together behind her back and held by a hook from above that forced her body forward. However, her long blond hair was tied with a cord that, in turn, was pulled back and tied to the hook so that her head was held up and she could see directly ahead to the wall and the fire in front of her. A leather gag had been forced between her teeth and tied around her neck so she could not speak. Her bosom hung loose and sweat trickled down her body and dripped from the long red tips of her breasts.

The mistress was dressed in stockings with suspenders and a tight black corset. Around her neck she wore a silver chain. She approached the girl and kissed her gently on both cheeks.

Delicately, she ran the tip of a riding crop round the back of her long neck, across her shoulder and down to the nipples of her hanging breasts. 'Welcome to the house of pleasure...' she said '... and of pain.'

'Do not worry. We will begin soon. First you will be beaten on the buttocks and the soft insides of your thighs. The pace will be slow but regular and there may be some intervals. I will undertake to do this but the three gentlemen who are here for this meeting may join in.' The girl's eyes shifted. 'Oh, yes, they are here now, watching. You will not see them, even though they will possess you completely.

'How long will it last? It will last much longer than you can bear it. But you *will* bear it. I will decide to stop when your body has felt completely sated, full. When there will be no point in continuing as continuing would have no further effect. It will be a feeling you will have never had before. I can assure you of that.'

She walked round to the front of the girl so she was directly in front of her face.

'Of course, that is what you are here for, is it not?'

'Well, in a moment we will begin, slowly at first. As we proceed, remember that you have chosen to be here, as I have. Tomorrow you may take my place, and I yours...'

I looked up at Ashbee. I didn't know what to say.

He smiled. 'There are, of course, many different themes, sapphic, uranian, coprological... in fact, just about all the varieties of amatory prose that you can imagine,' he smiled again, 'and perhaps some that you can't.'

I didn't know whether I should express outrage or ignorance. Instead I just said, 'But I have no experience of these things.'

He gave a little snort. 'Experience isn't necessary, only imagination. I am old enough to be able to tell you with authority that the vast majority of what is reported as amatory experiences between men and women owes a great deal more to imagination than experimentation.'

'But I don't think that makes it *right*!' I said. I somehow felt obliged to express some indignation. 'It isn't decent and Christian.'

He frowned a little. 'I would not have decided to talk with you,' he said, 'if it were not the case that some of the samples of your work I have seen indicate to me that you have the correct *aptitude*. Also, I can assure you that the clients for this work that I do are among the most decent and Christian gentlemen in the country.'

'I'm afraid that you are completely wrong, Mr Ashbee,' I said. 'I don't think I would have any skill at this at all. And this is just not what I am intent upon writing.'

Ashbee looked at me with a little smile in an almost paternal way. 'Please think about it for a while. There is such a sufficiency of material required that I wouldn't need to ask you to do anything that you would find too, let us say, distasteful.'

'You have been very courteous,' I said, 'and I will consider what you have said, but I can assure you my answer will be the same.'

'Very well.' He called for the butler to show me out and shook hands heartily, seemingly unoffended by the point I had made about the writing.

'I wish you the very best with your writing, Mr Ledbury.' He came to the library door. 'But I will tell you that I leave for Paris in a week. I need someone to start immediately and I will pay in advance.'

As I sat and waited for Superintendant Ord, I pondered. The prospect of immediate payment from Ashbee, I can't deny, was attractive. I had scant savings left and very little expected income. Yet, I could not accept such work. What would Dorothea have thought? The answer to my problem, I felt, was in crime. Since the Whitechapel murders the public could not read enough about it. If, perhaps, I could learn more of the investigative methods employed by the police, I could write a series of factual articles, or even fiction, but of a higher standard than the mere penny dreadful.

I had not yet met Superintendant Ord in person, but I had spoken to him on the candlestick telephone at the police station. Unlike my expectation of a police officer, which was of someone who was officious, even intimidating, Ord seemed personable and put me immediately at ease. I realised later that it was his habitual manner when meeting someone for the first time and that, when a degree of intimacy was accepted, he could then get most people to cooperate as fully as possible. As I was to discover later when I spoke to the desk sergeant, Ord was a Scotsman from Perthshire in origin and still maintained the bluff congeniality of that breed— but he had long been in the capital and his manner and dialect were cosmopolitan.

After a while, there was a knock at the door. I answered it to a coachman who requested that I join Superintendant Ord in his brougham, as there was an appointment to meet. I fetched my coat and spoke briefly to Mrs Merrilees (I had informed her of my appointment with the Metropolitan Police in basic terms and she seemed quite excited by it all—if a murder victim had suddenly appeared in her parlour, I thought, she would have been delighted!)

When I entered the carriage, I was surprised to see that there were two occupants—Ord and a young lady. He beckoned for me to sit on the foldaway seat facing him.

Ord made the usual preliminary greetings. 'I apologise, Mr Ledbury, but I am rather behind myself today. This is my daughter, Isabella, and I must drop her at an engagement before I can speak to you at the Yard.'

Ord's daughter was of no more than medium height with a slender waist but a fully-formed bosom. Her long neck was accentuated by a broad steep collar of mauve velvet and her hair was auburn, thick and luscious piled up in the pompadour style with a few locks hanging around her ears. She wore a broad-brimmed hat. She had appealing big quite dark blue eyes, some little freckles on her cheek and a smallish mouth with pink lips. For a moment I thought she was like a little girl dressed as a woman.

'Good morning, Mr Ledbury,' she said, and offered me a delicate little hand in a white satin glove. 'I told father I could get a hansom cab, but he wouldn't let me.' She smiled. 'I'm going to the lecture at the Galton Institute.'

'Isabella is a student at Bedford College.' Ord said, 'She wants to go into business.' He frowned a little and Isabella looked sideways at him and smiled. Then, surprisingly she leaned forward towards me and had, for a moment, to put her hand on my knee to steady herself.

'Father,' she said, 'is a bit *old world*. He doesn't really think a woman should be allowed to read a book or smoke a cigarette!' Ord looked slightly embarrassed.

'But,' she added, 'he will let me do what I want.'

'Och,' said Ord, sounding more Scottish than before, 'she will be the death of me.'

I was slightly distracted as, while he was speaking, I became aware of a young man running alongside the carriage.

Ord hadn't noticed. He turned towards me and said in a

conspiratorial way, 'Her poor mother died when she was wee.' For a hardened police officer, his sensitive side seemed to have suddenly surfaced.

The coach suddenly came to a halt.

'Are we here?' asked Isabella.

Ord opened the door.

'No,' he said, 'the carriage has been halted by a messenger boy.' It was the young man who had been running alongside. Ord alighted, exchanged a few words with him and was given a small folded sheet of paper which he opened and read. He nodded a little as if the contents did not come as a surprise to him.

'Mr Ledbury,' he said, 'I must apologise. Something has occurred. I cannot continue our engagement at this time. I will instruct the driver to take you home after my daughter finds her engagement.'

'Father,' said Isabella, 'you cannot send Mr Ledbury home just like that. It is obvious. He must come to the lecture with me! He will enjoy it.'

She turned towards me and smiled. 'You *will* come, won't you.' Looking into her wide blue eyes I realised why her father would let her do just what she wanted.

The lecture hall at the Institute consisted of about 200 seats arranged in a curve with two aisles. It was mostly full, but an usher directed us to the front of one of the side sections where there were free seats. This also seemed to be where the ladies, of whom there were only a few, were seated.

At the front was a lectern and behind it a screen directed towards which was a lantern. From this I gathered that this was to be an illustrated talk.

There was no introduction. A bearded gentleman in a flat cap came out and sat on a small stool to the front. I surmised that he was the lanternist. Then Galton came out. He was a man of average size with balding hair and a wrinkled face. He was not an imposing figure, but when he spoke, his voice resonated across the aisles.

'Gentlemen,' he said, and then, glancing towards the front rows, 'and Ladies, I, with some assistance,' he beckoned towards the lanternist, 'am going to give a little insight to the developing science of eugenics and, as some have called it, criminology.'

The first part of the talk, I have to say, was not of great interest to me. Taking an analogy of fallen fruits in an orchard, Galton demonstrated that, taken at a certain time, some would be ripe and some would be rotten, but most would be somewhere in between, with only a few completely ripe or completely rotten.

He then developed this model to apply it to a population of people, for example, the people of a city like London. Some would be fit and able, others weakly and infirm, but most would be, again, somewhere in between.

Galton now moved on to the meat of the talk.

'And now we come to the problem of the common criminal. If our population we take to be the labouring classes of London, then we can only assume that at one end of the spectrum we will have those who are hard-working, Christian and devout and at the other end we will have a proportion of consummate scoundrels!'

The audience seemed to have appreciated the emphatic way in which he made this point.

'The criminal,' he continued, 'commonly has three peculiarities of character: his conscience is deficient, his instincts are vicious and his power of self-control is very weak. The question is whether these peculiarities of character can also be detected through his physical appearance.'

At this point he made a sign to the lanternist who uncapped the apparatus, projecting two beams of bright white light onto the two screens.

'The technique that we shall employ is that of the photographic image. Of course, you will all know that the recording of convicted criminals has become more and more commonplace over the last fifty years. However, where my method differs is that I have established a large collection of images of all classes of the labouring society, from the sober and upright through the idle and imbecilic to the criminal. Thus I have been able to make some observations as to all their physical characteristics.'

There now followed a show of pictures in which, using the two screens, Galton compared the characteristics of, I suppose you could say, the good and the bad of society, emphasizing certain physical features that were common to certain groups such as the Jew, the sexual pervert—I winced a little at the thought of Isabella and the other ladies looking upon this—and, most notably, the common criminal.

'Here we have,' said Galton, 'an archetype of the common criminal in which all the characteristics we have identified are shown. Note the têtes montonnes, the handlebar ears, scaphocephaly and trigonocephaly caused by the assymetry of the wormian bones in the lambdoid, the superficial position of the gyrus cunes caused by adhesions between the dura matter and the vault of the cranium. If we could see further we might note the excessively large canine teeth, the pigeon breasts and prominent arcolae, the prehensile feet. The general pallor of the skin and a continual flinching of the body—like a cur who has been whipped!' Again, he emphasised the point and the audience reacted.

'You may be interested in the scientific methods that have

enabled this enlightening study to take place. My associates have developed that machine that allows various profiles to be taken at the same time.'

He then showed us a photograph that consisted of a young man, shaven-headed and naked to the waist seated in and strapped to a chair. Above and on either side there was a system of mirrors, and in front of the whole there were two plate cameras. I have to say that the whole seemed more like an instrument of torture than of enlightenment.

'Gentlemen,' he had now perhaps forgotten that the ladies were present, 'to conclude my address I wish to introduce and commend to you the new science of eugenics.'

The conclusion was somewhat delayed, however, as he at first deviated to discuss the work of the Italian doctor Lombroso. Lombroso had, he noted described the criminal as exhibiting 'enormous jaws, handle-shaped ears, insensitivity to pain, excessive idleness, love of orgies, and the irresponsible craving of evil for its own sake, the desire not only to extinguish life from the victim, but to mutilate the corpse, tear its flesh and drink its blood'. To the amusement of the audience, Galton explained that the English criminal exhibited traits a good deal more subtle than his Italian counterpart!

Now he came to his more serious conclusion.

'Help for the weak and sympathy for the suffering is the natural output of a merciful and kindly heart, yet it is necessary to breed out those we have identified as of feeble constitutions. They shall be treated with care as long as they maintain celibacy, but if they continue to procreate children, then they may be considered enemies of the state, who have forfeited all claims to kindness.'

He had one final hurrah, however. Using the technique of composite photography, in which several images are merged together to produce one, he showed us images that claimed to show the type of the common criminal both male and female, and then of the 'ideal' type, both male and female. I can't say that it didn't strike me that this ideal couple did seem, in no small measure, to resemble a little myself and Isabella, but I kept this thought to myself.

When we gathered outside and some of the crowd had dispersed and other small bunches of men lit cigars or pipes, I asked Isabella what she thought of the science of eugenics.

'I greatly pity those whom Mr Galton regards as enemies of the state,' was her first response.

'Do you not think, then, that his photographic methods are reliable?'

'If they were, I suppose it would make my father's job all the easier. But I am sure that there are some very saintly-looking people who have done some very wicked things.'

We were then interrupted, however, as two men came into sight. I saw that it was Superintendant Ord with another man; a shorter man, about my height but broader, with a full short beard and dark eyes that shone through a ruddy face.

'Isabella... Mr Ledbury,' Ord said. 'This is George Holdsworth— Inspector Holdsworth—he is assisting me in the Kilburn case.' Holdsworth nodded to us both.

'My dear,' said Ord to Isabella, 'I'm afraid I must now take Mr Ledbury away from you.'

'But we were so enjoying our conversation,' she said.

'Nevertheless, duty calls.' He pursed his face as if tasting something quite unpleasant. 'I will get a constable to call you a cab.'

Isabella had a little embroidered bag and she took from it a silver card holder. From it she extracted a card and with a little silver pencil that slipped out of the edge, wrote something on it. She gave me the card and said, 'Thank you so much for your company, Mr Ledbury. I hope that you have learned something today.'

I was contemplating what I had learned as we got into the carriage and headed off, so I said nothing for a while. I felt good for some reason. The little engraved card nestled safely in my jacket. My wallet was full although my pockets were nearly empty.

Holdsworth was the first to speak.

'You have been to one of the entertainments proffered by Mr Galton, I believe.'

'Yes,' I replied, 'It was certainly interesting.'

'Mr Galton believes he can study madness with a yard measure. Do you truly believe that is possible?'

I didn't really have an opinion on this matter yet. So I simply said, 'The presentation seemed to be very convincing to the audience.'

Ord interjected at this point. He had been very quiet, lighting his pipe and puffing in a contemplative manner.

'The detective branch of the force is no longer the Cinderella branch. No less than the Home Secretary has requested that Mr Galton address a committee to enquire into the best means of identifying habitual criminals... '

'So,' I said, 'maybe his solution is part of the answer to seeking out the criminals in the country that you are looking for.'

Superintendent Ord considered this for a moment, stopping to tap his pipe out on the corner of his seat. He looked perplexed and, I thought, a little sad. For a moment I felt something that may have been a little like pity, for I knew that quite recently Mr Punch in his periodical had referred to the detective department as the defective department and chided it for its inability to bring to justice rogues such as the infamous Whitechapel murderer.

Ord, sucked hard on his pipe and said, 'Let us just say that there are many photographs in my rogues gallery of the greatest rascals who also most closely resemble the best people in the country.' I was struck by the way Ord's opinion seemed to echo that of her daughter.

Ord now said nothing until we had reached our destination.

After a while the carriage slowed, as we entered a maze of streets. Holdsworth turned to me.

'Mr Ledbury, you must swear not to reveal one whit of the scene that you will see in here. The journal men may get hold of it in due course—but not if we can help it. They may think that the purpose of Scotland Yard is only to entertain the masses with tuppenny dreadful tales of gruesome murders—but I can assure you that neither myself nor any of my colleagues hold that view.'

They had taken me by carriage to an area of London with which I was not well acquainted. We turned into a comely enough street in a plainly residential area. The terrace was plain but seemed well-furnished, speaking of a genteel and reasonable living. We stopped in front of the steps at number thirty-one. A police constable stood at the front doorstep.

'I can delineate the story in brief to you,' Ord took my arm to ensure that I realised the full necessity of my attention and spoke in a lowered voice. 'The victim was discovered by the maid-of-all-work this morning. That poor girl is still in shock and her story is barely intelligible. Elizabeth Southall was a young lady of twenty-seven years—handsome enough but renowned, apparently, for a frosty temperament and for her frugality. According to the good folks in the neighbourhood ne'er an uncovenanted ha'penny would escape her purse. Until a few months ago she took care of her elderly father who had a pension from imperial service in Afghanistan. Since the old fellow departed this earth she has been little in society. There are rumours that, for her good standing, she has been courted by sundry gentlemen but has rejected them all.'

We turned to enter, but Ord hesitated and frowned. He addressed me directly, 'Ledbury, I am sure that you are a gentleman of wit and discretion.' He put one hand on my shoulder. 'What we have here is an unco thing—such like even I have never seen before. I… I have a duty, an estimable duty, to see what lies behind this door, but you do not. I would not have asked you to come here with me if I did not have an instinct that you can help find the progenitor of this awful affair.'

His eyes met mine and for the first time in his company I shifted uncomfortably as if we had shared or were about to share an embarrassing secret.

Then Holdsworth said, 'Are you prepared to steel yourself to look upon a sight that no Christian should see?'

I gathered that comment was superfluous so I simply nodded my affirmation and followed him into the parlour of the house. With the blinds drawn the hall was in semi-darkness, fusty and airless. For the first time I detected another odour both sharp and sickly that was new to me at that time. It was the smell of blood.

The room had no light of its own and the blinds were drawn, but it had been lit by lanterns placed around the walls. Several policemen were in the room and there were two large plate cameras attended by men who were not in uniform. On top of the table what looked like a small tent had been set up to receive the plates from the cameras.

The room was basically furnished with a chair and settee with antimacassars. There was a paisley-style carpet in the centre of the floor and, at the centre of that, there was the naked body of a girl. Her eyes were open and staring—her body pale, and on her body there was a symbol inscribed in blood, like a circle with a cross in it, and in the centre of the cross a sort of figure.

I had a flashback to my dream of the last night, the human figures stretched across their cells. It felt cold in the room. I didn't want to look. Suddenly, the business of crime did not seem so promising.

Holdsworth addressed me. 'As you know, she was discovered when a servant lass calling at the house next door heard the door thudding in the wind. With the naïve curiosity of the young, she investigated and this is what she found. The rooms were let to a gentleman called Aubrey Nicolson. Nothing is known of him. We are seeking him.'

Ord interrupted to introduce me to another member of the party whom I previously hadn't noticed.

'This is Dr Geoffrey Manners. He is schooled in the science of pathology and something of an expert on scenes of crimes such as these.'

Dr Manners was a man in his forties of small to medium height, slight, clean-shaven and with short greying hair. He was dressed in a neat grey pin-stripe suit with a waistcoat and gold albert. He was bare-headed. He did not offer to shake hands as he was wearing gloves, presumably to aid his investigation of the body. He began to remove them.

'Good afternoon, gentleman, we have a pretty little scene here!'

I didn't think that 'pretty' was an appropriate term for it.

'Can you give us your summary of it?' asked Ord.

'Well, the girl has been dead for some time. She seemed to have been placed here, so the death may have occurred elsewhere. There are no indications that she has been in any form of struggle. The only marks on her body are uniform small bruises on her wrists and her ankles. We have found nothing in her hands, her fingers or her mouth. We have taken photographs and are testing the floor and the furniture for fingerprints.'

I couldn't take my eyes off the bloody marks on the girl's stomach. I couldn't help but speak my thoughts.

'What kind of diabolical sadist could have done this?'

Manners looked at me for a moment.

'Diabolical, perhaps, but not a sadist.'

'What do you mean?' asked Ord.

'Well, there are several contradictory indicators. For example, the girl seems to have been well nourished. The body is clean. She has been washed and combed, presumably recently.' He indicated some features of the photographs he had taken.

'On the other hand,' he continued, 'she has been whipped by, perhaps, a leather strap—but then, it seems, the weals have been soothed and cleaned by some sort of lotion… '

'But what about the blood?' I interlocuted, looking at the most graphic of the photographs.

'Oh, the strange marks on the torso. That is not the girl's blood.'

'Whose blood is it, then'

'It is sheep's blood—readily available from the local abattoir. It can be bought by the bucket. The poor use it for making puddings and pancakes.'

Ord looked perplexed. 'What then,' he asked 'can be determined as the cause of death?'

'Hmm. Not absolutely clear. There are no signs of strangulation so my best guess is that she has been smothered. A cloth or even simply a hand held firmly over the nose and mouth to disrupt the breathing.'

We all paused to contemplate for a moment and peruse the rest of the photographic prints. Eventually Ord said 'She was discovered naked.' He paused. 'Has she been… abused?'

'It does not seem so.'

'Is she… virgo intacto, then?'

'No, no… but there are no signs of forceful abuse or forced entry of any sort.' He added, 'In any of the orifices.'

Ord looked at me and at Manners and at the photographs. 'What exactly,' he emphasized the word exactly, 'has taken place here?'

'Well, in short, the young lady seems to have been held captive, physically punished, but also well tended to, then dispatched in an efficient and relatively painless manner. It's an enigma.'

'If the captor cared for her, then why did he kill her?' I asked.

'Who knows, perhaps she had outlived her usefulness, perhaps he was afraid of being caught, perhaps, even, she died accidently in some kind of play-acting… '

Ord humphed and pointed at the photograph of the bloody insignia. 'That, however, is no accident.'

Some words of the letter I had received from Jeremy suddenly came into my head. I started.

Ord noticed that my expression had changed. 'What is it, Ledbury?'

'I have an idea.' I hesitated. I did not know if Holdsworth had been told of the letter.

'Well, man, what is it?' Ord said.

I decided to state it plainly. 'The sign on the body is a message… along with the letter… '

'A message to whom?' asked Ord.

'A message to… ' I thought for a moment. 'A message to Sherlock Holmes!'

Blacklock stared blankly, not seeming to comprehend.

'Or, perhaps,' I added, 'a message to us.'

I was enthused with these thoughts but suddenly I came to realise that I was facing Ord, Holdsworth and Dr Manners and that two constables had come to stand, one either side of me. I looked around, almost in a panic.

Ord looked at me and at Dr Manners and then he beckoned the constables away.

I was horrified. 'Surely you can't suspect me of any thing to do with this,' I said.

Ord slowly lit his pipe. 'Mr Ledbury, if you think of it carefully, why should we not do so. Only you brought us the letter. We did not know where it came from.'

'Then, why did you invite me along here?'

Ord spoke slowly. I think it was at this moment that I realised that his approach was a lot deeper than his manner first indicated.

'It was necessary to see how you would react,' He looked me straight in the face in a very blunt way.

I did not know what to say.

'Forgive me,' he added, 'but let me assure you that I am now certain that you have had nothing to do with the events of the last few days.'

'And how do you know that?' I asked.

He turned to Manners. 'What time do you estimate the girl's death?'

'I would suggest fifteen hours ago, certainly not more than twenty.'

Ord now addressed me. 'Why do I know that? I know that because my constables have been following you since you first revealed the letter to me,' he said, 'so you could not have done this terrible thing.'

I suppose I was relieved but, for the first time, the seriousness of the situation became clear to me. I was a writer, but the sight in front of me was at the very edges of my imagination, as was the amatory literature of Mr Ashbee.

'Come,' said Ord to Manners, 'I have an idea!' I was unsure what to do. Ord looked at me. 'Mr Ledbury,' he said, 'it is best that you remain with us for now. We will interview you at the Yard and explain to you the precautions you must take to ensure that no unauthorised news of this case escapes. That,' he said in a heavy serious voice, 'would be very unfortunate indeed.'

After a while in the carriage, I found we were heading south down Gray's Inn Road. Myself, Ord and Manners. There were some terraced houses, carriages and gentlemen walking to their employment. A few serving girls on errands. In a little while, we came to a tall brick wall on the right, higher than one could reach the top of, with a few doors in it. We stopped at one in the centre. It was painted a dark red, but there was no number or sign on it.

'You have acquired the key?' Ord asked Manners, and the doctor took a key from his pocket, inserted it into the keyhole and opened the door.

Inside the door was a long garden with a few cherry trees, out of bloom now, and some benches. Five or six young ladies—girls really—were sitting in their shawls, a couple reading.

'What is this?' I asked. 'Is it a school.'

'Oh no,' Manners replied, smiling, 'it is a brothel!'

We came to the door of the terraced house set back from the main road and rang a bell. To the left of the door was a board that seemed to constitute a type of tariff:

	for member	by member
Rodding	£1 10s 6d	£1 15s 0d
Flogging	£1 10s 6d	£1 18s 0d
Fustigation	£1 18s 0d	£2 10s 0d
Nettling	£1 10s 0d	£1 10s 6d
Curry-combing	£1 10s 6d	£1 15s 0d

Ad valorem quotations on request

The doorbell was answered by a matronly buxom woman of about forty with a dark complexion. She did not look particularly pleased to see us.

'Good afternoon, Mistress Ring?' said Ord.

She nodded 'Come in,' she said. 'One of our rooms is available for you. But please be speedy.' She humphed a little. 'Several of our members are upstairs waiting to be entertained.'

Ord frowned. 'I'm sure that the anticipation will only serve to heighten their experience.'

The inner hall was dark and only lit by the sparse light from the stained glass above the door. There was a strange but not unpleasant smell. As my eyes became accustomed to the dark, I saw that it emanated from a series of large jars to either side in which strips of birch twigs were soaking in some sort of solution.

She led us and we entered a room on the left. It was surprisingly well lit although the windows only occupied the top third of the walls. Around each wall there was a framework of wooden bars, as in a gymnasium. At one end, hanging from them, a selection of belts, harnesses and other leatherwear that you might see in a saddlers. Against one wall was a rack containing different sizes of rattan canes and another with sundry whips and riding crops.

In the centre of the room was a remarkable apparatus. A chair or a stool or, in fact, more like a series of chairs or stools linked together with hinged parts and attachments of padded cushions and leather straps.

Mistress Ring patted the seat of one part of it. 'This is our horse. Made for comfort. A tribute to our late founder, Miss Berkley.'

Manners had brought a briefcase with him. He took some photographs out and showed one to Mistress Ring. It was the Kilburn girl.

'Has this girl ever been in your employ, or ever visited here?'

She looked at it, but showed no sign of recognition. 'I've never seen her. Not our type, anyway. Too old.'

Meanwhile, Ord seemed more interested in an examination of the Berkley horse. He had taken one of the photographs and I realised that he was comparing the photograph of the marks on the girl's ankles and wrists with the bars and straps with the brass buckles on the horse.

'You manufacture and sell these instruments, do you not?' he asked Mistress Ring.

'We do. Perhaps some of your officers may be interested in a purchase?'

Ord ignored this jibe. 'Then I presume that you have records of who you have sold them to?'

She shook her head. 'Oh no, no, our members require complete discretion. There is no written record of any of our transactions.'

'But you have worked here for some time. Surely you have some memory of who has purchased them?'

'Oh no, no memory at all that I could reveal. Our gentlemen wouldn't be happy at that at all.'

'Well, perhaps they would be if it were a request of the Metropolitan Police in the course of investigating a murder?'

'Oh no, no!' This seemed to be her favourite expression. 'One of my gentlemen would not like that at all.'

'I wonder who could that be then?'

She drew him closer and down a little with a hand on his shoulder and whispered something in his ear.

Ord was, I knew, a stoic Scotsman. He merely pursed his lips very tightly He grimaced for a moment then he straightened up and moved away

'We'll take some measurements,' he said to Manners, 'if you have a measuring tape.'

'However,' he again addressed Mistress Ring, and I detected a combative tone to his voice, 'this instrument will have to be taken away… for further investigation.'

'Please do,' she said, 'I have two more next door and two under construction. My carpenter has never been so busy.'

'And,' she added with a mischievous grin, 'I shall send the invoice to the gentleman we mentioned.'

'Hmph,' said Ord, and turned and walked vigorously away.

Manners and I followed him down the long garden. As we did so, I saw a man enter via the red door. He walked up the path towards us carrying a bundle of books under his arm. As he passed, he nodded, it seemed, at all of us. I recognised him immediately. It was Henry Spencer Ashbee.

Excited, I waited until the door was closed behind us and immediately button-holed Ord and Manners.

'I know that man,' I said.

'What, Ashbee?' Ord said, 'Almost everybody in London knows something about him, although it is scarcely spoken about.'

"But I know something important about him,' I was sure I was on to something. 'He makes books… '

"Yes, he brings them here for distribution.'

I wasn't sure how to express myself. 'But, well, he is here at this place, and I happen to know he has literature about… well about women and men and things… '

'Of course he has, that is what he does!' Ord didn't seem to see my point. 'Are you, by any chance, one of his clients, Mr Ledbury?'

I was horrified, so I just blurted out, as coherently as I could, the story of my involvement with Ashbee. 'And,' I added, 'he had a book, that he had written, I think about… about the degradation of women, just like we have experienced in this case!'

'Look, Mr Ledbury,' Manners intervened. 'There are many men in London who may like to read or write about the degradation of women. The police don't have time to investigate them all.'

'But some of his work involves the tying up of a woman and a beating on the behind.'

Manners smiled. 'That, I'm afraid, is a very common preoccupation of a great many men including some of those who sit in the greatest houses in the land!'

I must have looked surprised. Manners smiled.

'Yes,' he said, 'There are some at ease in the most senior seats who bear the marks of Mistress Ring on their eminent backsides.'

'And in their minds,' I added. They looked at me quizzically.

'Surely the memory of pain leaves an indelible impression on the mind also,' I explained.

Ord smiled. 'You sound like some of those queer German books my daughter reads!'

'But what about Ashbee,' I asked.

'Look, let me make this clear,' Ord interjected. 'Ashbee has his little amusements—he writes and he collects things and he invites gentlemen to his library for evenings and to have brandy and cigars. But he has never hurt a woman. He has never hurt anyone. He is a fantastist! I can vouch for him. We are members of the same lodge.'

Something came to me and I looked at Ord. He must have detected a strangeness as he said 'Something has come to your mind. What is it?'

I hesitated.

'Come on, laddie, out with it! Straight talk is always best.'

'I was just wondering… just wondering… '

I decided to grasp the thistle and state my point plainly, 'how you came to know of this place, and how you had a key to gain entrance.'

Ord showed no sign of dismay at this comment. He simply shrugged.

'Ah, you think that I or Dr Manners may have had some dalliances with Mistress Ring and her entourage.' He shook his head slightly. 'Well, I would not be the only person in such a position as I am to have jeopardised himself in such a way.' He shrugged. 'But I can assure you that it is not the case. The reason we have a key to that establishment is that we protect it to some extent. Many important people frequent it. They are entitled to do so of their own free will and to do what they wish when they are there and they are entitled to what protection we can offer against, for example, blackmail. That is the reason that I am familiar with the place and the good doctor has had to be consulted from time to time with some issues.' He paused.

'And,' he continued, 'the reason that we came here today is that I have come across similar marks to those we found on the girl in an old case—in fact, one of the first that I worked on here, when I was a detective sergeant.'

'Oh.' I was sorry I had questioned him. Even though he had arranged to have me followed, he had, after all, established my innocence. 'What case was that?'

'You will have heard of it. It was the Whitechapel murders.'

I took a hansom cab, ordered by Superintendant Ord, to my home. I don't think that ever in one day had I seen so much and had so much to think about. My mind was fogged and I ached for my bed. Ord wanted to see me the next day. He had once again emphasised the necessity of absolute secrecy regarding the matter of the letter and the Kilburn girl—although, I supposed that that would not be her moniker until the press got hold of it. He had promised that some of the Holmes letters would be returned to me, but it would not be prudent, he stressed, for me to continue to reply to them at the moment.

When I arrived, Mrs Merrilees was busy in the kitchen, preparing a supper for Mr Bartholomew. I had thought it was much later, and I determined to refuse anything since it had been a long day and difficult day.

As I ascended the staircase to bed, Mrs Merrilees shouted on me.

'Oh, Mr Ledbury, are you not be having your supper with us tonight?'

I was too weary to sit with Mrs Merrilees and Mr Bartholomew in the parlour that night.

'It is very good of you, but I have dined out tonight,' I lied.

'Perhaps a little supper, then. A bit meat or cheese?'

I considered. My stomach was empty.

'Could I have a little bread and cheese in my room?'

She looked pleased.

'Of course. Oh, I've put your bundle of envelopes on the desk.

A constable brought them.' I had told Mrs Merrilees, reluctantly and roughly, about the police interest in some letters I had received or would receive and asked her to take care of anything delivered for me. She had been delighted, as if it were a little more adventure in her otherwise humdrum life. At least, I thought, some of the Holmes letters had been returned which might be a small step towards getting my little industry up and running again. It was one way of earning a crust, preferable to constructing the amatory scenes that Ashbee had asked of me, I thought. Then I wondered why I had thought of him at all.

She turned to go, then remembered and took something from the pocket in her apron.

'Oh, Mr Ledbury, I almost forgot, there's this one too. I found it by the door. It must have fallen out of the bundle or been delivered separately. I kept it here. I thought it might be from your young lady, Dorothea.'

I took the letter from her and opened it in the privacy of my bedroom. I immediately recognised the handwriting. It could not have come from the carefully tied bundle.

One thing was certain. Jeremy might have thought that I was Sherlock Holmes, or Arthur Conan Doyle, or a conduit to the police, but he or someone on his behalf had delivered this letter directly to my door—and whoever that was knew where I lived!

Chapter Five

A PROFESSOR OF GRAND DESIGN

I have come to believe that the whole world is an enigma, a harmless enigma that is made terrible by our own mad attempt to interpret it as though it had an underlying truth.

Umberto Eco

There are strange flowers of reason to match each error of the senses.

Louis Aragon

Itook the letter to Superintendant Ord in the morning. He read it carefully:

Dear Mr Holmes,

You will now be aware of the culmination of my first adventure. I hope that you and the plodding Superintendant enjoyed my work.

Naturally, I did not expect anything of you so soon, but you will have further opportunities to play in this game. Soon you will be delivered of the Kensington girl.

For the moment, I will leave you with a riddle.

My house is like a prison,
And sometimes in a spin,
I'm always going out,
But I'm ever staying in.

Jeremy

'Hmph,' said Ord, and looked at me. 'Do you have any idea why this was delivered directly to you?'

'Not at all.'

'It was delivered yesterday. He cannot have been aware that shortly afterwards you would actually be accompanying us to the initial discovery of the girl.' He paused. His brow was knotted.

'Since he seems to know of our involvement in the case, It is safe to presume that he would know that any correspondence addressed to Sherlock Holmes would come to this office directly.

Therefore, we can only presume that he must want *you* to be directly involved in the case. It is perplexing.'

'Perhaps he thought that it make more of an impression if I brought it straight to you.'

'Perhaps, but perhaps he thought it would further incriminate you and lead me to suspect you yourself as the writer of the letter or perhaps he thought you would be too frightened to bring it to me. I just don't know.' He frowned. 'However, you did bring it me. That is on your side.'

I was a little worried now. 'But do you still suspect me of being involved with the murders?'

'It is not your handwriting. We checked that. If there is a second murder you couldn't have had anything to do with it as we are aware of your movements… ' He grimaced here as the mention of the 'second' seemed to suggest a sequence ' …and you would have to be the world's biggest numskull to come here to Scotland Yard with this if you were involved.'

He pondered for a while.

'Nevertheless, for reasons unknown you are personally involved in this affair. I must ask you not to leave the city and I want you to come here every morning. I may have some tasks for you.'

'But can we wait until the morning? Shouldn't we be looking in Kensington if a crime is to be… has been … committed there?'

'I'm afraid Kensington is a large area, the size of many a town. We will inform our local men, but it would serve little purpose sending more men there just now, and it might excite alarm.'

Well then,. is there not anything more to be found at the scene of the Kilburn crime. Maybe we could take bloodhounds?'

'Bloodhounds are unlikely to help,' he said. 'As for the scene of the crime, we have discovered Mr Aubrey Nicolson,' he said.

I was surprised at this unexpected revelation. 'Where did you find him?'

'At his home, He returned last night.'

'So' I said excitedly, 'is he the perpetrator of this terrible crime. Is he Jeremy?'

'Unfortunately not,' said Ord. 'He is merely a businessman who works in the shipping trade. He travels a lot. He had been in Amsterdam. His rented accommodation was sparse as he is seldom there. It was locked, but the lock can be easily picked. All we have learned is that the person that deposited the body there, unless he chose the place at random, was aware that Mr Nicolson would not be there.'

'But could he not be an accomplice in the crime?'

'Extremely unlikely. Why would he return so readily to the scene? And he seemed genuinely shocked.'

'Well, surely we can trace who would have known of his absence.'

'He is an agent in a public office. Their business is open. All the agencies are touting for custom these days, it is a hectic business. Anyone could have called to ask if he were present or abroad on a trip. His lodgings hold more interest, but his address was common knowledge in the office in which he worked. Nevertheless, we are following that lead. A constable is interviewing staff at the shipping office and checking for any police record for any of them'

'Have you questioned the landlady any further?'

'Yes, but it has not been very helpful. Although she seems a respectable woman. In this city, with its comings and goings, most landladies have come to the conclusion that it is too onerous and not necessarily in their interests to know too much about their lodgers.'

I thought of Mrs Merrilees. She always took an interest in the wellbeing of Bartholomew and myself and attended to us as well as she could, but she did not ever enquire over duly into our personal histories.

I had followed carefully the new developments as Ord had delineated them, but I was frustrated by the lack of progress. 'But surely we must do something else right away. Another girl's life may be in danger!'

'Laddie, do you not think we are doing something! I could do more if we weren't also so preoccupied with the trouble at the docks. I have all the constables I can spare questioning everyone in the vicinity of the discovery of the body, I have a list being compiled of everyone who was likely to know of Mr Nicolson's lodgings and his absence from them. I have had samples of Jeremy's handwriting taken around newspapers and periodicals to see if it matches any oddball letters they have received recently.'

At this point, there was a rapping on the door.

Ord rose to attend to it, but first he turned to me.

'I have two persons who may now be here to consult on another aspect. It is as well that you are here as it is an aspect that may appeal to your rather vivid imagination! '

Ord opened the door and Holdsworth ushered in a lady and a gentleman.

'Mr Ledbury, let me introduce to you Mrs Annie Besant and Mr Arthur Waites.'

I had heard of Mrs Besant, her brother-in-law was the famous essayist. She had become rather infamous for her involvement with the Secular Society, her advocacy of the control by women of birth and her campaigning for the match girls. She was a tallish woman with white hair and dark eyes with which she looked straight at you in a challenging way.

He exchanged pleasantries. Waites was a tall, well-groomed gentleman with a luxuriant moustache. I immediately noticed that his speech had a American intonation.

Ord explained. 'Mr Waites and Mrs Besant are experts in symbols. I have asked them to offer their interpretation of this.' He indicated the photographs of the bloody sign. 'And,' he added, 'this… '

Ord had a small paraffin lamp on his desk. He took the letter he had just read and, for a moment, I thought he was going to set light to it, but he merely passed it over the flame once or twice and, amazingly, a symbol appeared on top of the handwriting!

'A cheap trick,' he said.

'But how did you know it was there?' I asked.

'I didn't, but we are more advanced in the sciences in our profession than perhaps you imagine, after careful examination by our laboratory men we found exactly the same on the first letter. Jeremy is clearly testing our application.'

Waites and Mrs Besant looked carefully at both the photograph and the letter.

'Let us first of all state the obvious,' said Waites. 'Both these signs seem to consist of a circle—or actually at oval, it is slightly taller than it is broad—divided into four quadrants with radial lines that could indicate cardinal points. In the centre is a shape which is indistinct, but could represent an eye.'

'Or, perhaps,' added Mrs Besant, 'the body of a person. In one way it is reminiscent of Leonardo's drawing of the Vitruvian man, his limbs stretched to the edge of a circle. It is in Venice, but I've seen it illustrated in a book.'

Something struck me in this suggestion, but I decided to hold my tongue for the moment.

'However', Waites added, 'it is always the tendency of man to see himself, or parts of himself, in a design. It is an effect of our mental dalliance by the earthly world.'

'Is it possible, then,' asked Ord, 'that this symbol is of the spiritual world? Can it be related to a church, a religion, or a religious group?'

Mrs Besant looked at him keenly. 'Many symbols have an established role in the church or everyday worship. They are all around us.' She hesitated. 'However, the interest of our society is more arcane. Theosophists believe that there is a body of ancient spiritual wisdom that we have partly lost. We are often called Buddhists but we do not believe in the Buddha or any one god. All religions may retain elements of this wisdom but we attempt to put it together. Only through the completion of this quest can we individually attain spiritual union with the world.'

'Could then,' I interjected, 'this symbol be very ancient?'

'Yes, it could,' Waites said, 'It is not a symbol that in itself is known to us, but it does resemble many others. We could suggest what it might mean, but that might be misleading. There are two things as to which I should caution you. Firstly, symbols do not necessarily mean what they seem to at first! For example, the tarot card denoting death is often taken as a dark symbol, but it can also be light, it can mean the death of woes or troubles, it can mean a rebirth or a renewal.' He hesitated.

'And the second,' said Ord.

'Well, the second is that a sign can have more than one meaning, depending on who interprets it. A cross may have no meaning or an entirely different meaning to a savage from a far desert.' He took a card, a little larger than a carte-de-visit, from his top pocket. 'Here is a well-known sign. What does it mean to you?'

He showed it to us. It consisted of a white rose within the centre of a red cross.

'Pray tell us,' requested Ord, who seemed a little exasperated at this diversion.

'Well, it is the rosy cross, the symbol of a group I have studied with some fervour.'

'And what does it mean?' I asked'

'Well,' Mrs Besant interjected, 'some think that the cross represents salvation and the rose the purity of body and mind that will enable us to attain salvation.'

'On the other hand,' added Waites, 'if we do accept that symbology derives from man himself, the cross could simply represent the body and the rose the mind.'

'Or,' Besant said, 'if we take a more basic interpretation, 'the cross and the rose could represent, respectively, the male and female reproductive organs.'

I blushed, quite shocked such a lady could mention such things!

'Mrs Besant smiled. 'Men are often unaware that so many monuments and monoliths they erect are essentially phallic in nature.'

Ord seemed keen to bring this line of enquiry to an end.

'So you say that the sign or symbol we have examined may have many different meanings! Is it then possible, that the perpetrator of this wickedness may have devised a meaning to it all of its own?'

Waites frowned. 'Ancient symbols are there to teach us wisdom, but sometimes wicked people suborn them to their own uses. I have a student in the Society, Crowley, who wishes to misappropriate our signs to his own uses. I will not let him. Esoterica, the subject of our studies, must be handled carefully in order to impart its wisdom for the benefit of us all.'

At that juncture, it seemed that Mrs Besant and Mr Waites had no more to add. So, after some pleasantries and leave-taking, they left us alone.

Ord addressed Holdsworth, who had remained silent throughout the whole conversation. 'What do you think?'

'Well, the sign could mean something or nothing, or something to one person and something else to another. That won't help us find a murderer.'

'No… ' Ord nodded. 'Well, if the spiritual world is of no assistance to us, perhaps the world of medicine will be!'

He looked at Holdsworth. 'You have made the meeting?' Holdsworth nodded.

'We are going to visit Professor Blacklock,' he said. 'An expert, I am told, on certain medical conditions.' He raised his eyebrows and sighed a very little as if he had some considerable doubts.

'You will be available later today, he might want to quiz you?' It was an instruction rather than a question.

'You may return home,' he said, 'but remember, as I said, I have had my special constable trailing you. I should also have kept a watch on your house. You will notice when you return some work taking place on the street. There will be a workman's hut and a brazier opposite your door. That will be where my man will be posted.'

I left Scotland Yard but I did not return home.

The tearoom of Joseph Lyons & Co in Piccadilly was a busy place. Here just about anyone could come, relax—free from their daily business or shopping—and read a newspaper or talk about the day's events. Unchaperoned young ladies could sit alone or even invite a male companion. It was here I was to meet Isabella, as she had requested on the card she had handed me the day before.

I can't say that I wasn't pleased that Isabella had wanted to meet me again and to talk more about the lecture we had been to. I had been thinking about Galton's ideas and prepared a few questions about them that could lead to further discussion, but when I met her she didn't really seem to want to talk about that at all.

'Galton is an ass,' she said, 'lost in the last century. What I want you to tell me about is the affair of the Kilburn girl!'

I paused. 'But surely your father will have told you about that,' I said.

'Practically nothing at all,' she said. 'Father is very dear to me, but sometimes he is such a presbyterian, masonic boring old fuddy-duddy!' I was surprised at her vehemence and when she saw my expression she laughed a little. There was a pause while we stirred our teacups.

'But why do you want to know about the Kilburn affair?' I asked.

'I have been studying the workings of the criminal mind. I want to know more. But nobody thinks a woman has any right to be involved in such things!' She looked a little exasperated.

I thought about this. 'Well, maybe they are right,' I said, 'it is an unsavoury case, the perpetrator is a sadistic monster.'

She thought for a moment, placing her hands together and bringing them to her lips, almost as if praying.

'You are aware of the term 'sadist' which is derived from the writings of the Marquis de Sade. Have you heard of the term 'masochist'?'

I admitted I had not.

'It is a term taken from the writings of an Austro-Hungarian writer. It means someone who takes pleasure in pain. I mean in receiving pain'. She looked at me, 'Can you believe that such people exist?'

I didn't really know the answer to this. I said, 'I suppose it is possible, but there cannot be very many of them, can there?'

She laughed. 'And you have been to the establishment established by the late Miss Berkley?'

I tried to look uncomprehending about this.

'Don't worry,' she said, 'I know all about that *and* about the recreations of Ashbee and his circle!'

I was genuinely surprised. 'But how can a young lady know about such things?' I asked.

She smiled. At least she seemed to be enjoying my company.

'I am very clever and very observant,' she said, looking pleased with herself.

'Have you also heard of the term 'misogynist'?' she added.

Again, I had to admit my ignorance.

'It is a term that refers to someone, usually a man, who hates women,' she said.

She looked at me closely. 'You don't hate women, do you?'

'Oh, no. Not at all,' I said.

'And you don't believe that intelligent women should be excluded from taking an interest in things that are usually confined to men?'

I shook my head. Then she took my right hand in her little gloved hand and looked at me again with her deep blue eyes and I realised that I was going to tell her what she wanted to know about the Kilburn case.

So I sat for a while and spoke slowly and told her most of all that I knew. It was quite difficult, not least when I had to mention some of the details about the way the girl was found and the conversation with Dr Manners, but she prompted me when I hesitated and, in due course, I suppose, I had told her just about everything I knew.

Afterwards, she was quiet for a while, obviously digesting all the information I had given her. Then she said, suddenly, 'You say her hair was washed, her face powdered and her body perfumed?'

'Yes,' I said, 'that is what Dr Manners told us.'

'And did the good doctor say any more about that?'

'No.'

'Are there any of the photographs you mentioned of her face and hair?'

'I suppose so.'

'Men,' she said, 'may not notice the most obvious things! If a women were to look more closely at the girl—even at the photographs—she could tell so much more.'

'Like what?' I said.

'Like, for example,' she replied, 'whether the make up of her face or hair was done by herself, or by a man. Like whether it was completed when she was still alive or after her death! Don't you see, that might be important.'

'But who would have done her hair when she was imprisoned unless she were coerced?'

'For obvious reasons, women like to always look good, for other women and for men.'

'But not, surely, for the kidnapper!'

'That is not necessarily so. You said the kidnapper also treated her with kindness. Children will always return to parents who beat them if that is the only way they know.'

'She was a grown woman and not a child.'

'Who knows how some people will react when put into situations they don't understand. Anyway, it would still be good to know about the make up.'

'Perhaps I could look at the photographs?' I suggested. 'If your father will allow me.'

'It probably won't be any good,' she frowned. 'It won't show the detail required, and it may have been changed by the movement of the body. It would have been best if someone had looked at it right away, preferably someone who knew her.'

'Well, I could mention it to your father.'

'Oh no. Don't do that. You mustn't tell him you have told me this. He wouldn't like that.'

I hesitated, then I asked, 'And that I met you for tea, would he not like that?'

She look perplexed. 'I don't know,' she said. Then she laughed. 'Well, maybe he would think that that was more normal than my studies and some of the other things I do!'

I thought it wise not to enquire about some of the other things she did.

'I could mention it,' I said. 'I will see him this afternoon, when we go to see Professor Hezekiah Blacklock.'

'I know of Blacklock!' she said excitedly. 'He is a noted alienist. He was director of the Asylum at Hanwell for some time. Now he is professor of medical jurisprudence at University College.' He may be able to help you with your case.' She had seemed quite excited but now a note of gloom hit her voice. Perhaps because she thought that the case was now receding from her.

'Do they teach you all these things at Bedford College?' I asked.

'Unfortunately not. Father gives me a generous allowance for my studies and I have an excellent dealer who acquires things for me.' She gave a little smile. 'Perhaps father isn't familiar with everything I read! I have an account at a little bookshop and the bookseller recommends things that are new. Sometimes from the continent.'

'Really.'

'Yes,' I can read German, you know. And a little French.' She looked proud of herself.

'You are a very modern young woman,' I said.

I thought for a moment. 'Do you approve of the suffrage movement?' I asked her.

'Perhaps in some ways,' she said. 'What do you think of it?'

'I think women will benefit greatly from it. It has already been established in New Zealand and may be soon in Australia. Women will be emancipated and, I hope, the world will be better for it.'

'It is all very well,' she said, 'but what will it benefit the girls of Mistress Ring's circus who take down their drawers for the perverse pleasures of men?'

I winced a little, shocked at her forwardness. She smiled, a little coyly. 'Well', I said, 'surely, that is another matter. The poor often have to be in the service of the rich—man or woman.'

She pondered for a moment.

'What I think is that in this imperial city, money rules everything as it does throughout the so-called civilised world. When women are allowed to make a decent wage from a respectable job as do men, then they will have a form of liberty!'

She seemed quite incensed. I was surprised. I had a little experience of women, but I had certainly never met a woman like her. Clever and opinionated, and quite passionate—but charming and feminine and a little vulnerable when, as often happened, the expression on her face gave away her feelings.

'Would you like some more tea?' I asked her. It is Lyons special blend. All the way from Kerala in India.'

'Please, I love tea. It is one of the great benefits of the Empire, is it not?'

I frowned a little. 'I'm not sure. It somehow doesn't seem natural. The leaves are harvested by coolies in India who are paid next to nothing, then shipped here by seamen from far-reaches of the world and unloaded by dockers who claim that they are so badly paid that they intend to withdraw their labour. All to make rich profits for merchants who sell the tea to Lyons & Co, who sell it to us for a higher price to keep them in business.'

'Well, is that not the way of the world, everyone serving their purpose?'

'Perhaps, but it is not like things used to be. In the old English village, everyone had a function. The farmer reared his sheep and cows. The maid milked the cows, the shearer sheared the sheep, the wheelwright made wheels for the carts that the carters pulled with the aid of harnesses made by the saddler. The oxen ploughed the land and sowers sowed the seeds. The miller ground the grain and the brewer brewed the beer. Everyone fitted in and all were happy. The world revolved around the farming season and there were festivals that everyone celebrated together.'

I stopped for a breath, as I realised this had been rather a long speech. Isabella was looking at me intently.

'Why, Mr Ledbury,' she said, 'you have told me two things about yourself. 'You are a countryman… and a romantic! Like my father.'

I protested. Not least because I had not previously thought of Ord as a romantic.

'No, no. You *are* definitely a romantic. You would prefer to live in the past.'

I felt myself growing a little embarrassed, but she put her hand on mine as if to comfort me.

'Of course, I don't blame you,' she said. 'The world is changing very quickly, too quickly for some.'

'I am aware of that, but how are we supposed to deal with it?' I asked.

She looked serious.

'I don't know,' she said. 'It is a dilemma. Each of us may have our own ways of dealing with it. But, whatever we do, we can't ignore it. Look at how things have changed in the last few years. First we had Mr Bell's electric telegraph, now everyone wants a telephone in their home. We have steam trains that take us anywhere through great underground tunnels, type-writing machines, lamps lit by electric cables. I have heard that a gentleman in Paris has invented moving photographs! Is that not quite extraordinary? I find it so hard to believe.'

'I will grant that many of these innovations are for the good,' I said, 'but outside the city people are not so dependant on them. Much of the population of England still lives in the old ways and that is maybe what we forget in London.'

She thought about this for a moment then changed tack. 'Tell me about the country, then,' she said, 'about where *you* come from.'

I felt relaxed, so I told her a little about myself, everything much, in fact, except the terrible events of the last few years.

I had been born in the old parish of Godalming, Surrey. It was a pleasant part of the English countryside. Near the Hog's Back pilgrim's trail to Farnham where the Bishop of Winchester had a retreat. It was a literary part of the world too. Not far away was Waverley Abbey, immortalised in the works of Sir Walter Scott, and also Moor Park, once the home of Jonathan Swift. And also the country home of the pamphleteer and parliamentarian, William Cobbett.

When I was a boy, I remember warm summers, fresh milk from the churns, walking barefoot down the river and Brimstone butterflies racing over the water meadow. I remember frosty winters and silver cobwebs in the hedgerow. I remember a croaking squab that had fallen from its nest and how it found its wings again when we threw it upwards. I remember the paint-like patterns of snails' shells and the slimy trails they left on tiles.

Life seemed like an idyll, but I was only a boy.

School was not quite so idyllic. The master was strict, but not cruel. He would rap us over the knuckles if we were caught dreaming, but that was seldom as he gave us many things to keep us interested if not amused. He seemed to us like an old man but I now realise that he was not so old and his dark eyes always sparkled as if he was revealing to us some knowledge that was very special.

While I was relating this, some memories came back to me as if a little sluice had suddenly opened. I remembered some boys asking me to go to the river dam with them to drown some puppies in a sack. Later on, when the master asked us to write something for him, I wrote a little story about one of the little puppies in the sack; of how he had escaped and his adventures is the woods and the fields and the town. I think that was the first thing I ever really wrote.

I did not tell Isabella this as I feared she would find the premise too cruel.

While we sat with our china cups and wafers, she listened keenly. When I had finished I asked her to tell me more about herself.

'Oh, there is not too much to tell. I was born in the country too, in the parish of Wolfhill in Perthshire, Scotland. My father was the local policeman and precentor in the church. But my mother died when I was only three. I don't remember her at all and, sadly, I don't remember Scotland at all. My father's sister had married a man who had done well in the business of rubber plantations and they lived in London. We moved here when I was five so that my aunt could help look after me when my father was at work. That is when he joined the Metropolitan Police. I did well at school. Three years ago my aunt died and left a small inheritance for me. It helps me go to college.'

She paused.

'And that's all really. I read a lot at home and sometimes father takes me to the opera or the ballet.'

'And do you have many friends?'

'Some schoolfriends and the girls at the college. I sometimes have tea with them and with Mrs Manners, the doctor's wife.'

'But not with other young men?'

She laughed. 'You are very privileged, Mr Ledbury!'

I said I would prefer it if she called me John.

There was a moment's silence and then I said, 'Tell me about the books you read.'

'Oh, I read everything. I always have a book. I read for my studies and other areas I'm interested in, medicine and science. I read poetry. I like Christina Rossetti and Robert Browning. And I read novels. I have recently read Mr Stoker's *Dracula*.'

I was quite surprised at this. 'Do you like it, the novel, I mean?'

'It is only a story, but it reminds us to be wary of evil. And Mina Harker—she is a very proper character.'

I determined to re-read Bram Stoker's peculiar story with special attention to Mina Harker.

That afternoon, Ord and Holdsworth picked me up in their carriage. University College was very near my lodgings.

'What do you know of Blacklock?' asked Ord.

'He is a noted alienist,' I said, quite pleased with myself. 'He was director of the Asylum at Hanwell for some time. Now he is professor of medical jurisprudence at University College.'

'That is correct. Medical jurisprudence. Some call it Forensic Medicine, or, indeed, Forensic Science. It is a developing area. Blacklock focuses on just one area of it, the human mind.'

'Is he not a medical man, then?'

'Oh yes, indeed,' Holdsworth interjected. 'He trained as a surgeon and served the Empire in southern Africa, but from 1881 he was director at Hanwell, a sort of Bedlam, and introduced many innovations there in the treatment of lunatics. For the last twelve years he has taught at the University of Vienna and took up his appointment in London only last year.'

Dr Hezekiah Blacklock was an impressive man, tall and large-boned. He stooped a little as he shook hands, pulling you, gently, a little closer to him so that you were immediately fixated by the stentorian voice and the intensity of his large dark eyes. He was slightly ruddy, more like a farmer than a physician, and his hair fell a little erratically over his smooth brow and surprisingly delicate eyebrows. In all, there was still something almost boyish about the great man, as if a young man had suddenly bolted into this august authoritative figure without losing some of the bloom of youth and enthusiasm.

His office was also impressive. It was large, with a huge desk as its central feature. The east and west walls consisted of shelves of books and the north wall, whilst accommodating two small windows at either side, contained a large semi-circular glazed bookcase, the glass of which was curved to fit. The room, however, was not dark as it was lit by four globular electric lamps. His books were manifest. So many of them in a variety of languages. Although I did not have the opportunity to inspect the volumes in detail, I couldn't help but make comparisons with the equally splendid, but different, library of Henry Ashbee.

Another man came forward to meet us with Blacklock. He was

young, probably no more than twenty-five, stocky, of medium height, clean shaven with fair hair. He looked at each of us then smiled pleasantly.

'Welcome, gentlemen,' said Blacklock, shaking hands with us in turn. 'This is my assistant, Bob Knowles. He takes care of my library.' He gestured around him.

'It is very impressive indeed,' said Ord. 'Are you the college librarian?'

'Oh no,' he said. 'I just help the professor. I can read German, my father was from Germany, and so many of the new books are in German.' He looked around him. 'I like books,' he added. 'I also sell them at a small bookshop.'

'I am familiar with a great deal of my collection,' said Blacklock, 'but the study of the human mind is growing so fast that it is hard to keep up. I couldn't do without Bob.'

He seated us all at a round table which, presumably, he used for his tutorials. 'I will get us some brandy. Please light your pipes or take a cigarette.' He pointed to a box on the table.

He returned with some glasses. Blacklock's manner was calm and relaxing and I felt that his students must have enjoyed coming here.

'Professor Blacklock,' I asked, feeling I should speak as I had not yet done so, 'you are an expert on the human mind?'

'I became interested in the human body at an early age,' he said. 'It is a remarkable machine constructed of a skeleton of 206 bones, 649 muscles and several large organs wrapped together in a great amount of skin. It consists of about 65% hydrogen, 25% oxygen and 10% carbon. Yet, I can tell you, it has only a fraction of the profundity and complexity of a lump of greyish matter weighing about three pounds that we carry around in our heads.'

'So how can you study something so small yet so complicated?'

asked Ord.

Blacklock tapped his fingers on the table for a moment, then spoke.

'There are many techniques which can be applied to the mind of a human being. A colleague of mine at the University of Vienna, Dr Freud, has developed a technique which can be applied to any person. He calls it psychoanalysis. Many gentlemen have volunteered for it. My speciality, however, has been with lunacy and degeneracy. Therefore, I am somewhat of an authority on the criminal mind.'

'That is why we are visiting you,' said Holdsworth. 'I presume that Sergeant Timms has given you the case file.'

'Indeed. It is most interesting.'

Ord leaned forward. 'Of course, this is a very sensitive case. It has not been released to the public in any form. We are afraid that there may be further incidents. That it is the work of a criminal lunatic. That is why we are hoping you can help us.'

'I believe, said Blacklock, 'although there are many who would disagree with me, that it is possible not only to adduce how a patient might act according to his psychopathy, but also to deduce, from certain actions, what that person may be like from his actions. We can, if you like, construct a sort of profile of the person who has committed certain actions or certain crimes.'

'And have you thought of what the profile of the criminal in this case might be?'

'I have, but you must realise that we have only limited material to work on at this stage.'

Ord nodded. I noticed that both seemed to assume that this was only the start of the case we were investigating.

'Let us make some observations,' said Blacklock.

'Firstly, the person, or *suspect*... let us call the gentleman S.' He hesitated for a moment. 'Of course,' he said, 'we are making an assumption right away that it is a gentleman.'

'Surely a woman would not commit such a crime,' said Holdsworth.

'There are cases of such excesses committed by the female gender in my casebooks,' said Blacklock. 'However, they are comparatively uncommon.'

'Let us presume, for a start, that it is a man,' said Ord. 'Mr S. Can we identify him?'

'Let us try,' said Blacklock. 'Firstly, he exhibits the characteristics of egomania. He regards himself as very important and probably above the law. This is a trait that is usually demonstrated by someone of high intelligence and ability, but someone who has not, perhaps, because of some impediment, succeeded or been recognised as much as he thinks is due. He may demonstrate a contempt of society and regards himself as unrestrained by its usual rules and restrictions.

'Secondly, he is likely to be someone who spends a great deal of time alone, perhaps obsessed with his work or his studies. He wishes to be intimate with someone but he is not secure enough to do so through the usual channels. He selects his victim according to some attributes she has that he admires.'

'But if he is often alone, how does he select the girl?'

'He will not actively pursue that. It is likely that he will choose someone who he has seen regularly, perhaps in the course of his business.

'Thirdly,' he continues, 'he treats the victim in a way that he believes will allow him maximum control over her.'

A thought occurred to me. 'How does he regard the girl. As his lover, his wife… '

'That is a very interesting question. Dr Freud, for example, believes that all men are obsessed with a sort of mother love. That in their subconscious they despise their father because he intervenes between them and their mother. In adult life they may be obsessed with seeking a sexual partner who resembles the mother.'

'Does he procure these women for the purpose of carnal relationships?'

'It is possible. It is also quite possible that he cannot perform natural relationships and that is why he turns to complete control of the object of his desires.'

Holdsworth expressed some surprise at this. 'So, he could be impotent?'

'That is possible, but, of course, there are degrees and types if that condition, as my casework demonstrates. I have encountered men, for example, who can only spend when watching a woman passing water or a woman caked in oven black. There are many such afflictions and, also, there are many disreputable houses that cater to them.'

We sat for a while seemingly digesting the substance of this new information.

'You have been most helpful and hospitable to us,' said Ord, after a while. 'I would be obliged if I could perhaps call on you again, if required, when more comes to light of this case and we have more information as to the nature of the culprit.'

We rose to leave but Blacklock rose at the same time. It was not to usher us out, it turned out, but to lead us in another direction.

'Please do not take your leave quite yet, there is something I want to show you!'

We looked at each other, puzzled.

'Come, gentlemen, it is only a few corridors to walk, and I very much wish to introduce you to someone!'

Ord queried, 'Who is it you would like to introduce us to—another doctor perhaps?'

'Well, not quite,' he replied. 'Come with me, gentlemen, 'I wish to introduce you to Jeremy!'

Chapter Six

SUNBEAM IN MANOEUVRE

I consider that a man's brain originally is like a little empty attic, and you have to stock it with such furniture as you choose

Sherlock Holmes

The boundaries which divide life from death are at best shadowy and vague. Who shall say where one ends, and where the other begins?

Edgar Allan Poe

What Blacklock showed us was extraordinary. It was a man but not a man. Like a man stuffed with straw.

'This is Jeremy. Jeremy Bentham,' said Blacklock. 'He has been here some time and mostly resides in the same place except when he attends meetings of the Council.'

I was aware of the arcane traditions of some of the university colleges, but it was impossible to think what purpose a sort of stuffed mannequin could contribute to their business.

'If you are not aware of the fascinating history of Jeremy Bentham,' Blacklock continued, 'perhaps I can furnish some of the rudimentary details.' He then outlined some of Bentham's controversial contributions to liberal philosophy with which, I am afraid to admit, I had only a distant acquaintance: his utilitarianism, his promotion of equality of the sexes, his invention of the panopticon prison or hospital, his role in the founding of University College in 1826, and then, finally, his donation of his own remains to form the stuffed figure or, as he called it, auto-icon, that stood before us.

While he continued in this vein, we gradually became aware of other artefacts including plans of Bentham's design for the panopticon, that were collected here.

'The panopticon,' Blacklock continued, 'was a circular institution with the cells gathered on the outside. Thus the subjects could be examined at any time from a unit in the centre allowing complete transparency.'

He pointed to some framed prints on the wall beside him. One showed a man supplicant before some bars and a bright light in the background.

Blacklock pointed to this image.

'I cannot help but detect a certain similarity to this and the symbol that you gave me a photograph of.'

It was true. There was a similarity and, suddenly the image seemed to appear burning in my mind, as a sort of memory of what I had seen in a dream. In the rushed course of events I had almost forgotten my nightmarish visit to The World Turned Upside Down and the frantic machinery that now seemed to take the form of a panopticon that I now viewed in the image before me. Now the dream came flooding back as vividly as when I had awoken. But how was it possible? Had my subconscious mind somehow what would come before me here?

'But Bentham is long dead,' said Ord, breaking my reverie. 'What could he have to do with it?'

Manners answered his query. 'Bentham still has his many followers who promote his beliefs. Benthamites. Could the murderer be one of them?'

'I seem to remember something I have seen about that. In *Notes and Queries* recently,' said Blacklock. 'Bob, fetch it from my library. The last volume.'

We leafed through the volume for a while and then found a short entry titled 'The Panopticon Society':

There is a rumour that among the ranks of committed Benthamites there is a dedicated inner core who form the Panopticon Society. These fellows will have it that the Panopticon is a model for the world as a whole and not just the criminal undergrowth, and that only through exercising a strict overall system of surveillance over the working people will society flourish

'Is it possible,' I asked, 'that one or more members of this

Panopticon Society are behind this?'

'If so,' said Ord, 'why? Why are they abducting women. Does that make their point in some way? Why write to Sherlock Holmes? It doesn't make sense?'

'But surely that is it. If it is the work of a madman, it needn't make sense to anyone but them!'

'Nevertheless,' said Ord, 'it needs to make some sort of sense, no matter how mad, if we are to catch the culprit.'

'Can't we find out more about This Panopticon Society?' I asked.

'I did note that the article said their existence is only a rumour,' said Blacklock. Still, we have the initials of the contributor. I'll see what we can find in my library and in the College.'

Later, in Ord's office we discussed our interlude with the professor.

'Is there anything is this matter of the society of Benthamites?' Ord asked.

Holdsworth shrugged. 'The connection seems at best tenuous at best. Unless anything else can be found I don't see how it can inform the investigation.'

I hesitated a moment then I said 'I think there may be something in the image. The man contained within a circle.' I didn't want to mention my dream for fear of ridicule.

Ord reflected. 'Our learned friends have perhaps already confused us enough regarding symbols. I am reluctant to put much import on it at this time when it could, possibly, mean so many things.'

There was a moment of silence then Ord continued. 'However, let us come to the business of finding suspects. I fear that the suggestions the professor has made regarding the nature of the felon are limited in their practical use at this time. The records we have of criminals, thanks largely to Messrs Galton and Ellis and their French and Italian counterparts, consist of photographs, fingerprints and measurements. There is nothing much of their history, their habits and nothing at all of how they think. There may be a great many egomaniacs around, but we have no easy way of detecting them.'

'However,' added Holdsworth, 'we can eliminate many of them immediately.'

'Of course, this is not a common scoundrel. He... '

'Or she,' I interjected. 'Blacklock said it could be a woman.'

'He or she, then, is literate, intelligent. We can dismiss the usual petty thieves and street ruffians, for a start.'

'Apart from Blacklock's suggestions, what do we have?'

'Very little. The possible connection with shipping, which we are investigating and... ' He thought for a moment.

' ...And the connection with you, Mr Ledbury!'

He had come up with something and for a moment seemed more enthusiastic than dogged.

'I want you to go out in the city. Go to public places. Go to public houses, pie shops. There is a chance Jeremy might try to contact you directly.'

'Will we have him shadowed?' asked Holdsworth.

Ord thought for a moment. 'I think not,' he said. My special constables are good, but not one of them is Sherlock Holmes. They may be detected.'

Holdsworth nodded.

'Besides this is a long shot. Worth trying, but a long shot.'

'But what if he tries to harm me?' I asked.

'I can't see any reason why he would.' Said Ord, 'Besides we have to take that risk.'

Clearly, he had taken that decision on my behalf.

As it happened, I had occasion to venture out into the city later that day. Some time ago I had approached several periodicals with samples of my work with a view to finding some paid employment. Only one had replied. Clement Shorter, the editor of *The Sphere: An Illustrated Newspaper for the Home*, had agreed to see me. *The Sphere* had just been founded and I had some hope that Shorter would be on the lookout for new talented writers.

Shorter's office in Paternoster Row was relatively small but was more cramped through the piles of papers and books that seemed recently to have been deposited there.

Shorter himself was pleasant enough but fairly blunt. After a few introductions and a brief account of his intentions for the new journal he came to the point.

'Mr Ledbury, I have invited you here because I detected some ability in your writing. However, I have to tell you that the samples I have perused are not themselves of any use to me. To be frank the public are not interested in country life anymore. They are interested in the future, the steam engine, the wheels of industry, the triumphs of our engineers. Then they are interested in the unusual, the offshoots of Empire, the exotic products of foreign shores, the great mountains and rivers of the world.'

He paused to light his pipe.

'I am talking to you and other young writers because I need new ideas. The South African war is providing a great deal of interest for our readers at the moment, but it will not last forever. We need new topics. Topics that reflect the new century, the *modern* world. I need stories about innovation, change, great engines, the hives of modern industry, fantastic discoveries, the wonders of the undiscovered world... '

I thought about this for a moment. I knew very little about industry or engineering and I did not have the means to travel to colonial shores. I wished that I was an adventurer, an innovator; that I could discover and reveal new wonders to the reading public, but I had chosen, perhaps unfortunately, to inter myself in the by-ways of literature. Then I had a small idea.

'What about crime?' I said.

He smiled. 'Well,' he replied, 'the public has a great interest in crime. It has been the case ever since the Whitechapel affair. But we are not in the business of Grub Street. The penny dreadfuls may present the more lurid details of crime.'

'But the public may be interested in the more considered approach. Perhaps what turns people into criminals.'

'Hmm,' the criminal type.' He nodded sagely. 'There has certainly been some interest in the work of Mr Galton and Mr Ellis, but their ideas are a little too rich for most people. Still, the general public are equally abhorrent of and intensely curious about the criminal underworld of the city. What take would you have on it, Mr Ledbury?'

'I have recently been conducting some enquiries into the workings of the Metropolitan Police... '

'Ah,' this caused him to start, 'I must caution you immediately that the public have little time for the police force in this city. Their reputation has hardly increased since their dismal failure in the case of the Whitechapel murders. The people would much rather credit the science of detection and criminal justice to the veritable, but unreal, Mr Sherlock Holmes!'

At this point I was aching to reveal my own connection with Holmes and Arthur Conan Doyle, but I was hamstrung. I could imagine the reaction of Ord if I revealed even the tiniest detail of our recent adventure to the popular press!

'Perhaps,' I said, 'the adventures of Sherlock Holmes, although they are purely fiction, might have some relevance to modern crimes. Perhaps his methods *could* be applied... *are* being applied to the detection of crimes at this very moment.'

Shorter considered for a moment. 'Mr Ledbury, I appreciate your enthusiasm and I believe that you have some talent. However, I am not convinced regarding your proposal. Perhaps if you consider and write it up more fully, we shall speak again.'

'And,' he added, 'in the respect of any real life crime, your sources will have to be reliable and open to scrutiny. *The Sphere* answers to the law of the land despite the workings of some less reputable publishers'

I took my leave. I realised that my only opportunity of selling a story on crime would probably rely on the successful completion of the pursuit of Jeremy. And even then, It might still be impossible to articulate my part in the story.

In the morning I rose and had my usual breakfast with Bill Bartholomew. Bartholomew was an American from one of the mid-western states. How he had found his way here was not quite clear to me as he was spoke in a mysterious way as to his origins and intentions—'transatlantic bonhomie brought me across the waves,' he would say, 'to serve some of my time in the service of this great country. Today, he seemed in an exuberant mood which I found surprising as his usual demeanour was more morose and he spent a considerable amount of time lamenting his fortunes in the shipping trade in which he was employed, I believed, as a small time negotiator of transports. I listened to this with a jaundiced ear and seldom questioned him about his comings and goings and general business, but it had, occurred to me, on more than one occasion, that it was odd that he should be so beleaguered while working in the biggest port with the largest trade in the world.

'Are you working at home today?' he asked.

'No,' I said, 'I have to go out—to see a contact about a writing job.'

'Oh, is it for one of the magazines you talk about?'

'Yes,' I said rather abruptly, trying to make an end to the conversation. 'It's a series of pieces. About people... about people in London. I have been commissioned by a new periodical, *The Sphere*. It is very topical.'

'*The Sphere*? I think I have seen that in the stances. It is very popular, is it not?'

'Yes,' I replied, 'it is very popular with many like-minded individuals who wish to read about the turn of the century and the beginning of the modern world. It is a magazine for innovators, adventurers and those interested in the mechanics of the developing world we live in.'

'And you writing about all these exciting things?'

I thought about this. 'Well, yes. I am writing about the new science of psychology. It is very popular in Germany... and other places.' I couldn't think of any more to say so I gave Bartholomew a stern look and threw open my hands as if to indicate I had said my piece.

Bartholomew gave me a queer look.

'I will look forward, then, to reading your next piece,' he said.

At this moment Mrs Merrilees came in with some toasted teacakes and I took the opportunity to make an excuse and take my leave.

One hour later I was indeed discussing a writing commission, but not with Shorter—I needed more time to think about that. I was, in fact, sitting with Ashbee in his library. My rent was due and, since I had invited Isabella to dine with me at the Corner House that evening, all the cash I had was committed. It would surely do no harm to undertake a limited amount of work for Ashbee. No-one need know. My suspicion that he might be involved in the murders had been scotched by Ord, but I salved my conscience a little by assuring myself that learning a little more about the letches of his readers might also inform me a little about the minds of the criminal classes. So I had come to visit him before his departure to Belgium. We sat round the desk and he brought me some aereated water from the gasogene.

'I'm glad you returned, Mr Ledbury. It had occurred to me that perhaps the sample of work I showed you last time was maybe, well, a little too robust for your tastes.'

I smiled a little.

'Well, flagellation is one of my most popular topics. The French call it 'le vice anglais'! Between you and I,' he gave me a look that was almost conspiratorial, 'I sometimes wonder why English gentlemen are quite so obsessed by the female buttocks!' He added, 'when there is so much more to admire in the female form.'

He opened a drawer in the desk and took out some paper and what looked like a few cartes de visite and handed them to me. 'I have something else for you that I think will interest you.'

I looked at the material. They were not exactly cartes as they had no inscription or photographers name on the back. They were all images of ladies of the salacious type. One showed three women, naked from the waist up, smoking, one showed one girl on the back of another baring their buttocks to a stern-looking mistress, one showed a girl, completely naked and smiling, sitting on the ground resting back on her arms with her legs apart while another girl, dressed in a bodice but showing her bosom, was inserting something into her, another showed two girls in tutus but bare-bottomed. One was beating the other with a carpet-beater and using a type of stencil to imprint the number 60 on her backside.

'Do you sell these too,' I asked Ashbee.

'No, I do not. That is not my profession. There are others that do that well enough. These are not of great value. You may keep them. I'm showing you them partly to give you some ideas, but also as an example of what I regard as the opposition.'

I looked puzzled.

'I will explain in a moment,' said Ashbee. 'Please read the typescript I have given you. It is of a different type from the first you read.

I read it:

In the centre of the room was a large bed, laid out with a crimson flannelette sheet and pillows. The bed was contained within a wrought iron frame that consisted of a grid with hoops strategically placed within it. There were windows at either side of the room that admitted a suffuse light through the foliage of willow trees. Against one wall was a washstand under the window and, against the other wall, farther back, a wardrobe and a valet stand.

The mistress said to the maid, 'Help me undress.' The maid helped her take off her dress until she was in her bodice and suspenders. Then she unclasped her bouffant hair and, with a hair brush, stroked it down her back.

'Now,' said the mistress, 'I will undress you. I do not want you to assist, simply to do as I say. For example, if I ask you to raise your arms above your head, please do so.'

The maid was small and dark with dark hair curling in ringlets by her face. She had dimpled cheeks and luscious little lips.

The mistress undressed her slowly and carefully, lifting her shift to reveal full round little breasts with dark teats. Then she removed her stockings and drawers until she was completely naked. The maid was docile, but her eyes were shining and bright.

The mistress looked up and down the naked girl and then kissed her once, gently, on the lips.

'Now, it is time to secure you,' she said.

From the wardrobe she took four leather bands with buckles and a steel ringlet attached. Kneeling, she attached two to her ankles, then the other two to her wrists.

'Lie on the bed,' she said. 'Place your head on the pillows so that you are comfortable.'

She took the girls left arm, pulled it taut and fastened it to a hoop on the frame at one side of the bed with a metal clip. Then she took the second arm and secured it at the other side of the bed.

She looked at the girl. She said nothing, although there was a ghost of a smile on her face.

'There is something more to be done.'

From the washstand she took a razor, opened it fully and sharpened it on a strop.

Then she took a little jug of water, some soap and a badger hair brush and made a little lather. Straddling the girl, carefully, she shaved the little black hairs from under the armpits of the tightly drawn arms. Then she turned herself around.

'Stretch your legs apart,' she said.

Then she shaved, delicately, all the hairs from around the girl's quim. The girl allowed her without demure, although she did wriggle a little as she felt the tickle of the blade.

'Now you are almost ready,' she said.

She took one leg and pulled it backward. 'Relax as much as you can,' she said. 'It will not hurt, although you will feel some pressure.'

She pulled the leg taut and fastened it to a hoop at the top far corner of the bed. Then she took the other leg and pulled it hard towards the other side of the bed. The girl winced and made a little sound.

'Relax,' she said. 'It is just a little further. Then putting all her weight on the leg, she pulled it taut and fastened it to the other side of the bed, a little above the fastening of her arm. Her buttocks were now fully exposed, each full and quivering as they were pulled apart.

The mistress stepped back and examined her work. 'Now you are fully open,' she said. 'Your body is mine and I can give you pleasure or pain.'

From the washstand now, she took another implement. It was a long stick. At the end was attached a feather.

She drew the feather down the girl's cheek and along her arms, carefully, from her wrists to the shaved underpit of her arm, then she performed the same on the other side. Then she drew the feather, slowly, from the girl's toes to the sole of her foot, down her thighs and around the lips of her quim, then she did the same at the other side. While she was doing this the girl gasped and made a little squeaky sound.

'There is much more that I can do before we are finished, but first I must expose your body a little more.

She moved the foot of the bed. Standing there was a half plate camera on a tripod.

'Now you will be recorded so that others can possess you as I will.'

I looked up at Ashbee. I was not sure how I was supposed to respond.

'Now, Mr Ledbury, you will see, in order to succeed in this profession' He seemed to roll his tongue around the word 'profession', although I found it almost humorous that the activity we were engaged on would receive such an accolade. 'You must try to understand the expectations of the reader. Here you will note from the sample I am giving you to take away, the gentleman concerned has callipygian tastes, that is, a deep regard for and appreciation of the female buttocks. You will also note that, in his imaginings, the frolics do not involve any other man. That is because he wants to be the sole possessor of his objects of lust.'

'The most important thing that we must understand in our profession,'—I noted the manner in which he comfortably used the term 'we'—'is that our readers are all individual. Now what can you deduce about the tastes of the gentleman who requisitioned this piece?'

I thought for a moment. 'Well, the physical contact is only minimal, but the girl is completely helpless.'

'Yes, and why do you think she is exposed to the camera?'

An idea struck me. 'Is it to make her even more helpless, her whole body can be photographed—even the most intimate parts—and made available to anyone.'

'Yes, you are beginning to see.' He looked pleased. 'The gentleman concerned is a what the French call a voyeur. He likes looking at the female form, but under concealment. He is not directly involved! And why do you think the photographer is not a man?'

'Perhaps because he likes women with sapphic tendencies and wishes to imagine them together.'

'That is part of it. But also, remember, he is not present at the scene. He wishes to possess the girl in a way, but, as we said, he does not wish any other man to possess her even in an indirect manner.'

'Of course,' he added, 'other clients might enjoy that particular thought, but not this particular gentleman.'

He explained this with obvious relish. I looked around at his library and his treasured collection. I realised that, in a way, Ashbee was also collecting, classifying and cataloguing his clients.

'One last thing,' he said, 'before I give you your tasks to take away.' He picked up a leather folder from the desk. 'And, of course, your advance,' he added.

'Why do you think our client commissioned us?' He still seemed to want to stress that we were partners of some sort. 'Commissioned *us* to do this work rather than an actual photographer?'

I had to confess I wasn't sure.

'Think of it. The photograph you look at. All is there, everything is recorded of that one moment of time. You look at it, then it is finished, you look at the next. It is like smoking a cigarette. It is perfect, but it is finished. All you can look forward to is the next one. Each time, however, that you read a passage of writing, you create it afresh in your mind. You can fill in the details that are missing, imagine the settings, add more details to the description of the characters. You can create in your mind a past and a future for this little story. Each time you read it, it exercises your imagination again. It is the same, but also different!'

He seemed happy with the little lecture he had given me, and I cannot say that he didn't express himself clearly and well. However, although I didn't comment on it, there was a contradiction between his enthusiasm for reading the same story several times and his earlier confession that he could not supply enough new material for his clients.

He pointed to part of his library. 'Cervantes invented what we now call the novel. He conjured it up from nothing. In a much more humble way, we are also inventing something. A new type of literature—each individual piece tailored for its purpose, so that it can be read again and again and offer fresh nuances each time it is read.'

I returned to my room for the afternoon and sat at my desk trying to write the material that Ashbee had commissioned from me in my notebook (he had assured me that this was sufficient and that either I or an assistant could finish it on the Type Writer later). Then, he explained, depending on the scope of the work it would either be bound as a pamphlet or, if it were more substantial, go to a printer he had in his employ to be made into a book).

At first the words flowed quite quickly, but after a while I found I was just staring at the page and I realised something else was on my mind. It was this: if Ashbee had the aptitude of recognising his client's preferences and character from the work they commissioned, would it be possible to recognise Jeremy from the letters he wrote and, even more importantly, from the crimes he committed! Perhaps the clues he offered us could be read like a sort of book and the author of it be identified from the text. After all, Sherlock Holmes could look at the scratches on a man's pocket watch and identify that he had served in the colonies or had contracted a rare fever. But that was fiction, what we had to deal with was fact.

So, I sat and I thought. What kind of man was Jeremy? Well, he had a grand opinion of himself. So much so that he thought that he could challenge the great Sherlock Holmes.

Then I thought of something else. In order to challenge Holmes, or me, or the police, Jeremy was in fact revealing something of himself. We had already seen that there were clues in his letters and his strange symbol, even though we could not yet decipher them. Jeremy's own vanity was the key. He believed that he was smarter than us, could taunt us. However, the more ebullient he became, perhaps, the more he would give himself away! This train of thought was enticing but the hard reality of the matter was that we were no nearer understanding the meaning of the letters, nowhere close to identifying a suspect—and there was the distinct possibility that others might die while we were pondering. I was lost in this line of thought when I realised that time was pressing and I had to be on time for my most important engagement of that or any other recent day. On my desk sat a copy of the *London Illustrated News* opened at a page of advertisements including various activities in the city: Atkins's Ghost Illusions; The Hide of Chummy, the Extraordinary Elephant; Real Moving Waxworx. For one night only: Mr Williamson's Popular Entertainments.

In the early evening, Lyons Corner Shop was busier than our previous visit. The pendants of five globes shone brightly in the twilight and there was a constant buzz of customers entering and leaving fresh from the offices or shops nearby. We had to squeeze into a seat by the wall opposite the windows.

'Tell me all about your meeting with Professor Blacklock.'

I had anticipated this question from Isabella and was prepared. Since the professor's contribution to our discussion had had no real impact on the case or changed our perception of it, I saw no harm in relating some of the general principles of alienism he had outlined.

'Well, he believes that egotism is a key characteristic of a criminal such as Jeremy, a belief that they can do whatever they wish and exercise complete control over the victim.'

'That would certainly fit in with what we know of the fate of the first victim,'

'Yes. However, we cannot see how it is possible to detect such characteristics of the personality of the murderer unless we can personally interrogate them.' I realised I felt comfortable expressing myself as if I was part of the company of the police investigation.

I continued, 'The man or woman… '

'Woman!' Isabella's eyes lit up. 'Are you saying that Blacklock believes that Jeremy may be a woman?'

She was clearly excited`. I wondered, ironically, if it was an aid to the argument of suffrage if women could emulate all the achievements of men—even sadistic murder.

'Yes, he did mention that… but I'm afraid there wasn't much else he said that was of any great help to us.' I didn't want to discuss Jeremy Bentham and the Panopticon if possible. I seemed difficult and obscure and I wanted very much to move on the latter part of our evening and the surprise I had prepared for Isabella.

Isabella considered. 'There are many contrary opinions of the modern alienists and their theories. Some think they are merely attention-seekers and the more ludicrous their suggestions the greater chance they have of achieving the attraction they crave.'

"Certainly,' I observed, ' Blacklock seems to have a way of

drawing attention to himself and his ideas that is very powerful.' I had been quite taken by Blacklock and his theories and I wondered now if I had been duped.

'Yes,' that is likely. 'Dr Freud,' I believe, 'has the same effect.' His students are much taken by him.'

'Are you, then one of his students?'

'Oh no.' She blushed a little. 'I don't know very much at all. He has released a new book but it is almost impossible to get, even in Germany. I know only a little—my bookseller gave me a review of it.'

'Is it about the criminal mind?' I enquired.

'Not at all, it is about dreams, but it has proved quite controversial.'

'Dreams, how can that be controversial?'

'Well, it has often been thought that dreams have a spiritual origin—visits from angels, if you like. They can give us guidance or foresee the future. If they are nightmares they visit us perhaps because we have sinned in some way or have had bad thoughts. Dr Freud doesn't see it that way. He believes that dreams are the subconscious communicating with us—telling us things in a roundabout way that our conscious mind does not want to hear— things that comes from our deepest instincts and desires.'

'What kind of instincts and desires,' I asked. The last thing I wanted to think about this evening was my own experience of dreaming, but perhaps the new theories of Dr Freud could help explain some elements.

'Well, they could be a desire for power, or wealth, but mostly, Dr Freud believes, they are *sexual* desires!'

I didn't know what to say. Isabella was a very unusual young woman but I couldn't think that this was a proper topic of conversation for an evening soirée. Also, I had realised, since the first mention of dreams, that I did not want to discuss my own strange dream with anyone, not even Dr Freud if he were to somehow transport himself to our company.

Isabella laughed, clearly noticing my discomfort. "Perhaps that is a topic that would take too long to discuss this evening when we have other things to do.'

That, luckily, gave me the cue to move on. I explained to Isabella the excursion I had planned for us.

'We are going to see actual moving pictures! That is so exciting.' She thought for a moment, then, smiling, said, 'I hope that they are not in any way salacious, Mr Ledbury, or inappropriate for a young lady like myself.'

'Oh no,' I assured her, 'they are going to be very proper indeed.'

The Alhambra Theatre in Leicester Square was a very impressive building with three cupolas above an ornate facade. As we entered I noticed a plaque on the wall denoting the foundation of the theatre. It noted that it was originally called 'The Royal Panopticon of Science and Art'. *'Panopticon'*, I thought. That seemed to be a recurrent feature of my adventure and my dreams!

When we were seated, a small gentleman in a tuxedo with a large handlebar moustache came forward and gave an extravagant bow.

'Welcome, gentlemen and ladies,' he said, 'to tonight's programme of the very latest kinematography from Brighton and other parts of the United Kingdom.'

He indicated a gentlemen among the crowd in front of a complex-looking machine. 'Gentlemen, Mr Williamson with his bioscopic apparatus!'

Then the lights went down and the machine began to flicker and whirr and images appeared on a screen in front of us.

First there was a short sequence of a clown putting on various faces. There followed photographs of the University boat race, some fishing boats leaving Yarmouth harbour and, finally, faces in a crowd going into Lyons Corner House. Isabella gasped when she saw these.

The programme did not last very long. When it was completed Isabella thanked me for the evening's entertainment. She said that she had enjoyed it very much.

'Is this going to be the future of entertainment?' She asked.

'I think so,' I said. These are very simple moving images, but soon, I suppose, they will be longer, and tell stories.'

'Like the theatre or the opera?'

'Yes, but, of course there will be no sound, so the actors will have to mime their parts. And we will always have the opera as long as men love music. The phonograph cannot replace that experience.'

'You mean men *and* women, do you not!'

'Yes, of course, I'm sorry. Men *and* women!' 'Or women *and* men', I added.

'You are learning very rapidly, Mr Ledbury... John.'

I thought for a moment of my correction of her father regarding the suspects. The whole business of what men and women should respectively do seemed to be getting more confused!

There was a moment's silence.

'Now you must walk me along Coventry Street to Piccadilly Circus. My carriage will be waiting for me.'

'Oh,' I was surprised, 'You have booked it already?'

She laughed. 'My father insisted. I am a very modern young woman, but I'm afraid there are times when I must still bend to his will.'

'Your father knows where you are, then... ' I queried, '...I mean, with me... ' I had, of course, wondered about this but now felt a little embarrassed.

'My father knows just about everything—and I suspect just now that he is taking a keen interest in where you are!'

At this moment a carriage pulled up beside us and she seemed to recognise it. 'I must go now'. She leaned across and gave me a little kiss on the cheek and suddenly she was gone before I had the wit to say anything at all.

I arrived back at my lodgings still in a state of excitement. So much had occurred in only one day. My mind was buzzing with thoughts of Ashbee's posed cartes-de-visite, Isabella's enthusiasm for the German alienists, the shadowy images of real people in Mr Williamson's entertainments, and, of course, the little kiss on the cheek from Isabella at the end of the night. So I lit my little oil lamp and, sitting in my bed, began to write some of my submission for Ashbee, but with a new idea in my head. I had completed almost seven pages before sleep overtook me with my pen still in my hands.

I was in a feverish dwaum, but not of the totally unpleasant kind I had had before, when a loud knocking at the door woke me in the morn. Ord had sent a carriage for me. The driver was taciturn and all he would tell me was that there had been another 'discovery'. He did not head for Scotland Yard as I expected but headed across town towards the west end of the city. I had hardly had time to awaken properly as I rushed to wash and get dressed and the dream was still turning round in my head. Isabella had said that dreams could tell us about our innermost desires so while I sat in the carriage and, as it began to bob along the cobbled street, I closed my eyes and brought it back to life.

Once again, I was standing at the door of The World Turned Upside Down, but this time when I opened it I wasn't inside the tavern but instead in a little room lit with candles in a central chandelier. The room seemed to be a library. It was octagonal and was shelved from bottom to top with books. When I closed the door that too was shelved, so I was in a central location completely surrounded by the books. If it was a library it was not like the libraries of Ashbee or Shorter as here the books rather than the reader took presence, hemming me in on all sides.

I scanned round and focused on one shelf. There was no doubting what I saw there. Thick volumes bound in buckskin all featured the little logo employed by Jeremy on their spine. I reached forward to grasp for one, but as soon as I touched it the bookshelves swung open and I realised they formed an entrance to another room of exactly the same constitution as the first!

I turned round again and another shelf caught my eye with, again, a row of volumes with the little sign. But this time there was another, thinner, volume lying horizontally on top of them. In the candlelight I could just make out the title which was, in fact, my own name in little gilded letters! I stretched out for it but in my haste it fell from my fingers down the back of the shelf behind the other books.

The gap was not quite wide enough for my arm so I pulled out some of the other books. They began falling on to the floor, then, as if in a chain reaction, the other books followed them, from floor to ceiling engulfing me in a sea of books. Strangely, however, in the dream I did not panic. I was too excited in search of my prey. Then I felt my fingers fold around it and I rose, almost swimming, above the books, triumphantly with my prize in my grasp.

Then I woke up.

'You have decided to join the land of the living, I see.' Ord was staring at me and did not look too pleased.

' …And you *have* been venturing out onto the city streets?' His face creased into a frown and it was not clear to me whether this was intended as a question.

Eventually the carriage drew to a stop—but not at some seedy lodging house. We were in the borough of Islington and we stopped at an impressive terrace of town houses.

Ord outlined the situation. 'Mr and Mrs Crichton-Hall returned from their country residence only this morning to find their daughter Euphemia. Well, you will see… '

And after a while, the photographers arrived and set about their business.

In another darkened, sparsely furnished room, in another nondescript street in a more prosperous but still unheralded part of the city, lay another naked girl, quite dead, with a bloody sign on her body, lit spasmodically in a pale white and dark red as the photographers lit their flash powder which emitted a slight smoke and an acrid smell. It was like a sort of scene from hell worthy of one of my more extreme dreams. I began to shiver. Reality, my dreams and the imagined little tales that Ashbee had introduced me to all seemed to mell together and I realised that I was confused and afraid. Where had my dalliance with literature led me?

However, I pulled myself together and remembered what Isabella had said.

'I wonder,' I asked Ord, 'if it was possible to get some photographs of the face to show a friend?' 'A friend,' I added, 'who is somewhat an expert on facial features'.

'What! You don't mean that charlatan Galton?'

'No, no, I meant… ' Ord was looking at me quizzically, so I drew away.

'No, silly idea.' I moved towards the woman. Her face looked composed, her cheeks red, but her curly hair well enough arranged.

I suddenly had a vision, impressed upon me by the maid in Ashbee's story. I felt a little dizzy. I think the blood drained from my face and next I knew Dr Manners was beside me.

'Mr Ledbury,' he said, 'you had better come to sit in the carriage. I have some salts that will benefit you'.

I sat in the brougham shivering. I was aware that my mind was beginning to wander. I seemed to be drifting out of fantasy and reality. Perhaps my brain had tried to absorb too much. And the effect seemed to be that I lost touch with reality. I thought of the partial whirring images of the moving pictures. Everything that was going on in my head just now seemed like that, as if it was a secondhand trick of a beam of light.

I wished fervently that there was someone to whom I could relate all happenings: my impression of the murdered girls, my liaison with Ashbee, the strange dreams that took me into another world, the aptly named World Turned Upside Down. Perhaps I could have confessed it all to Dorothea, but now who was there? I had to be very careful what I told Ord. And Isabella! What would she think of my employment with Ashbee? I could not bear to think of it.

I needed a rest and was neither surprised nor discontent when Holdsworth instructed the driver to take me back to my lodgings. I sat silently on the way. The next waking sound I heard was a small but persistent knocking on my bedroom door.

Chapter Seven

THE INTENTIONAL AND AFFECTIVE FALLACIES

Footfall echo in the memory,
Down the passage which we did not take,
Towards the door we never opened

T S Eliot, *Little Gidding*

Bid us sigh on from day to day,
And wish and wish the soul away,
Till youth and genial years are flown,
And all the life of life is gone.

Samuel Beckett, *Watt*

There was a light but persistent knocking at my bedroom door. I hadn't pulled my curtains and I noted that it was light outside and there was some slight sunshine. Which meant, in the Scottish winter, that it must be late morning.

Reluctantly, I put down the notebook and answered the door.

It was the concierge.

'Mr Nowell?'

I nodded.

'It's ten o'clock. I'm afraid you've missed your breakfast. It's check-out time.'

I realised that I had only booked in for two nights.

'I need to stay longer,' I said, 'at least one more night.'

'Oh dear,' he said, 'we need this room for a couple coming down from Inverness. We are quite busy.'

'Don't you have another room?'

'Hmm… ' He pondered. 'I could maybe put you in the attic room. It's small but it has a *restroom*,' he emphasised this word which he had obviously learned to impress his American customers, 'on the landing just below,' he added.

'OK,' I said, not wanting to consider the alternatives too much.

'You may leave your bags in reception.'

'Can't I go there now?'

He looked dismayed. 'It's not ready. Check-in time is usually three o'clock.'

'Could we not make it *unusually* early today.'

He tutted a little. Then he said, 'I'll ask the maid if, *specially*, she can have it ready by twelve.'

'Can I have a coffee or something?'

'There are some places in the town.'

I took my briefcase and left my overnight bag in the hall. A couple of minutes later I realised I been sent out into a freezing Scottish winter day. The sky was a deep grey. Little flurries of rain stung my face. I wrapped my overcoat round me and cursed.

I wandered towards the city centre, through the imposingly terraced Charlotte Square into George Street, then I turned up right into Rose Street, a narrow cobbled street between the grander shopping streets, George Street and Princes Street. There were a few shops and many public houses not yet opened. Some were getting deliveries of kegs of beer through cellar hatches in the street. Luckily, after a while, I found a small cafe. It was pleasant enough, with bright lights, vinyl chequered tableclothes, plastic bottles of red and brown sauce and a bowl of white sugar patterned with drips from coffee or tea. I ordered a mug of coffee and a fried egg roll and after a minute or two, my body began to warm, so I ordered another coffee and another roll and sat back to think.

What was I doing here? I thought about Ledbury, a young man who wanted to be a poet, then I thought back to myself, a young man who went to Harvard wanting to be a scholar.

My time at Harvard had been pleasant enough, although perhaps not as exhilarating as I had at first imagined it would be. I went to classes and did the other normal things that freshmen do— shooting hoops, playing pool, eating pizza and looking at girls. I went into Boston to see the Red Sox sometimes. I'd sit in the bleachers and watch Yastrzemski and Conigliaro field under the shadow of the green monster.

School went well and I developed a proficiency at completing my assignments without too much effort which allowed me time to wander around town taking in the day-to-day happenings and to read a lot. My reading extended far beyond the reading lists from my classes. The big debate of the time concerned the intentional and the affective fallacies. Two professors called Wimsatt and Beardsley had identified these as key problems in literary criticism. The intentional fallacy was when too much emphasis was placed on what the author intended to do with the text. The affective fallacy was too much emphasis was placed on the reader's interpretation of the text, leaving it open to the subjective impressions of the individual. A truer criticism would free the text—a poem, say— from both these extremities, concentrating instead on the inherent structure of the text itself.

Engaging with these ideas made me realise that literary studies in the United States, and in the English language, owed something to European scholars, so I enrolled for a French class and that is where I met Nancy Gomez, who was my girl for most of my junior and senior years.

Nancy was a sophomore from Colombus, Ohio. She wore big spectacles and had curly hair. Nancy was fun and she always seemed to be having fun—she even embarked on her essays with a sort of delighted enthusiasm. She started taking the pill and her breasts grew large like melons. We made love every day in the little bedsitting room I had rented for the semester.

Nancy was not really a scholar but she loved French. She believed the French viewed the world in a completely different way from most of the Western world and she, too, had a quixotic way of thinking about things, often making surprising connections and observations

It was Nancy who introduced me to *Histoire de la folie*. This was a literary study by the French philosopher Michel Foucault. There was a copy in translation in the library, published in England and titled *Madness and Civilisation*. Foucault's thesis was that there had always been those who, in various societies, behaved in a mad or illogical way. However, it was only fairly recently, at the beginning of the nineteenth century, that society had begun to identify and classify various types of madness and to use that classification to lock away the afflicted or at least put them apart from normal society.

I was sitting in the bleachers as usual watching Yaz slug a homer over Williamsburg, when something occurred to me. Literature was often about madness, either in real or constructed forms. Characters in literature were outsiders, mad in that they were at odds with conventional society. In extreme forms this is manifested in extreme pathologies, as in *The Justified Sinner, Jekyll and Hide* or *Crime and Punishment*. But also it is evident in less direct forms throughout a range of European and American literature. I didn't realise at the time, but this was a thought that would preoccupy me throughout the rest of my literary career.

I had enrolled on a class called The Twentieth Century Novel and Society which was quite adventurous as it opposed both aesthetic and textual approaches to literature, looking to find different ways of contextualising them in historical discourses and themes. Our first assignment was on George Orwell's *Nineteen Eighty-Four*, a work that the English, for some reason, seemed to loathe as much as Americans seemed to love it.

Trying to find a new tack on what was a well-known and much-analysed work, I had originally decided to focus on the context of the Reformation. Orwell reflects Martin Luther's proclamation that man could only answer to God, not the church, the state or Big Brother, in Winston Smith's intransigence.

However, now, instead, I decided on a different tack. I would regard Winston Smith as a sort of patient in a clinic. Using this context, I would ignore the question of whether the context of the novel was as a political polemic, an overt criticism, in fact, as usually suggested, of Stalinism.

So I looked at it this way. The world is illusory and unimportant, only represented partially by the flickering image of the television screen. If Winston Smith is effectively a patient in a form of clinic then the outside world is only part of his treatment or therapy. Smith is a madman because he cannot speak the same language as others in society. He has to be cured through the psychological apparatus that allows him to learn to speak as a sane man. Two fingers equals three fingers is, therefore, the key to his recovery as it is the true logic of the world, not the illusion he has adopted.

This viewpoint gives the lie to the intentional fallacy, as it doesn't matter what the author intended it to mean, and the affective fallacy, as it doesn't matter either what context the reader wishes to put the work in.

I was pleased with the essay.

I got it back. It received a delta minus.

This was my lowest mark by far, so I thought I had better ask one of the faculty what I had done wrong. So I went to see Elmore Belling. Professor Belling was nominally the course leader for the course I was on, although he didn't teach on it, concentrating his efforts on the graduate school. Belling was reasonably well known as an innovator in literary theory. He had written a polemic article attacking the lack of adventure in literary criticism provocatively titled 'How the twentieth- century influenced Shakespeare' which had incited degrees of condemnation and enthusiasm.

'There are many good things about your essay he said,' after perusing it. 'However, it seems the professor who assessed it didn't think that it quite addressed the question set.'

I frowned.

He laughed a little. 'I can see that you don't agree.'

The expression on my face must have revealed that I did not.

'Listen,' he said, 'what you have done is excellent. The mark is irrelevant. You have taken your own point of view and you are beginning to learn to be a true academic. You have great potential.'

After this, Professor Belling took me under his wing. 'Never give up,' he said. 'Attack every assumption. Be daring. Learn to be wrong, then you may find that you can be right!'

'Fail again, but fail better, do you mean?'

He smiled. 'You've read Beckett. Good.'

In my senior year, I wrote a long essay comparing *Gulliver's Travels* and *Candide* in which I constructed a sort of taxonomy of reason through which madness or transgression from the normal world could be measured. Professor Belling liked it and encouraged me to join the graduate school. And so, still armed with the funds from my father's insurance and the sale of the business, I embarked on my PhD.

I didn't have many close friends, but, as a graduate student, after Nancy had gone back to Ohio and we had said fond, but final, goodbyes, I hung out with Al Gilbert.

Al was interested mostly in early American literature, the folksy stuff especially. He thought my interest in Europe was a sort of aberration. 'There's too much of it,' he said. 'And it isn't all in English.'

'Most of the world doesn't speak English,' I said, He frowned but nodded slightly. 'And arguably half of America,' I joked in riposte.

'It's way too heady for me, anyway,' he said.

'You've never been to Europe anyway!'

I had taken a tour of European cities after my sophomore year

'It's not natural, all that travel,' he said, 'for us mid-Westerners. Hell, most of my family don't even know where *Boston* is!'

'Well, that's a sad reflection on American education, is it not?'

'Didn't somebody say that world wars were started to teach Americans geography!'

I laughed. I liked Al. He was quiet and unambitious, unlike many of the Harvard postgrads, who had quite inflated opinions of themselves. Yet I felt that he had an intuitive understanding for university politics that I probably lacked, but the good thing for both of us was that we could keep our own council and do the things needed to get by.

Al, then, as a sounding post for my ideas, was essential to my development into the graduate student.

For my PhD I had decided that the period I was really interested in was the late eighteenth and early nineteenth century. So much happened then, the birth of the modern world, the move from the rationalisation of the enlightenment to the passion of romanticism. The title was 'Madness and intransigence in the European novel: 1764-1818. The dates I took from the release of Horace Walpole's *The Castle of Otranto* until the publication of Mary Shelley's *Frankenstein or the Modern Prometheus*.

This turned out to be a successful venture as, when I had finished my PhD, I extended the thesis and called the book *The Gothic Novel and the Invention of Insanity*. It was published by Indiana University Press and was moderately successful. My sojourn at Harvard had proved successful! And so it happened that I was fortunate enough to be given an assistant professorship at Pittsburgh. A post which, of course, had proved satisfactory until recent events.

As I mused on the past, the cafe door opened and some young folk came in chatting away. A little wind blew in from the open door and a paper napkin fell off my plate on to the floor. I realised my remaining coffee was cold and my plate was empty. It was not yet time to return to the hotel but I felt that I had to move. My legs were stiff and I was impatient to get back to my reading.

I walked a bit down Rose Street and took a turn left. On the corner was a basement bar called Milne's Bar. The bar was down a set of well-worn steps on a corner. Below the level of the sidewalk, there was a rough stone cast wall painted white and the doors to cellars on one side and the entrance to the bar on the other. It was open as I saw a young woman go in, so I followed down the steps and entered. Inside it was dark, but there was a fireplace with a blazing fire at one end. The bar and gantry was typical of Scottish pubs, polished mahogany with hanging lights, beer pumps and ranks of bottles beyond.

'Could I have a scotch?' I asked.

'We have a range of malt whiskies,' the barman said, nodding towards the gantry. 'You are privileged, most shops around here have little more than a Bell's or a Whyte and Mackay's.'

Something came to mind. 'Do you have an Aberlour?'

'We don't,' he said, 'but there are other Speyside malts, a Tomatin, a Macallan, a Balvenie. Or maybe you'd like something a wee bit more robust, an Islay malt perhaps—a Laphroig or a Caol Ila?'

I'd heard of the Macallan, so I ordered that. I didn't ask for ice.

There was a little tap for water at the end of the bar and I added a little.

There was only one man at the bar, wearing an old macintosh and nursing a pint of Guinness.

'Are you here on holiday?' he asked.

'Sort of,' I said. 'I'm doing some research into a poet.'

'You've come to the right place,' he said, 'this is the poet's pub! They all come here—Hugh MacDiarmid, George Brown, Tom Scott, Stella Cartwright... I'm not sure she's exactly a poet, right enough.'

I looked at my watch. Thirty minutes until I could get back into my hotel room.

'I bet your poet had an eye for the ladies!'

'Pardon,' I said.

He looked surprised that I had addressed him so directly.

'Och, I didn't mean to offend you. It's just that all the poets seem to like the women. They say they need to have a muse.'

He had a point. Ledbury's poems did seem to refer to sort of muse. A women held on a pedestal. I wondered if this was the Dorothea he referred to?

'Do the poets who come in here... do they write love poetry?'

'Oh yes, some of can be a wee bit, you know, fruity! There's the kimmers o' the Coogate and all that.'

I thought of the collection of amatory literature of Henry Spencer Ashbee.

'Some of it sexual, then?'

He chuckled. 'You could say that! Some of it is about the whures and the hellfire clubs in the Old Town. That Goodsir Smith, especially.' He smiled broadly, although he didn't have any teeth to show. 'Oh yes, he's a lad for the ladies, and he's not the only one,' he added.

I thought about this as I headed back to the hotel. Ledbury had an eye for the ladies; he was a poet with a fanciful imagination; he wrote amatory literature. How accurate was his account of the events in his notebook, and could he, in fact, have had more to do with the amatory affairs of Ashbee than I had thought from his own revelations?

I wondered why Ledbury had chosen to write the story of his involvement with Ashbee if he was trying to hide it. But he had, and he had written out in graphic detail some of the amatory adventures. However, he had also written out his dreams in detail. Was he just a fastidious writer, determined to record every detail of his experience?

But then I baulked a little. The predominant methodology that I had learned was to always focus on the text and analyse it from within itself. Key concepts were the intentional and the affective fallacy. The first was the fault of focusing on the imputed intentions of the writer instead of the text, the second was the fault of focusing on the response of the reader instead of the text. Perhaps there was another way of getting to his story, looking at the structure of the text itself.

But I was too far ahead of myself, I still hadn't finished my reading and it was now time to continue. I walked up on to Princes Street and past the West End on my way back. The rain had lapsed but the wind blew full in my face. I bought a newspaper from a stall on the corner. When I arrived back at the hotel the room wasn't ready. The concierge said 'Just five minutes, Sir.' So I sat in the lobby and read my newspaper. One short item caught my attention and I froze in shock:

Police are investigating the sudden death in a flat in the city of a postgraduate student, Amelia Gammack, from Banffshire. Her death had gone unnoticed as her employer, a bookshop proprietor, had recently passed away. The alarm was called when she failed to turn up at a city centre pub where she was occasionally employed as a barmaid. The door of the flat had been securely locked from the inside and the student was found dead in her bed. A Lothian and Borders police spokesman said 'the death is unexplained but, at the moment we are not aware of any suspicious circumstances.'

I thought of Amelia soft and yielding in my arms and of her pale and lifeless in her bed. How had this come to pass? My concerns about the validity of the text and the truth of Ledbury's account seemed pointless now. That was in the past. This was the present, and people were dying. For the first time, perhaps, I realised that I was involved in something more than dry academic research. The book that I had sought and obtained illicitly was associated with two deaths! And I had been very close to both of them.

Chapter Eight

JUST ONE KISS

Hell is a city much like London.

Percy Bysshe Shelley

London, as taut and meticulous as a cobweb

Martin Amis, *London Fields*

Heavy riddles lie in this,
Sorrow's source in every kiss.

John Millington Synge

I awoke in the morning again sweating, my heart pounding and my eyes stinging in the morning light. Ord and Manners had despatched me from the crime scene with a carriage and police constable when it became clear that I was unwell. I had tried to rest as they suggested but I spent the night with a fever and still plagued with outrageous imaginings. Then Mrs Merrilees had knocked to ask if I would like some breakfast. She seemed concerned about me, but I refused and explained that I had a headache which was probably due to too much writing.

Why, oh why, was I cursed with these dreams? Dreams not of the great imperial showcase that could be London, but dreams of a different London. The city in a fog with a black vapour over it, rivers and brooks dark as ink, common sewers, draining from dunghills, the refuse of hospitals and slaughter houses, lead and soap works, mills and manufactories, street sweepers, beggars and herring hawkers lurching out of yellow fogs, rookeries, collapsing houses of lath and plaster, malodorous gases, the smell of rot and decay. All these seemed to populate and oppress my gloomy reverie.

I recalled the latest in a sequence of dreams. Once again, I had found myself at The World Turned Upside Down, but it was altogether darker and colder than before. In the main bar there were scenes of debauchery. Ladies letting their bosoms hang out of their frocks, drunken men with dead eyes and filthy matted hair, One woman was splayed over the piano which played discordantly as a giant of a man seemed to have entered her from behind and was playing her to his own particular tune.

'Good evening, sir,' said the man behind the bar. 'It is a festival night for the dockers. They have at last declared their cessation of work!'

I didn't respond and made my way through to the back. But the back room seemed elongated and even darker than on my last visit. And it seemed to have transformed into an opium den! Along each wall, figures sat or lay hunched over pipes. There was a rancid smell and occasional whispers or moaning sounds.

However, as my eyes accommodated themselves to the gloom, I could make out the outline of His Nibs. He was seated in a sort of oversized captain's chair, almost like a throne, and smoking a large calabash pipe.

'Mr Holmes, it seems that the announcement of your death, as of mine, was premature. We return to grapple yet again!'

I began to speak words, but words that did not seem to be my own.

'I am not aware that my death was ever pronounced abroad. You see I am alive here now in front of you.'

'I see you and, as you see, I too am here in front of you. I trust you know who I am?'

'I know you well. You are the great spider that sits motionless in the centre of this great city, but your web radiates outwards to every corner and you can feel every quiver of it, every crime, debauchery, every evil that infests the city comes from you.'

'I see that you have not lost your gift for melodrama. But, come, let us to business. That is what you are here for.'

'My business is that of every other good citizen—to uphold the law.'

'Hmm, I will take you at your word for that.' He held out both hands in front of him.

'Give me what you have promised and you can have the girl.'

I suddenly realised that I was carrying my little briefcase. I put it on the table in front of me. He took out a ledger and a long quill pen, wrote down a few words in a ledger and opened the briefcase.

Then the scene all seemed to fold in on itself and the briefcase fell apart and seemed to form a door from a cellar. And then arose from the cellar two men with dark hooded faces and deep bloody eye sockets. They were carrying some books and as they passed behind His Nibs there were following them some women, all young and attractive.

'These were not promised to you,' I said.

He looked at the ledger and laughed.

'It appears they are all forfeit, for you did not fulfil one part of your bargain.'

'And what is that?'

'Here it is,' he said. He held the ledger in front of me and pointed to a portion of it.

'To be delivered to me for my absolute possession one person. To whit, a sinner, a lecher and a pornographer, Mr Holmes, or should I say, Mr Ledbury!'

Then something seemed to push me forward into the cellar opening and I was falling, then standing in the same dark alley from my earlier dream. The old hag was there. It's Mr Ledbury, she said. 'Look over there, there's something for you.'

There was a bundle wrapped in rags. I bent down on to my knees and looked. It was Dorothea. She was pale and worn and completely dead. On the wall behind her in gaudy black blood was the symbol!

I lifted her in my arms. She weighed practically nothing. I didn't know where I was going. The feeling then that came over me was like nothing I had experienced before. It was as if all hope or joy had been sucked out of me, but not life. Life and suffering had to go on. There was no end to it. And that was not just me at that moment but the whole world for all time. Any illusion of life or any belief in redemption was gone, it had never existed, lost in this dark chasm where seemingly only death had its dominion.

But, then, just as it seemed I was sinking further into the abyss, I shook myself fully awake!

My head hurt at the temples. I was afraid, but at least I knew the answer to the riddle!

When I arrived at Scotland Yard, as promised when I had recovered well enough to go abroad, Ord seemed in an unusually foul mood. He cast a newspaper in front of me. I read it.

HAS THE RIPPER RETURNED

We are in the possession of reports of two foul murders that have returned to once again shame our city, seat of the Empire. The Metropolitan Police Force are currently investigating the evil and atrocious slaughter of two young ladies whose names we cannot make available to the public. We hope, however, that further details will be available in the near future. It is believed that the victims are Christian women from the respectable ranks of society rather than women of fallen virtue or east end slavies who have too often been the target of the vile and unnatural instincts of the beast.

Since the Whitechapel murders and the lamentable failure of our detective forces to bring the felon to justice, many have lived in fear of the return of the wretched monster who went by the moniker of Jack the Ripper.

However, some reports say that the bodies of the unfortunate ladies have been marked with blood in a way that may bring past circumstances to mind.

It continued with more sensationalist details about the Whitechapel murders and murder in general with some barbed comments regarding the inefficiency of Scotland Yard and the detective branch of the police.

'Laddie,' this was a term that Ord used when he wished to be overbearing, 'I hope that you haven't divulged anything to anyone!'

I thought briefly of Isabella. 'I have not,' I lied.

Holdsworth looked at the newspaper and interjected. 'They only seem to have some of the facts. They could have come from a variety of sources. Even a clerk at the Yard. The more widespread the enquiry, the more know about it.'

Ord seemed to mellow. 'Well; I suppose it was inevitable. George, prepare a statement. Include most of the salient facts, but think of those we must withhold. Perhaps the public at large have something to say that will help us.' He sat down.

'But prepare the constables to receive any number of communications from the confused and the deluded.'

'I know the answer!' I interjected.

'The answer to what?'

'The riddle. I dreamt it, last night.'

'Well, what is it then?'

I recited the riddle again:

'My home is like a prison,
That's sometimes in a spin.
I'm always going out,
But I'm ever staying in.

'The answer is a spider. The spider sits in the centre of his web which radiates outwards. He spins his web to catch flies, so it is a prison to them. It is an analogy that Sherlock Holmes uses when he is describing Professor Moriarty, the Napoleon of crime.'

Ord nodded. 'It makes sense, but how does it help us?'

'I don't know, but Jeremy wants of think of himself as like Moriarty, in the centre of this whole affair. And it relates in some way to the Panopticon, the prison. I suppose that it too is like a giant spider's web, the prisoners trapped by the filaments that tie them to the centre.'

Ord paused and deliberated. 'Laddie', he said, 'Return home and await my summons. If this affair is to do with the fictional exploits of Mr Sherlock Holmes. If... I say... ' He frowned a little. 'Then perhaps it is time to approach not the monkey but the organ-grinder!'

I was returning home but not immediately. I had recovered a little from my earlier dreams and intended to continue as before. The pressing and unusual circumstances I found myself in were no cause for a faint heart.

I had determined on completing two tasks that day. Both were in the vicinity of my lodgings, so I would walk between them, although the weather was dull. There was a wet mist about and the cold seemed to seep into the soles of my feet. Nevertheless, I plodded on, clutching a small briefcase with a lock on it that was employed for the security of my latest work.

I had concentrated for some time on my latest commission from Ashbee. The problem with this sort of writing, I decided, was that there were a limited number of scenarios that one could use. On the other hand, I realised, that the clients—gentlemen—would be happy to read them time and time again, like children who ask their parents to repeat the same fairy tale. So I wanted something similar to the sample I had, but also different.

I sat at my desk and read the passage in the sample again. Then I remembered the photographs that Ashbee had given me. I took them out and pinned them to the wall in front of me, hoping they would lend me inspiration.

I had to ring the changes in some way. So, I thought, firstly the dramatis personae. They were to be only female. So, three ladies, I thought. Perhaps not in a bedroom, so a drawing room, I thought. I would have to focus in the dress and the method of undressing, which, I thought, should be gradual to build to the climax. Would there be penetration? No, or only minimal at most. I was pleased with myself for managing all this thinking in such a short time!

Of course, the key feature was the voyeurism. The sample used the photograph as the method of exposing the body to the maximum. Could I use that again? Then I had some inspiration. Monsieur Lumiére had invented the moving picture and Isabella and I had only recently seen some products of the invention albeit of a simple nature. But could the mechanism of the cinématographe be applied in some way to amatory prose?

I would have to give this some thought. It was not of the temperament of Ashbee to pressurise my writing, but he had indicated some urgency. 'I have five clients at the moment who have requested new work. One is the scion of a well-known family, one a writer to the signet, one a manufacturer of ear trumpets, one a bookseller, one a member of parliament for a northern constituency, one a shipping magnate and one a country doctor of good stock. They all have similar but slightly different tastes,' he had told me. I wondered which client this new work was; for the lawyer, the manufacturer of ear trumpets? I knew, however, that discretion would not allow Ashbee to tell me. He had hinted that some of the best known gentlemen in England were amongst his clientele, and that they relied on his absolute discretion! I had decided to use the same characters as before, the mistress and the maid, but in a slightly different way. Once again they are in a room with a washstand and a bed, but this time there is more light. It is an attic room and light floods in from a clerestory above. Also, there is an apparatus on a tripod set up facing the bed.

The mistress strips first until she is dressed only in her stockings and suspenders and corset. Then, as before, instructing the maid to do exactly as she says, she strips her, starting with the slippers from her feet and continuing, slowly and carefully, with each item until she is completely naked. She tells her to lie on the bed and ties her hands together behind the central spar of the bed frame quite loosely so that she can move and pull her hands apart to some extent although she is still confined.

I was aware that often it was preferred to have the subject completely bound and unable to move with the sensual parts of the body fully open, but for my new idea, movement was necessary, indeed essential.

The mistress now removes her bodice to fully expose her bosom. Whereas the points of the maid's comely young breasts are quite large and hard and dark and round like raisins, the paps of the mistress are more pointed and the tips small but quite long and pink and set in a rosy aureole the size of a florin.

She leans over and kisses the maid fully and passionately on the lips so that her hanging breasts touch the maid's a little. The maid gasps and smiles, stretching her arms so that the bonds are pulled taut.

The mistress is now completely undressed apart from her stockings and suspender belt which are both a pattern of crimson and black reflecting her full auburn hair and rosy breasts. She says, 'now it is time to introduce you to Charles!' From under the bed she takes a codpiece made of leather. It is seven inches long, stiff and of a regular thickness, stitched finely around a solid core and pointed slightly at one end. It has two straps attached to the blunt end with which the mistress fastens it around her thighs so that it extends outwards from her pubes. She also finds a small tub with a screw top which she opens and takes a smear of an oily substance with which she anoints the member, making the brown leather darker and more glossy.

'This is Charles', she says, 'he is determined to give you pleasure!' The maid says nothing, she simply looks at the member, raising herself as far from the mattress as her binding will allow her and opening her mouth a little. Her lips are luscious and wet, her eyes gleaming as if almost in tears.

The mistress kneels on the bed causing the mattress to sag a little. She takes the legs of the maid and forces them apart, holding them high on both hands then resting the heels on her shoulders

Then, in a smooth movement, using both her hands, she pulls the lips of the maid's quim apart and inserts the member into the maid. The maid writhes and emits something like a squeal. She flinches, then seems to almost fall back as if submitting to the pressure that forces her whole body backwards and into the sheets and the mattress, her hands forced into the wall behind the bed.

The mistress says 'this is what we both want, more than can be imagined!'

Then, rhythmically, she forces herself into the maid causing her buttocks to rise from the bed, her legs to flex, her back to arch, her bosom to rise and fall and her mouth, silently, to convulse with her shrieks and cries. The mistress's eyes shine with a sort of fiery lust. Her lips are taut. She is giving all her attention to the maid, every move she makes, the stretching and compressing of the folds and tucks of her body, the creasing of her face and, especially, the sound, somewhere between a sigh and a scream, she makes each time the member is forced deeper inside her.

The cinematic apparatus, with whirrs and clicks, in a similarly rhythmic war, records every motion.

As soon as I completed this, I contemplated for a moment. I had stressed the sounds that the maid had made, and yet that was something that would not be recorded by the camera. Of course, the written word could do that. It was all powerful, almost omniscient. It could record what people looked like what they said and even what they thought. That was something the moving image could never aspire to.

Ashbee was pleased with the work I had returned to him. Hmm,' he said, 'your work is well written and genuinely original; not something for which my business is noted!'

I was delighted by this.

'The use of the moving pictures is a work of genius,' he declared enthusiastically. 'I must admit that my reservations about the efficiency of photography are partly confounded by this.'

'Why is it different?' I asked.

He thought for a moment. 'I think it is different,' he said. One photograph is a document from the past. It is a moment in time that is over. You cannot revive it. The moving picture, however, is here and now, you are experiencing it. I would like to live to see it perfected.'

'I am sure you will,' I said.

He paused for a moment and then he shook his head. 'No, I am in the rotting season of my life. I have been aware of that for some time.' He paused for a moment then returned to the matter of the manuscript.

'However,' he declared, 'the true test if its merit will come when it is presented to my client. He is a younger man, although well appointed, so I suspect he may understand the new apparatus better than I.'

He looked thoughtful for a moment and smiled.

'I like your work very much and I will increase your payment by a shilling for each episode.'

He opened a drawer of his desk and took out two sheets of foolscap. I noted that they have been typed on with his machine

'Here are the profiles of two other clients. You will see they are identified only by numbers. The names are known only by myself. Suffice it to say that one is a well known artist and scientist and the other a titled gentleman from the country.

'In the case of one, his obsession is that he is attracted to women smoking cigarettes. The other is a lech that is rather rarer and which has no name that I know of. He is attracted to women of the lower classes, but not whores. Women who are skivvies. Women who clean floors and ovens and hearths. In short, women who delve in dirt!'

Although this was rare something made me think that I had

heard of the condition myself before.

He gave the sheets to me.

'You must return these, but use your imagination, Mr Ledbury. Choose one or the other. I'll be interested to see what you can do!'

I had one more call that afternoon. When I arrived at the College, Knowles was there to greet me. 'Professor Blacklock is attending the General Council of the College,' he said. He will be back presently. I have a delivery of books from the continent to collect. Please feel free to use the library. All we ask is that you ensure that you return any book exactly to its place. If you leave before the professor returns, the servitor will lock the office.' Aware of Isabella's fascination with the strange foreign books in Blacklock's library, I had thought that it might be useful to have a closer look.

I really didn't know where to start. Many of the books were in languages I could not read. I wished I had Isabella with me to decipher the German titles, but I knew her father would not permit it. Unsure what to do, I selected some titles at random and perused them. I wasn't really learning anything but the very act of opening and closing the books seemed like a form of progress.

I was so engrossed in this that I didn't notice Blacklock had returned. But then I felt a presence and I turned round to see that was standing, silently, watching me.

'I'm sorry,' I said. 'I'm intruding on your time and your private study.'

'Not at all,' he said. 'Do you think I would have accumulated such a collection just for my own use? That would be a very peculiar hobby. My students and my acolytes are always welcome in my library. I hope that, eventually, it will help advance scientific thought.'

'It is very good of you,' I said. 'I'm afraid that I'm not much of a student. Many of these books are incomprehensible to me.'

He laughed and beckoned me to join him at a seat at his round table.

'Some of them are unknown to me too. The true scholar doesn't aim always to accumulate knowledge. Sometimes it is enough to know that it is there.'

'I would like to have a library also,' I said. 'Some day when I am more settled.'

'You should have,' he said. 'I believe you are a writer yourself.'

I was surprised that he knew this.

'A writer, yes,' 'I said, 'but not a scholar. I write for some magazines, and I write poetry.' I didn't know why I was telling him this, but Professor Blacklock seemed to create a comfortable silence in which you could speak.

'I am not a poet,' he said. 'At least not in the conventional sense. I am a sort of scientist. But don't assume that there isn't an art to that.'

'The art of comprehending the human mind. That is quite an art.'

'I think it is, at least. It is not at all like conventional medicine. In surgery we can remove the ailing part of a body to better protect the whole. That is not possible with the mind.'

'Is there no cure, then, for the insane?'

'Some of my colleagues like to talk of a pathology of mental illness, so that by identifying a condition they can then seek a cure. I am not so sure.'

'What is your philosophy, then?'

'The mind does not work like a human body in which each bone or muscle has a function. It operates as a whole. It is a closed box.

We cannot access a part of it, only the whole.'

'What is Dr Freud's theory, then. I thought it was that through treatment we could access parts of the mind that have previously remained hidden?'

'That is one way to look at it, but I myself, do not prefer that model. Granted I agree that there is a conscious and subconscious component to the mind, but I don't believe that they can be easily separated. My method is distinct. I concentrate on behaviour. That is something that we can measure. We can impute that if a person behaves in a certain way, then his mind will be constructed in a certain way. If we can change the way a person behaves, then we may, in turn, change the way his mind will influence his behaviours in the future.'

'And is it possible to change someone's behaviour?'

'Ah, that is not difficult at all in simple ways. If you can train a dog to do tricks, you can train a man too. The techniques are actually basically the same.'

'And have you done that, in your experiments?'

'Not exactly, but remember that for many years in the asylums for the incarceration of the mentally ill, behaviour was controlled almost solely by the bill whip. I introduced more enlightened and humane ways of ensuring the patients could keep their behaviours in check. In time, with the better patients, it was possible to help them control their baser thoughts.'

'And how can you do that?'

He thought for a moment. 'It is complicated but, if you don't find it laughable I can probably give you a very basic example.'

'I'd like that,' I said. I felt that I was privileged to be receiving a sort of personal lesson from the great man.

'Well, suppose that you—I mean any person—has a problem that you cannot solve and it making you unhappy and also that your mind is fixated on it. You cannot solve it but you cannot think of anything else. Do you see?'

I nodded.

'Well then, I ask you to say to yourself 'I will solve this!'

I was a little puzzled.

'I know that it sound like nonsense,' he said smiling, 'but it is a very simple example.'

'But how will that help if the problem is insoluble?'

'Well, it may not be! We are not assuming that. But if you say that to yourself, or even out loud, eventually you will find that you are training your mind to counter a negative thought with a positive thought. Eventually it will become automatic for your mind to work this way and, if your anxiety is allayed, you may actually solve the problem!'

'I know someone who would very much like to acquire that sort of knowledge, if convention would allow.'

'Well, why don't you bring her here, Mr Ledbury. I don't allow convention to impede the acquisition of wisdom.'

For some reason I did not question why he had said 'she' rather than 'he'. I thought that perhaps the professor could read my mind. Then I thought about Isabella. There was nothing I could imagine that she would like more than to see Professor Blacklock's library. But that would require some further thought.

'I am indebted to you,' I said, 'for the use of your library, your elucidation of your theories and your kind words.'

That evening I met Isabella again at Lyons and we sat watching some slivers of rain on the window pouring a little milk into a new brew from Kerala.

I had brought some of my poems to show her.

'None of them have yet been published,' I said. 'I would like to make a little volume of them in due time, but they maybe need more work.'

She read several of them and focused on one:

In this place lies all I love,
That I have taken pains to name,
Yet nothing now remains the same,
The meadow below nor the sky above.

The budding glory of the trees,
The voice of water that softly speaks,
Whispers of wind from distant peaks,
The golden treasure of the bees.

For all of you is found in all of this,
The church stones singing a sacred word,
The trembling heart of a captive bird,
And all is lost in just one kiss.

'It's lovely,' she said. 'You *are* a romantic!'

I was pleased.

'Oh!' she said, and shook a little as if a chill wind has suddenly hit her.

'A sweetheart,' she said. You must have a sweetheart!'

I didn't say anything, but my hand must have moved to my pocket watch.

She held out her hand.

'Will you show me? Please.'

As always, I could not deny her. I opened the watch. In it was contained an image. It was an ethereal sort of image, fading to the edges, of a pretty young woman dressed in a simple frock with a lace collar.

"What's her name?'

'Dorothea… Dorothea Woodburn.'

'And she is your sweetheart?'

I shook my head.

'No. She is dead. I killed her.'

There was a pause. Isabella sat back and looked at me, frowning.

'You must tell me everything,' she said.

So I did, and this is the story I told:

'I was born in the ancient parish of Godalming, in west Surrey. My father was a wheelwright. He would work all day, making wheels the old-fashioned way, nailing the strakes on to the fellows one by one, although the blacksmith would also make round irons which could be hammered on and would cool on the wood.

'I liked to sit in the workshop when I wasn't at school, watching my father. It was just him and I; my mother had died giving birth to me and I had no brothers or sisters.

'I was a fit and agile young boy. I could run like a whippet hound and leap like a flea. But I was shy and retiring. I liked walking in the countryside and I loved writing and drawing. The rhythm of the seasons seemed natural to me there was a time to flood the water meadow and to cut the osier willows to make baskets and the plants and butterflies would blossom and appear in tune with our taskmaking..

'As I grew older I began walking out with Dorothea Woodburn. I knew her from school. My father liked her. She was the daughter of the local brownsmith.'

Isabella gave me a slightly strange look so I moved on.

'And then… and then my father died. Suddenly. One day I found him just slumped over his workbench. Stone dead.

'So I took over the business. I worked hard but it wasn't the same. Everyone was suspicious. They thought that I was too young, too dreamy to succeed. And they were right, it didn't succeed. Only a couple of months after my father's death—after toiling all day in the workshop—I continued the task of clearing out my father's little office. In one drawer of the desk I found a key. It opened another drawer that was partly hidden beneath the front drawer. In it were several papers neatly arranged. My father had been struggling to find enough custom for some time and these papers indicated that debts had been incurred which the business had no way of paying back.'

'I think that you must have very much felt alone,' Isabella said. 'Apart, of course, for your young lady.'

I must have paused, lost in thought. 'Tell me what happened then,' Isabella added.

'I sinned,' I blurted it out. 'It was behind the hay ricks. I got Dorothea with child. When we realised that she was that we also realised that we couldn't hide it. The parson expressed his disapproval, as did her parents in clear terms, but he agreed to marry us in the chapel at Milford.' I continued with the story:

'I sold the wheelright's workshop and paid off the debts as best I could. I made no explanation for the failure of the business but the townsfolk, I'm sure, blamed me absolutely.

'We rented a little cottage and I got some work bringing in the harvest. I worked during the day and spent the evening writing poetry and making sketches. We were poor but happy enough. One day, Dorothea said, we would move to the city and I would become a famous writer.'

At this point, I faltered. My voice had grown more feeble. I felt faint. But Isabella looks me straight in the eye.

'Take some water,' she said. 'Here, I will give it to you.'

I continued and told the rest of the story in the most concise way I could, concentrating just on the simple facts:

'The labour came weeks earlier than we expected. I called Mrs Gulliver, the midwife. It lasted some time. Dorothea was in terrible pain. Mrs Gulliver did all she could, and then we called the village doctor, but when it was over, Dorothea had not survived.'

I paused.

'And the baby… ' Isabella asked.

'The baby was born… ' I didn't know to express this.

'The baby was born… but it wasn't *right*. The head seemed to large and misshapen. The eyes were bulbous.'

Mrs Gulliver said 'please go and find me some more hot water.'

I said, 'We have used all of it; it will have to be drawn and boiled.'

'*Please* find it,' she said.

'When I returned. A little while later, the little baby boy was wrapped in a coarse white sheet, like a shroud.'

'There is nothing to be done now,' she said, 'other than call the Pastor.'

I looked at her. I thought I was going out of my mind. 'There is nothing you can do now,' she said, kindly, and led me away from the place.

'Afterwards, while I was still shocked and unable to do anything at all, Doris, the sister of Dorothea, came to me and said foul things. She said that I had killed my own mother. That I was cursed. That the child had been conceived in sin and that I had reaped the harvest of sin. The townsfolk believed it too, I was sure. They would look at me and whisper'.

I had little more to say. 'That is why I came to London and have never returned.'

Isabella sort of shook her head a little but not too vigorously as if trying to get rid of something that was bothering her.

She looked me straight in the face. For a moment I thought she was going to strike me

'You didn't do anything wrong', she said. 'The sister was just being wicked for her own reasons. Sometimes if people are ignored they say evil things just to get attention. Perhaps she was jealous…'

Her eyes were glistening a little as if they were tearful.

'No-one can explain why your wife and child had to die. It happens in the world because life sometimes can be cruel, but it can be kind too.'

She laid her hand on mine. 'Perhaps some day you will have another child.'

I didn't know what to say but I blurted out 'do you think *you* will ever have a child?'

She sat upright in her chair and frowned a little then she seemed to gain her composure. The tone of her voice changed a little.

'I believe that it surely should be every woman's ambition to experience it.'

She arranged her hair and organised her purse and things.

'I must go now, but nothing that has happened to you is your fault. I do believe that you are a good man.'

After Isabella had left, I felt a gnawing emptiness but also a great relief. I had never told anyone my story. I remembered shivering in the brougham wishing I had someone I could confide in, and now I had told at least a part of my story to someone and the result had not been disastrous.

Chapter Nine

MARKED BY DESTINIES

Crime, especially murder, is very pleasant to think about in the abstract: it is hearing blustery rain on the window pane when sitting indoors. It reinforces a sense of safety, even of pleasure, to know that murder is possible, just not here.

Judith Flanders, *The Invention of Murder*

If once a man indulges himself in murder, very soon he comes to think little of robbing; and from robbing he comes next to drinking and Sabbath-breaking, and from that to incivility and procrastination. Once begun upon this downward path, you never know where you are to stop.

Thomas De Quincey, *On Murder as a Fine Art*

At breakfast, Bill Bartholomew was being particularly fractious. 'The dockers are greedy,' he said, 'they fail to consider others, such as myself, who depend on their labour for their living. If they strike it could be disastrous for me.'

I spread some marmalade on my toasted teacake. I had long realised that Bartholomew viewed world events through a lens focused only on his own immediate prospects and well-being.

'They claim to be paid so little,' he added, 'yet I've heard say they thieve as much as they earn every day.'

I baulked at this. 'But they claim they are not even paid enough to feed their children and keep them out of rags.'

'Well, why should they have so many children that they can't afford to keep. Your government should stop it.'

I thought of Galton and his enemies of the state.

'Having a child is a precious gift from God,' I said. 'No man should have the right to deny it.'

'Well, if you say so,' he said. I think he detected the slightly higher pitch in my voice and decided he didn't want an argument. 'But something should be done those filthy closes and vennels they inhabit. They put off my customers coming to the docks.'

There was a pause in the conversation and I perhaps suggested by my demeanour that I had no intention of continuing it. However, he was determined to have the last word.

'Anarchists, that's who it is, causing all this trouble. Some young boy has tried to shoot the Prince and Princess of Wales. Would you believe it. And he says it's all because of the war with the Boers!'

I returned to my room. There was no doubt that Bartholomew's arrogance was excessive. Perhaps this was simply the nature of the American character, but there was also something in his tirade that seemed out of kilter. I wonderered if he himself had some undisclosed secrets.

I was musing on this when there was a knock at the door. It was Mrs Merrilees who requested that I join her in the parlour for some morning tea.

We sat in the commodious armchairs with their tartan antimacassars. For some reason she seemed to want to talk to me and she started making conversation.

'You must be very lucky having a home in the country,' she said. 'I was born in Bow, in the noise and smoky breath of the big city. Mind you, it wasn't nothing as big then.

'I was well done by with me husband Arthur. He was a clerk with the Russo Brothers, the importers of olive oil for thirty years since, but poor Arthur passed away, just after we moved to here. But I still got my Raph and Kathy, and Kathy's two boys. Her man's a foreman in the cooperage.

'What about your family, Mr Ledbury? You talk about them very little.'

'I'm afraid my parents are dead,' I said.

'Do you not have any brothers or sisters?'

'No.'

'I had my sister Lily, but I lost her. My brother Raph is still alive, he was a great example to young Raph. He lives in Portsmouth. He has contagion of the lungs. I want to go see him soon. I will ask Lily to take care of you gentlemen.'

'I'm sure we will be able to take care of ourselves,' I said.

'Oh no, I couldn't imagine that. I took care of my Arthur, all the time, right to the end.

She looked rather sad and contemplative and shifted a little uneasily in her chair.

'Do go home, Mr Ledbury,' she said. 'I know it is something you are feared of doing. I never go to where I was born myself, but it's not there. You must go home sometime.'

I realised now why we were having this conversation. Mrs Merrilees was concerned about the recent events. She was a caring woman and was concerned for me, I believed, but perhaps after the initial thrill of the police involvement, she thought it might be better if the affair could just disappear, and me along with it.

She rose from the chair. 'Oh, there is another letter for you.' She picked it up from the demi-lune table. 'But I don't think it is like the others.'

She gave it to me. It was not from Jeremy. The handwriting was small and neat.

'Mr Ledbury, you really should go home sometime and see your family. All this business with the police is wearing you down.'

She was right, but, of course, I had no home to go to. 'I am planning to… very soon,' I lied.

The letter was carefully written on perfumed paper with a little rose in the top corner. It was from Isabella. It said: 'Dear John, There is another lecture at the institution this evening at seven. I am going with Mrs Manners. Please meet us there if you can come. That is, if you don't mind being chaperone to two beautiful ladies!'

This was the sort of outrageous thing that I was getting used to Isabella saying. She seemed to enjoy being a little wicked in her conversation.

I had been summoned by Ord, I discovered, when a carriage arrived a little while later, before I had time to address the business of amatory literature.

When I entered Ord's office, unusually he was alone.

'Sit down, Mr Ledbury,' he said'

I did so.

'I believe that you have taken my daughter to an entertainment at the Photographic Society! It has become quite a sensation the city, I believe'

I had been meaning to mention to him that I had seen Isabella, but somehow I hadn't got around to it.

'She was interested and I obtained some tickets,' I said. 'I ensured she got the steam train at Waterloo. She told me her home is very near the station and that she travels often.'

'It is not as close to the station as I would like!'

He clasped his hands together and frowned slightly.

'I am getting to be an old man. I will be sixty shortly. Isabella is all I have and, you may understand, it is not easy for me to guide her. She is an extremely headstrong child!'

He shook his head ruefully.

'But she is not a child anymore. She is a woman.'

'Yes,' I said, 'she is very headstrong and a very attractive woman.'

I was not sure that I should have said this and I stopped, gazing open-mouthed at Ord waiting for him to speak. Eventually he did so.

'The tickets to the entertainment were three shillings apiece, I believe.' He paused, then he said, 'You will not object if I ask you what is the payment received in your line of business?'

'It is increasing all the time,' I said. This was true. 'I have a lucrative new commission, writing reports for gentlemen...

Technical reports.'

He nodded and rolled his tongue in his mouth. He took out his pipe and lit it.

'Have you told Isabella any details of the investigation we are undertaking.'

'It may have come up briefly in conversation,' I said, 'but, of course, I knew that she wouldn't incautiously reveal any details to anyone.'

'That is not what I am worried about,' he said. 'You may be beginning to be aware of the very great deal of evil that is all around us. I have dealt with it for too many years, but no matter how hard we work to combat it, it increases. London is a cesspool of vice.'

He shifted the seat at his desk as if about to rise.

'In the near future I intend to retire from this work. I hope to return to Scotland. To the country. Naturally, I would like Isabella to accompany me. But, as I said, she is a woman, she will find her own life.'

He leaned forward towards me.

'Mr Ledbury, you will not disobey me in this matter. You may continue to see my daughter only if you swear to me, on all that is good, not to speak another word about this business or any other crime.'

I had no choice but to agree.

Ord nodded slowly.

Mrs Euphemia Manners was not at all like her husband. She scarcely seemed older than Isabella, although Manners must have been a man in his forties. She was indeed beautiful, with full black hair, dark eyes, arched eyebrows, a full mouth and a radiant smile, but she didn't share the slightly chilly reserve of her husband. In fact, as I spent more time with her, I couldn't help but feel there was some sort of wild passion inside her that could at any moment explode.

'There may be a new college formed called Imperial College and they are of a mind to admit women to their medical faculty. Isabella and I may join them' she said.

'Oh, has Dr Manners suggested it?'

She and Isabella sharing a conspiratorial look which suggested that he had not.

As we gathered outside the lecture hall, a large man with an impressive mane of hair and beard swept past us. Mrs Manners recognised him.

That is Havelock Ellis, he writes about... ' she looked at Isabella again and smiled. ' ...he writes about intimate relations, yet it is said he lives with a women with sapphic tendencies and they don't... '

Isabella interrupted 'perhaps Mr Ledbury doesn't know what is meant by 'sapphic tendencies'.'

I thought of the work I was doing for Henry Ashbee and felt my blood rush to my face. The ladies were having grand fun at my expense.

'Oh, I'm sorry Mr Ledbury. It's just that I believe that you have been on some adventures with my husband, purely in the course of upholding the law, of course!'

Isabella nudged her. 'Oh, I forgot that your business is of the strictest confidentiality! I will be very quiet like a mouse.'

An usher called us from the anteroom into the lecture hall. I was very glad of this interruption as the conversation was taking a turn that was very difficult for me. After all, I didn't know what Dr Manners had told his wife about me.

I thought also that I didn't really know about Mrs Manners. I knew that Isabella was very clever and perceptive, but I felt that she was still a naïf compared to her companion. I felt for my pocket watch. I did not know too much about the female kind. The only one I had been close too was Dorothea. Now here I was in the company of two young women who were not of the country sort at all.

As I pondered on the nature of women and womanhood, I'm afraid many aspects of the evening's lecture passed me by. However, some images remained in my head.

At the start Ellis came out to the lectern with another man. 'Gentlemen... and ladies,' he said, thank you for coming once again. I trust that you enjoyed the first lecture, by our patron, Mr Francis Galton. Tonight we have a treat of almost such magnitude. I am delighted to welcome, from the United States, Eugene Talbot from Chicago.'

Talbot was a small man with an extravagant moustache. He commenced by showing four glass slides which he labelled: 'Brain Of A Paranoiac Criminal', 'Brain Of A Genius' 'Idiot Brain', 'Imbecile Brain'.

This was passably interesting, but he then laboured on with slight distinctions in a droning voice that I found hard to follow.

But then he continued and I found a topic closer to my heart.

'Shakespeare recognised that some who are perhaps deformed and marked by destiny are prone to mischief. Thus, in *Richard III*, Margaret calls Richard:

Thou elvish-marked, abortive, rooting hog!
Thou that wast sealed in thy nativity
The slave of nature and the son of hell!

'A popular expression in Shakespeare's day for a deformed person was 'stigmatic.' It denoted any one who had been stigmatised or burnt with an iron (an ignominious punishment), and hence was employed to represent a person on whom nature had set a mark of deformity. Thus in *Henry VI*, Queen Margaret says:

But thou art neither like thy sire nor dam;
But like a foul misshapen stigmatic,
Marked by the destinies to be avoided,
As venom toads, or lizards' dreadful stings.

And later Clifford says to Richard:

Foul stigmatic, that's more than thou canst tell.'

This idea rather took hold of me. Was it possible that some, let's say 'criminal' types were marked in some way, visible or invisible, from birth, and destined to follow whatever unfortunate path that nature led them to? I determined to consider this in more detail at a later opportunity.

The rest of the lecture consisted of a series of slides, similar to those shown by Galton but not of a composite nature, of various criminal types or with mentally defective conditions.

After the lecture, the three of us went to Lyons corner house for tea.

Mrs Manners was quite animated.

'We are very fortunate that medicine in England has made such great stride. Not so many years ago the only treatments we had were primitive. Now we have anaesthetic and antiseptic and… '

'Of course,' interrupted Isabella, 'those were not invented in England!'

'Surely they were.'

'No,' said Isabella, they were invented in Scotland.,

'Oh,' I forgot. She leaned over and put her hand on my arm. 'Isn't she just a perfect little Scotch lassie, Mr Ledbury?'

Isabella took in her breath.

'You are very rude, Phamie,' she said. Then she looked me in the eyes.

'Do you think I'm a lassie, John?'

I opened my mouth to speak but couldn't think of anything.

There was a pause, then we all laughed to release the tension.

'But, really, isn't modern medicine a wonder that allows us to treat poor unfortunates such as those we saw?' continued Mrs Manners.

'I'm not really sure they are being treated particularly well,' I said. I thought they looked rather like specimens, like the zoological discoveries at Regent's Park.'

'Perhaps we have to allow some experimentation on the most

unfortunate. For the common good in the future,' said Mrs Manners.

'But what about Galton's proposal for the sterilisation of the lower orders of society. Is that not inhumane?'

After I had said this it occurred to me that perhaps this was too delicate a subject to discuss with young ladies, but neither of them blushed.

'Yes,' said Isabella, 'no-one has the right to do that unless it can be proved that the children would suffer absolutely.'

'I do know that my husband would approve of it,' said Manners. He is a keen Galtonite and reads all the publications.' She paused and pursed her lips for a moment. 'My husband is at heart a theorist. He only works for the police for the thrill of the grisly cases he likes, and to be in the city. We live in the country mostly, near Oxford. I get to visit the city occasionally.'

'Dr Manners is of a noted country family,' Isabella explained. He chose to study medicine so that he could benefit the people of his parish. He does much good work.'

There was a pause in the conversation.

'Are you returning to Oxford tonight?' I asked Mrs Manners.'

'I am staying at the Ralston Hotel, in Montague Street. They know me there as I often stay there when I am in London unaccompanied. I will probably dine alone and retire early.'

Shortly afterwards we saw Mrs Manners to her carriage. As we had a few minutes before I had to see Isabella on her road home, I now had the chance to broach the subject of my conversation with Ord with Isabella. I was nervous. I anticipated that Isabella would be unhappy when I told her that I could see her on one condition, but, in fact, when I did get round to saying it, she didn't seem upset at all!

'No matter,' she said, 'I will find out from Phamie, apparently Dr Manners is not very cautious at all, especially when he is in his cups!'

I didn't really know how to reply to this.

Eventually I said, 'You would still like to see me, then?'

'Of course I would, 'you amuse me greatly!'

I wasn't sure if this was a compliment but I was pleased I could see her.

I had a late evening appointment. I passed by the hotel where Mrs Manners stayed. I suddenly remembered Ashbee's elucidation of his clients: ' …a country doctor of good stock'!

I entered into a little antechamber at the premises occupied by the Theosophical Society. A fire was lit so it was pleasantly warm. The interpretation of the literary stigmata had roused me to consider whether there could be any particular interpretation of my strange dreams. Therefore, I thought I would approach the expert on signs, Mr Waites.

However, the man I encountered was not Waites. Instead, it was a large man of about thirty years of age. He had a pleasant enough countenance but his head seemed a little too large for his body and his neck was very thick. When he spoke, his voice was mellow and sonorous.

'Come in and sit down, Mr Ledbury. I was expecting you.'

'Actually,' I said, 'my appointment was with Mr Waites.'

'Ah,' he said, 'they haven't told you. Mr Waites is on urgent business in the country. My name is Crowley. He asked me to see you.' He added, 'On behalf of the Society.'

I explained to him my wish to try to interpret my strange dreams and I outlined them in as much detail as I could remember.

'There are two aspects to these reveries that are easily explained,' he commenced. 'Firstly, many dreams are spawned from anxiety. It is said that we live in an age of anxiety because of the hectic pace of change that our new industries and ways of living have induced. I have observed that there is nothing so likely to cause among the learned classes as a fall from their position. The underworld of London you describe in your dream is exaggerated but it is also very real—many a gentleman has been plunged into it.'

Certainly, I thought, my current rather impecunious position was the cause of some anxiety, but the recent dreams were much more vivid than any before.

'What is the second?' I asked.

'The second is also obvious. Many dreams are a form of wish fulfilment. We can be someone in our dreams that is more than what we are. Some may dream of being a great horseman, a soldier, a diplomat, a lord or a lady. A person of standing or a hero of some kind. You are an intelligent and a literary man, so Mr Sherlock Holmes, perhaps, is the object of your fantasy, the one you most wish to emulate.'

We talked a little longer but I didn't feel that we were getting any further into the depths of my visions. Then he said 'Mr Ledbury, I do wonder what your interest is in our Society. Apart from the obvious there are other avenues of adventure into the hidden wonders of the world.'

'What type of adventures?' I asked.

'Magick!' he exclaimed. 'There are methods whereby we can conjure up worlds beyond that which we commonly inhabit. However, it requires us to lose many of the inhibitions that tie us to pure quotidian concerns.'

I was curious, so I asked him to explain his methods. His explanation I found quite shocking and beyond my immediate ken. However, I took my leave and promised that I would think carefully about a proposal he made to me. My encounter with Crowley I found not dissimilar to my first meeting with Ashbee, and that again caused me some concern.

I returned to my lodgings to encounter a visitor. Raph Merrilees was master's mate on the battleship HMS Royal Sovereign. He was very proud of the Queen's navy and of his post. He could recount the date of commission and the size of every ship in the fleet.

'The size of Her Majesty's Royal Navy is equivalent to the size of the navies of France and of Russia put together and is increasing all the time, although the Germans are also growing fast. The new thing will be massive underwater ships that will patrol the waters of the world unseen.'

When he was on shore, as an unmarried man, he mostly lodged with his sister in Houndsditch, but he often visited his mother, who he would refer to as 'Mater Marion'.

He would produce a bottle of rum and entertain me with tales of the strange places he had been and the tricks and caprices of his crew. These exotic little stories were a useful counterpart to the darker imaginings of Crowley and I had, rather unwittingly, become involved in his continuously more unlikely stories when a carriage came to the door. It was a messenger from Ord. They had discovered another girl!

This time we were at the east end of the city. Another, rather nondescript, terraced house. Apparently, on this occasion, the alert had arisen as the door of the property had been left open, blowing in the wind and had drawn the attention of a neighbour's maid.

Inside, the blinds were drawn in the room, as in the others. There was an overwhelming smell of wax as if everything had been recently polished. Then that seemed to dissipate and I could smell something else. Lavender, I thought. I was on edge. All my senses were over-reacting. The image of the girl seemed to be burning into my mind, like a photographic image etched on a silver-coated plate. I shook myself and tried to regain some composure.

Dr Manning entered first, then Ord and the rest of us behind. I saw the girl. She was naked like the others. I saw the outline of the symbol drawn in blood like the others. Manners was stooped over the corpse.

Suddenly he shouted. 'She is breathing. She is alive!'

It did not take long for the headlines to appear:

Scotland Yard have landed a remarkable coup. For once stripped of their blindfolds, they have actually saved the poor victim of a horrible crime. The girl was snatched from her certain fate at the hands of the criminal lunatic known as Jeremy by the constables at the moment she was sure to breathe her last. Out sources can only inform that the incident took place at an undisclosed location in the east end of the city. All England is waiting to be informed as to whether the felon has been apprehended

Chapter Ten

THE PHILANTHROPIC ASSASSIN

It is our semi-barbarous Code of Laws that makes Heroes of vulgar felons, by exciting the imagination and calling forth sympathy and pity for a poor wretch about to become the principal performer in a public Show. The Law, is the Newgate dramatist; the scaffold is the stage; the whole mixed public is the audience; and 'the moral' is, in its most extensive influence, that there is something *great* in a man who is to be hanged.

P H Horne, *The Philanthropic Assassin*

It is in death that the individual becomes at one with himself... in the slow, but already visible, approach of death, the dull common life at last becomes an individuality; a black border isolates it and gives it the style of its truth.

Michel Foucault, *Collected Works*

The next day I sat in my room contemplating. The result of the previous day had merely been a crushing disappointment. Ord had felt obliged to report to me as soon as the dealings at the crime scene were complete.

'The girl has been taken to a hospital, but it seems that she remembers nothing at all of her experiences. Amnesia. The doctors won't say whether her memories can be retrieved or no. I thought of taking her to Blacklock. He must have experience of such things! But her family and the doctors have insisted that she must be allowed to rest for a few days.'

I was disappointed, of course, but then I reflected that we should be grateful that the girl had not perished. This was surely good news and there was, of course, a glimmer of hope that her memory would return. In consideration, I was not unhappy at the moment. So much had happened in the last week that it felt like a month, or more. I was naturally chastened by the murders and puzzled by the enigma of the murderer, but part of me was coming alive, for the first time since I had left Godalming. Isabella was also the first young woman I had spoken to at any length since I had lost Dorothea.

I had not spoken to anyone about that and the account I had given Isabella, I realised, was delivered with brevity, so that I would not lose my emotional control.

I had been miserable and lost for a long time. As miserable, I thought, as any of the poor wretches I had seen in my nightmarish visions.

Many times I had thought of death as a merciful release from my woes. What kept me alive, I thought, was my poetry and, strangely, the job for Doyle. I knew that Holmes was an illusion, purely a creature of fiction, but the fact that so many felt so close to him, imagining him as a flesh and blood person gave me, in a way, some faith in people, and in writing. I enjoyed responding to the letters and had missed doing them since the police had suborned them. I admitted to myself that I was also enjoying writing the stuff for Ashbee. I was uneasy about it, but I excused myself with the fact that it was all just fantasy, anonymous and for private consumption.

But now I felt alive again! To what extent this was due to my adventures and what extent to Isabella was not clear. Well, actually it was clear! I was completely in love with her.

With the advance I had received from Ashbee, enhanced by the extra I had received for the sapphic episode, I had bought tickets for us both for another display of moving pictures at the Royal Photographic Society.

I was fascinated to see it as I had been imagining scenes photographed for my last amatory episode—thankfully not like the scenes we were watching today. Nevertheless, I couldn't stop thinking what Ashbee would have thought of such images, if he had ever seen such a thing.

The room was dark but in clear view was a young boy in short trousers and a striped shirt watched by an officious looking adult. He was swaying from side to side and bobbing up and down. He was boxing a kangaroo! Next were some scenes of a boat race, the oars rising and falling almost hypnotically.

Isabella was sitting close enough to me in the cramped room that I could feel her shoulder press against mine and smell her hair.

Afterwards, for once we did not speak about murder, or stigmata, or Galton's eugenic plan, We spoke about water and boats and fields and summer sun.

I thought we were happy together

The next morning I awoke after a reasonably refreshing sleep, troubled only by images of whirring cameras pursuing me through the streets of London. A minor discomfort compared to my too frequent excursions into the darker recesses of the capital.

I had refreshed myself with some muffins and tea when, unexpectedly, Ord called on me.

I was excited. 'Has the girl improved? Are we nearer to solving the case?'

'Unfortunately not.' His expression was grim. 'However, for want of any progress, we will follow another avenue in this tangled web.'

He explained.

'A constable has a brother who works at Wandsworth Gaol. He noticed a man who has a tattoo on the back of his hand that resembles our sign. We are going to interview him, but we have to be quick.'

'Yes,' I said, 'if he is the culprit we have to apprehend him immediately.'

He shook his head. 'No, unfortunately he can't be responsible for our cases. He has been in jail for some time. He is a buggerer and murderer of young boys and he is to be hanged for it at nine o'clock tomorrow morning!'

When we came face to face with John Evans, I must admit I was shocked. Although I had no truck with the theories of Galton and Ellis, I had to admit that he went a good way to fulfilling the picture of a criminal lunatic. His head was lumpish, his ears protruding and his canine teeth (his front teeth being entirely missing) pointed and large.

Ord had explained the sorry history of Evans. He had spent most of his thirty-five years in asylums, gaols or workhouses. Recently, however, he had found a job as a sort of Johnny-do-it-all at a poorhouse in Soho. Two boys had disappeared within a week. Then the body of one was found beneath some loose floorboards in a cupboard when a slavie had noticed a smell. The boy was naked from the waist down, his rear portion all bloody. His hands were tied behind his back with a bit of cord and his mouth gagged with a blue scarf that witnesses had testified had belonged to Evans. Despite questioning, Evans had never revealed the whereabouts of the second boy. The jury had unanimously agreed that he should hang. He was now awaiting that fate.

Evans did not look well, nor as if he had been kindly treated. There were bruises and cuts on his face, his eyes were bloodshot and his skin seemed stretched and taut on his bony jaw. He was confined in a strait-jacket made of duck cloth and his hands, which were tied, contained within large sailcloth mitts. Ord asked him his name and he replied in the affirmative.

Ord asked the warder if he would remove one of the mitts.

'Is it likely he will try to harm us?'

The warder looked embarrassed. 'Well no, it is for him not to harm himself.' He gave us almost a conspiratorial look, 'He... deranges himself. His own... private parts.'

Despite Evans's rather fearful appearance, his voice was gentle, almost effeminate, not refined but not coarse. We eventually persuaded the turnkey to remove the mitt and the jacket partially so that we could see the tattoo. He did so reluctantly.

'Where did you get this?' Asked Ord, indicating the back of his hand.

He looked puzzled. Then he said, 'I went to the well but it was too deep and the bucket broke.'

He held his hand out and the constable pulled the fingers apart, rather too forcibly I thought, but Evans didn't show any sign of pain.

'We need to know where you got this!'

'I followed the river to the sea. I hoped it would set me free. But all I found was a dark cave.'

The constable look exasperated. I thought he was going to hit him, so I interjected.

'Can you not remember a little,' I asked. 'It is very important to us.'

He looked more closely at me.

'What is your name?' He asked.

'My name is John Ledbury.'

'My name is John Evans.'

He frowned for a moment, but strangely it made his face seem a little more gentle.

'You have seen death,' he said. 'I can see it in your eyes. Will you come to see me die?'

'I would not like to,' I said. 'Why do you ask me?'

'No reason other than that I would like it.' He paused. 'It was a man, you know.'

'What man?'

'A man gave me it as a gift. He said it was a gift. I don't know why he gave it to me.'

'Who was this man. Can you remember anything about him?'

Evans shook his head. 'He dealt down by the docks in… I can't remember… ' He began to cough and splutter a little and to me, suddenly, he seemed to visibly shrink.

'Will you spare poor John some water?'

He took some water and then he fell back.

'I have now to begin to die.' He looked very strange and his eyes seemed to go up into his head so we could see mostly the whites. Then he began to tremble all over, not very violently but steadily.

'That's him gone again,' said the turnkey. 'You won't get any more out of him tonight.'

'Nor,' said Ord, ruefully, 'are we likely to tomorrow.'

'Stay with him,' Ord said to the constable. 'Note anything he says before the fatal tree.'

We left the poor little cell.

I was confused but I had to say something. 'I have an idea who he is referring to.'

'And who is that?' Asked Ord.

'I saw him in a dream,' I said, 'they call him His Nibs, but I think he is Moriarty.'

'Mr Ledbury, you are aware that you are referring to a character in the stories of Mr Doyle!'

'Yes,' I said meekly. I didn't know how to explain myself.

Ord looked at me as if he had had enough of madmen for today.

'Does this person you have met in your dream resemble anyone you have met in real life?'

'No,' I admitted.

'Then I don't see how it can be if any help to us.'

'I would like someone to explain my dreams,' I said. 'I have made some enquiries to the Theosophical Society.' I stopped. I didn't want to tell him about my encounter with Crowley.

'Well, your dreams may be the business of Mr Waites or Mrs Besant, but I'm afraid it is not the business of the Metropolitan Police.'

I had an idea, but I said nothing.

The next morning, I went down to the final scene. I had never seen a scaffold before

I was allowed to join two other gentlemen, who I believed to be of the Press. After a short while a procession came towards the gallows. It was led by the Chief Warder, the Chaplain, John Evans, his arms pinioned and almost carried by two warders by his side. His eyes were half-closed, his lips trembling and his mouth foaming a little. They were followed a little way behind by the hangman and his assistant. As they reached the gallows, the assistant hangman dropped to his knees to pinion the prisoner's legs.

The Chaplain approached Evans. 'Is there anything you would like to say?'

He coughed a little to clear his throat. Then he said a few words in his little voice.

'I would like Mr Ledbury to pray for my soul.'

Then the hangman placed a white hood over his head and then the noose.

As the court clock struck the hour, the hangman pulled the lever committing the body of John Evans to a drop of around seven feet and his soul to oblivion.

We left the scene leaving the body to remain suspended by the rope for the customary hour. As we left the bell began to toll. I found the sound distressing, playing on my senses in a peculiar way. As we exited, I gulped in the fresh air of the prison yard with relief.

The crowd dispersed quite quickly when the event was over, chattering and keen to get to taverns or coffee houses to recount their experience or, in the case of the press men, to get to their offices to write a lurid account of the hanging. Before I could leave, however, someone approached me. It was the turnkey who had introduced us to Evans.

'Mr Ledbury, Sir.'

I was slightly embarrassed at being there. 'Can I help?' I said.

'I was wondering if you would take the prisoner's possessions?'

'Doesn't he have any family to collect them?'

'Not that I know of.' He added 'There isn't much. I could just put them in the incinerator.'

I consented. It seemed wrong that no-one would recover them and I thought that there might be something that would give me a hint regarding the tattoo.

'Here we are,' he said a moment later. 'There is £11.6d mostly in copper, a bone comb and these... '

They were two small—no more than one inch long—crudely shaped coffins of a white substance with a little curved thing that looked like a baby inside each of them.

'He chewed bread them shaped them with his fingers and the wooden spoon we gave him to eat his gruel.'

I took them.

That night I thought carefully. Is it possible to pray for someone who has committed such atrocious crimes?

I didn't know the answer to that question, but I did pray for him. God is forgiveness, Isabella had said. I slept peacefully all night and had only one dream. I dreamt I was holding a small child in my arms. It was a child but it spoke like an adult. 'Hold on to what you have,' it said. 'Now is the time to rest, for soon you will see the future.'

Chapter Eleven

THE PAST IS
A FOREIGN COUNTRY

The world is full of obvious things which nobody, by any chance, observes.

Arthur Conan Doyle

I dreamed, and behold I saw a man clothed with rags, standing in certain place, with his face from his own house, a book in his hand, and a great burden upon his back. I looked, and saw him open the book and read therein; and as he read, he wept and trembled: and not being any longer to contain, he brake out with a lamentable cry; saying 'What shall I do?'

John Bunyan, *Pilgrim's Progress*

I stopped reading. The tale of the little bread coffins had brought a chill to my heart. I thought of the coffins recovered from Arthur's Seat and the story that they related to grisly murders just a little way from where I now rested. It was a dark and cold city and I felt suddenly cold. But then I realised that I *was* cold. I felt the radiator to the side of the bed. It was dead. I was sitting freezing in my bed in my underwear covered with a few blankets and, for the first time for a while, I wished I had someone in bed beside me, someone to hold on to. And I knew who I would have liked that to be—Sandie Gregor.

I reported the problem to the concierge and, since I had missed my breakfast again, went to the little cafe in Rose Street for coffee and a roll and sliced sausage.

It was the summer before I commenced my postgraduate study when I met Sandie. She was a Junior but the same age as me as she had taken a couple of years off after high school to work in a burger bar on the beach.

It wasn't hard to meet Sandie. She simply came up to me as I was leaving the library and said 'Hey, want to go for coffee?' And that was that.

Sandie was a wild child from California. Harvard at that time had a reputation in equal amounts for conservatism and rebellion. The year that I had arrived Timothy Leary had been sacked. I had never involved myself with drugs, but Sandie introduced me to smoking marijuana.

I found that quite pleasant but more pleasant still was sleeping with Sandie. She had long honey-gold hair that reached nearly to her waist. She brushed it all the time but I never knew her to have it cut or, indeed, wash it. But she liked to swim and it had a salty tang. Her body was slim and tanned, flat-chested but with little hard dark nipples. Her skin had a sort of sheen as if it were slightly oiled.

Sex with Nancy had been regular but routine. With Sandie, however, it entered a country I had not visited before. Her slender embracing legs, her long tongue, her delicate fingers, her lithe body…

We would spend long hours in bed, often listening to the radio or records on her little record player. Her favourite song was *California Dreaming*. She said it reminded her of home and she would sing along with it. I liked that. It seemed to transport me to another place, almost another time.

One day I remember especially. It was hot. We were high, I suppose. We were lying on top of the bed naked drinking Annie Green Spring's tonic wine. She was smoking a cigarette and I was trying to read the *Boston Globe*.

'There's a storm blowing in,' I said

'Yeah,' she said, open the window. Full.'

I did and the vinyl curtains of orange and blue flowers billowed in the warm wind. The radio was on. It was playing Simon and Garfunkel's *The Sound of Silence*.

Suddenly Sandie said, 'I want you to spank me.'

'I'm reading,' I said, thinking she was joking.

'No,' she said, 'Don't read. I want it now!'

She took the cord from my dressing gown pocket which was on the bedpost. Then she lay over my legs, shifting her legs apart slightly to accommodate me.

'Tie my hands,' she said.

I did as she instructed. I spanked her, successively on each buttock. They grew redder with each strike.

'Harder,' she said, 'harder and slower.'

She made some sounds as if she were in distress but when I asked her if she wanted me to stop she shook her head violently and rasped 'no'.

When it was over and I tried to untie her hands, she said 'no, leave me.'

I shut the window. It caught the curtains, so I opened it and shut it again.

A minute or so later, she said, in a quiet voice, 'I hate you.' She was still lying on her stomach on the bed. Then she began to laugh in a manic way. Then she said, 'you can fuck me now, if you want.' She added, 'You know the way I want it, don't you.'

I switched off the radio and got the vaseline out of the drawer. I lifted her red-gold hair from her neck and let it drop. Then I pulled her still tied hands up as far as I could so that her bony back with the groove in it was arched. Then I gave her what she wanted.

Memories are so fickle. We may have made love a hundred times, but that is the one time I remember, perhaps because it was the last with her.

Sandie did something that no-one had ever done before except, perhaps, my mother. She abandoned me. The next day I went back to the apartment with some groceries and found her with a man in an intimate position. She didn't seem unduly concerned. 'This is Harvey,' she said. And that was that.

After Sandie and Nancy, I felt that I had investigated relationships enough for a while. I had a few other occasional girlfriends. I didn't smoke pot again, but I regularly had a few beers with Al and other friends, and developed a fondness for an occasional scotch.

Nat Cohen and Bart Greenblatt were often my companions outside of school. They liked to embark on what they amusingly called two-fisting—that was, a different shot in each hand, to be downed one after the other, either in turn choosing the nature of the offering. And so a few weeks and months went by like this. But my main concern was with finishing my thesis. I had had no difficulty with the other classes that constituted my degree, but, amongst the beers and shots and lying in bed thinking, I had not been able to focus on a subject so all I had was a hotch-potch of notes and ideas and some rather disjointed arguments.

I needed new ideas, so I went to see Robert Lowell. He was America's most famous poet and he lectured at the University on and off, but rumour had it that he was mad, and was treated at the McLean Hospital in Belmont.

I couldn't follow some of his lectures very well. They were often about the confessional in poetry and made allusion to historic events and social conventions with which I was not familiar.

He ushered me into his study in a rather terse but not unfriendly fashion. He perused some of my work, reading and then peering quite intensely into space.

He made a few specific comments regarding my ideas and then he used a sort of metaphor he had taken from anthropology—the raw and the cooked. Poetry could be cooked, working through in a methodical, logical way, or raw, rough, experiential, immediate. The best poetry was a mixture of the former informed by the latter.

It was clear that he was obliquely suggesting that I need to spend more time polishing my own work. However, shortly after my encounter with Lowell, I took a different tack immediately compared this to my own developing theory regarding deviance and madness.

I tried to continue to read. The next paragraph concerned Ledbury's dream of a small child who spoke like an adult. I had to stop reading as the passage for some reason struck me so powerfully that I felt I had to think for a while and rest my eyes. Then I realised it would be foolish to return to sleep. I had to warm myself and eat, so I made my way to the little cafe on Rose Street.

As I walked along, I thought more about my time at Harvard. I was the sort of person that made friends easily, but tended to lose just as easily. I was not involved with societies and I thought fraternities, with their weird rituals, were farcical. I was a grouch and a lone wolf. I now realise that I was probably plagued with anxiety, but an anxiety that was based not so much on loneliness but on the state of being alone. I wished I could be as comfortable with myself as friends like Nat Cohen and Bart Greenblatt who could happily spend hours drinking or strumming a guitar or hanging out playing pool.

Also, after Sandie, for one reason or another, I had found that I didn't want, at least for a while, to have another lasting relationship, I found some clubs I could go to and I had fun of a sort, and I found girls that met my requirements, but I didn't want to live with a woman or even date one for very long. Besides, I had other matters to concentrate my mind. Financially, my future was not entirely secure. When I left the university, I would have to find a job.

Unlike everyone else I knew, I had no family. I was in reality an orphan. I suppose that I had my uncles and aunt, but, in honesty, it had never occurred to me to contact them. We didn't have the least thing in common. I had come to realise that I had more in common with my father than my mother, and he too had been a sort of orphan. Nevertheless, I determined to have a vacation in Scotland to see my father's birthplace. I flew to Edinburgh and stayed for a week. I saw the usual things: Holyrood Palace, the castle, the monument to Walter Scott. I travelled down to the Borders to see Scott's house at Abbotsford with its magnificent library. One night I went to Nicky Tams, a big busy basement bar with Scottish folk music. I met a girl from Glasgow who was studying at the university. I went back to her flat and we kissed and cuddled, but we didn't sleep together. I kept her number but I didn't call her. Then I walked up to see the Elsie Inglis Maternity Hospital where my father had been born, and I took a train up to Kirkcaldy, over the massive red steel Forth Railway Bridge and up the coast past Aberdour castle and Kinghorn where some seals basked on the rocks in some Scottish summer sun. I walked the length of the long town and saw pubs and shops, then I bought a fish tea at a busy little cafe, then I got back on the train.

And, a little later, I got back on the plane home. I had gone on vacation and I had had a vacation, but that was all. I had found nothing had helped me find out more about myself. There was a gnawing emptiness. The world was full of places to which I did not belong

I seemed to have lost everything too quickly! That was why memories of my past life were coming back.

'Are you OK, son?' The women in the cafe asked. Almost in

surprise I realised that, while in this reverie of the past, I had almost forgotten where I was.

'Yes,' I said. Then I added, 'could I have more coffee, please? Black.'

'Are you going to your work?' She saw I was still holding my briefcase.

'No. Well, yes, I suppose,' I said. So, I realised, I was once again in Edinburgh, but not this time on a journey into my family past, but on a very different quest.

I needed a drink, so I walked across the road and down the stairs into Milnes Bar and ordered a pint of eighty shilling ale and a scotch.

The barman looked me up and down. 'You were the one talking to Cockney John,' he said. He nodded towards the corner. 'He's in a bad way, hardly makes it down the stairs to the door these days. Emphysema.'

I saw the old man sitting at a table with his half pint of Guinness, leaning on his stick and breathing with difficulty. I went over to join him.

'Do you need any help?' I asked. 'Do you not need some medicine?'

'I've had enough medicine,' he said. 'I'm just sticking to this now.' He indicated his beer. 'Two half pints is the most I can manage these days.'

'You're not from Edinburgh,' I said.

'No, I'm English, but I've been here for nearly thirty years. My mother was Scottish and she always wanted us to return, but she died. I came up here and just decided to stay.'

'And do you like it here?'

'Oh, aye. The climate can be a bit challenging, especially for sassenachs and foreigners like yourself, but Scotland is the finest country in the world and its poetry the greatest ever written.'

'I'm not a foreigner,' I said, 'I was born in Fife.'

'Well then,' you'll probably agree with me. I come here because of the poets. I can't write myself, but I like to read it.'

'And do you read the poetry that's written in here.'

'I do. They may be a hell-raising bunch, but there is grand music in their voices. Listen to this:

The rose of all the world is not for me,
I want for my part,
Only the little white rose of Scotland,
That smells sharp and sweet,
And breaks the heart.

I admitted that it was a powerful verse. 'What do you think your poets use for inspiration,' I asked him, 'is it their country, history, the past?'

'I don't know,' he said. Then he added, 'I think most of them use other poets. And women, they like to use women.'

It was a dull and misty day, although the drizzle had stopped. The gloom made the lights in the windows of the stores seem incandescent and welcoming. I walked through the mist at the West End where the steeples of the Old Town merged into a half-obscured jaggy skyline I wandered under the grey wholeness of the winter sky until I found myself in St Cuthbert's churchyard.

Something, perhaps a memory from a book I had read drew me there. I descended some worn stone steps feeling the damp cold and roughness of the sandstone wall in my hand.

I made my way through the kirkyard but came to a dead end delineated by a tall wall. The blackened stalks of weeds, burnt out by winter frosts poked from the top of the wall. In the centre was an inscription:

Sacred to the memory of Thomas de Quincey who was born at Greenhay near Manchester, 15th August, 1785 and died in Edinburgh 8th December, 1839.

Of course, the English writer De Quincey, the 'opium eater'. Connoisseur of mental disturbance and visionary experiences. Very much in the spirit of Edgar Allan Poe.

And then something else came to mind. I sat in this old city and thought of another—London. Robert Louis Stevenson had wandered the streets of Edinburgh but had set his best known work in the equally dreary streets of its larger southern neighbour.

In *Dr Jekyll and Mr Hyde* he had created an archetype for the twentieth century, the two contrary impulses in man, good and bad.

Several connected or conflicting images seemed to be coming together in my head, lost in the mist and the confusion of history.

I stared ahead again at the memorial to De Quincey. Of course, he had written an essay on murder, of all things: 'On Murder Considered as one of the Fine Arts'. Great writers could be as obsessed as the general public with gory crime!

When I returned to my room, I realised that I had to steady myself. My own confusion and my own memories were fogging my mind and leading me away from my quest. I had to get back to the manuscript but, before that, I decided to go back to my first encounter with Ledbury, his volume of poetry.

There were fewer than twenty poems in the slim volume. Ten, I had already decided, were of no great interest.. However, one of the others, in the form of a sonnet, deserved further consideration.

Sweep away angels with angelic scorn,
The dogs that come with curious eyes to gaze,
And feast their curiosity upon,
This object in the decline of his days,
Who cursed the day he was ever born,
And wished away his errant ways.

Oh, raise the demons from the deeps!
Thou poor stigmatic with thy ailing ways,
No heavenly horde your company keeps,
No shriven soul intently for you prays,
No matter how you suffer no-one weeps,
But mocks with scorn your endless dying days.

For this the aged child within you stays,
And each and every word your guilt betrays.

I guessed that Ledbury had appropriated the term 'stigmatic' from Talbot's lecture for this poem. But why write it at all with its deprecatory tone. It seemed to harbour a deep sense of self-loathing. And then I noted the 'adult child' that featured in the passage I had recently found so moving.

So what of the character of John Ledbury? In reading the manuscript it had initially been enough to accept the story he told uncritically. But was there more to it? And was it possible that

Ledbury himself had something to hide? Was he himself in any way complicit in the murderous affair?

I realised that perhaps I had been too naïve in my acceptance of the narrative of Ledbury's notebook so uncritically. A closer and more critical reading was required.

I settled myself, took a drink of cold water and rubbed my eyes. And now it was time to finish reading the notebook in the hope that I could find some resolution to my confused thoughts.

Chapter Twelve

THE MAD, THE BAD
AND THE SAD

Prison offers the same sense of security to the convict as does a Royal Palace to a King's guest. They are the two buildings constructed with the most faith, those which give the greatest certainty of what they are—which are what they are meant to be and which they remain.

Jean Genet, *The Thief's Journal*

The human body enters a machinery of power that explores it, breaks it down and rearranges it...

Michel Foucault

People that were dirtying up the edges of things, those people that stood at the edges of photographs of nice people.

Sebastian Barry, *The Secret Scriptures*

The next few days were uneventful. Uneventful at least compared to the mad pace of those that preceded them. I was glad of a little relief after the unsettling execution of Evans. I had had tea with Isabella and walked in Hyde Park. She had even intimated that I might visit her home sometime although she didn't think her father was in enough of a settled state of mind for that at the moment. I thought for a moment that I could invite her to my lodgings, but that would probably not be considered proper and I didn't particularly want her to meet Bill Bartholomew or Raph Merrilees, or indeed Mrs Merrilees—I was anxious not to disturb my landlady in any way in case she were to reintroduce the idea of my moving back to the country. However, I was increasingly feeling more relaxed in the company of Isabella. One day, while we were boating on the pond she gave me a present. It was a tiny book, not even the length of my thumb.

'It is a miniature Bible. Printed on India paper by a printer in Glasgow. It is all complete, but you will need a magnifying glass to read it.'

But I didn't. In the bright light of the summer sun I read a passage out to her with my naked eye. She was greatly amused.

I had a little money from Ashbee, so I hired a carriage to take us to Isabella's station and before we alighted she gave me another little kiss—this time quite adjacent to my lips!

There had been no progress as regards the girl and her lapsed memory and the doctor in attendance had appraised us of the fact that her cognisance of the previous events might not return at all. However, I soon discovered what Ord's seemingly cryptic and quite rude remark regarding 'the organ grinder' referred to:

'Fortunately, through some connections in the Lodge and the Diogenes Club, I have managed to briefly contact Mr Doyle. He has made some suggestions and on the basis of those we have decided to interview some suspects.'

I sat in on the interview of a few possible suspects, but none seems even remotely involved in the mystery. The very last, a young costermonger dressed in macaroni clothes, seemed lost but responded clearly.

'I don't know why I am here.'

'To help us with our enquiries into the abduction, rape and murder of two young women.'

'I have never murdered anyone, and besides I couldn't rape no young woman.'

'How do we know that?'

'I can show you!' And she did.

Fifteen minutes later, Ord was pacing up and down. He was not pleased.

'I expect even my most junior constable to do better than that,' he said. 'Mr Doyle is clearly a talented writer but he is no Sherlock Holmes!'

He shook his head slowly but his meditation was soon interrupted by a knock at the door. It was Holdsworth and Manners.

'Come in gentlemen,' said Ord, 'we have progressed no further with this morning's interviews so, along with Mr Ledbury I thought it would do no harm for us to consider some general aspects of this case yet again.'

I suggested that we consider the symbol again. Ord didn't seem too pleased.

'Yes. It could relate to a society that follows the beliefs of a scholar whose body has been stuffed in straw and is kept in the corridor of a university, it could be the sign of an ancient Egyptian god, it could be from a lost scroll from the library in Alexandria, it could be the symbol immortalised by Leonardo and connected to the Illuminati, the Masons, the Priory of Sion or the Knights Templar. It could be a spider in the centre of its web… '

At this point he held his head in both hands as if it hurt.

Of course,' said Manners, 'it could mean all of these things.'

'What did you say?' asked Ord.

'I mean the murderer could be aware of all of them. Perhaps he is deliberately trying to confuse us.'

'In that case he is certainly succeeding,' said Holdsworth.

Ord decided to change the tack. 'Mr Ledbury, I trust you have been out and about in the city as I instructed you. Have you noticed anyone following you or any suspicious behaviour in your vicinity?'

'No, not at all.'

'But you have been walking in clearly visible places.'

'Oh yes,' I said. 'I have been walking in the vicinity of Bedford Square.' I immediately regretted saying this. The last thing I wanted anyone to know about was my visits to Ashbee—and it was also very near to the establishment run my Mistress Ring!'

'And various other places,' I added.

'It is not easy to be clearly visible in the city,' said Holdsworth. 'There is the matter, for example, of the London particular. There are days when set to work when you would struggle to find your own feet if you had lost them!'

'It was said that the Ripper moving in the miasma, but also that he, or she, was a familiar face in neighbourhoods they frequented, a doctor or a midwife,'added Manners.

Ord nodded, 'sometimes, it is possible to be very obviously somewhere but remain unseen.'

'In what way?' I asked.

Ord thought for a moment. 'Suppose I told you that there were hundreds of people abroad on these streets at this very moment but that no-one would ever look at their faces.'

'Are their faces covered in some way, like the cowls of Berber women?'

'No,' said Ord. 'I will give you a hint, I picked it up as I walked down Regent Street on the way here: Duncan's chocolate, the headlines from the *Evening Standard.*'

Holdsworth's face creased in incomprehension, but, perhaps because I too had walked up Regent Street that day, I knew the answer.

'Sandwich board men!'

'Yes. We see them but we don't see them as persons, only as the slogans they represent.'

'It is an interesting point,' said Manners. 'However,the abductions took place in the suburbs. They are quiet backwaters where people keep themselves to themselves, but they notice things. There are always curious eyes behind closed curtains. The felon couldn't take a chance of being noticed unless he was already a familiar figure in all of these areas, yet they do not have much in common.'

'It is a presumption, however,' Holdsworth added, 'that they were abducted from their homes. Is it not possible that they went to him?'

I had a sort of vision. 'Mr S,' I said, 'the spider. He sits at the centre of the web and his prey comes to him.'

'So,' added Manners, 'Mr S must be someone they all knew, or who they had a connection with.'

'It seems,' said Ord, 'that we come back to the same sticking point, what do these young women have in common. Let's look at the files again.'

After we had spent some time passing the files among us, Manners suddenly started and smiled.

'What is it?' I asked.

'Oh, I was just observing the limitations of photography. One thing that the photographs cannot reveal but I know having examined their bodies that no photograph could reveal!'

'What is that?'

'They had red hair—one ginger, two auburn—but definitely a touch of red.'

Ord looked unhappy but acknowledged the point. 'It is because of so many experts that our police records are inadequate. They are obsessed with measurements and comparability so everything must fit the same bland form. This business of the red hair shows us that simple human observation often suffices.'

'But what would it tell us if they did all have red hair?' asked Holdsworth.

'It might mean sometime,' I added, 'Doyle wrote a story called The Red-Haired League. It was one of his favourites.'

'However, once again,' said Ord, 'the hair is a mere detail. It is not uncommon. The colour of the hair may just be coincidence.'

'Umm,' said Manners, 'you may think it more common than it actually is. About one in every five people in Scotland have red hair, but in Anglo-Saxon countries it is much less common.'

'Could there be a Scottish connection between the victims?' I asked.

'We don't know that either,' admitted Ord. 'However, one thing is clear. We don't know enough about these women. My constables and sergeants are trained to construct these files but their training, unfortunately, stops them from thinking outside their own experience. We need someone with more imagination.'

I immediately thought that he was referring to me, but he addressed the others.

'Holdsworth, Manners, go back and talk to the relatives and anyone else who can be of use. We don't just need to know the details. We need to know everything. What were their interests, their hopes, their dreams? What did they read? Where did they shop? How did they dress? And, I suppose, the colour of their hair.'

I felt that he wasn't so enthusiastic about this, but his logic was that we had to move on somehow.

'It is best that both of you go,' he added. 'Since you are a physician, Geoffrey, rather than a member of the Force, it may serve to elicit more of a response. People trust their physician generally.'

I felt I had to interrupt. 'Can't I help. My profession helps me to understand people!' I thought momentarily about Ashbee's advice, but then dismissed it.

'No.' said Ord emphatically. 'Holdsworth and Manners will do it.'

'Can't I help then?' I felt disappointed that I was left out.

Ord thought for a moment. 'Yes, take the files back to Professor Blacklock and tell him what we have discussed. See if he has any ideas.' He added, 'And don't lose them!'

I wasn't sure if I was being fobbed off, but at least I wasn't being totally excluded.

'Sir,' Holdsworth addressed Ord, 'Are you not coming with us?'

'No, I might not be able to help. Besides, I have to think. Also, unfortunately, I have to see the Assistant Commissioner.'

Blacklock had suggested I meet at the Bridewell at Hanley which he attended once a week as a consultant. He read over the case files again.

'I fear I have nothing new to offer you with regards to this case, Mr Ledbury,' he said, 'However, with your quest to discover more about the criminal mind, it might be salutary for you to view some of the inmates herein. I can give you a brief view of some. At this time they are allowed briefly into the yard to sun themselves.'

He took me to the yard where there were a few sad souls, shuffling around or sitting motionless.

'Here is one case,' said Blacklock, pointing out a tall man leaning on a wall. 'This is Jacob Antrobus. He was a rapist of four or more women. He would enter their chambers by a variety of ingenious means when they were sleeping and force them to succumb by holding a razor to their face. When held in another, rougher, institution he would, if the opportunity arose, force himself upon the younger men or boys. He is the survivor of a great many lashings.

'His urges are controlled by an apparatus that is locked around his waist and contains his member. He has become a good Christian. He has a supply of tobacco which he is allowed to smoke after he has recited passages from the good book that he has consigned to memory. If there is difficulty, he is punished by the confinement of his pipes—not his tobacco, note, as its presence serves to remind him of the rewards of virtue. He has been docile for more than a year.'

Antrobus spied Blacklock and came up to him.

'Will you not take away this? It is all of me that is my poor body wrapped in my tomb.'

'Bide contented, Jacob,' said Blacklock, 'or you know the consequences.'

Blacklock now pointed out an old woman. 'Jane Grove was originally jailed at the age of thirteen for stealing bread, but rather than accept her punishment she became an incorrigible thief and liar. She is now an old woman but she is quite content, she believes that angels visit her in her cell. We encourage that as it is a harmless delusion that comforts her.'

Another man was standing nearby. Unlike the others he was soundly secured in chains

'That is James Scrope. He murdered his mother, his father, his two sisters and his infant brother with an axe. He is to be hanged but I brought him here pro tempore to examine him. He is an interesting case. He has no recollection of committing the deeds and believes himself completely innocent.'

As Scrope looked towards us, perhaps overhearing a few words, he began shouting and shaking his bonds. Within a few seconds two guards had apprehended him and dragged him away.

'He will be caned again,' Blacklock said. 'This establishment still believes in the rule of the rod. The prison or the hospital is not merely a place of confinement, it is an instrument of punishment also, so the prisoner must expect that they will experience a just measure of pain if appropriate.'

For some reason, a vision came to me of the gentlemen who were caned for their own pleasure at Mistress Ring's establishment. 'Surely such punishment will not subdue them if they cannot reason,' I suggested.

'Well, they are imprisoned within the Bridewell, but they are equally imprisoned within themselves. If we can modify the behaviour that makes them offend they may be of some use to society. A regime of punishment and reward may help with that. However, although we seldom succeed, we have to adopt different approaches, whether effective in the short term or not. That way we can learn about human behaviour.'

I thought of something. 'Do you often allow them to associate with other inmates?'

'Not very often,' replied Blacklock, 'but we do not confine them absolutely. A dungeon or oubliette hides the prisoner away, but now we believe that the opposite is necessary, the prisoner must be in plain view.'

'Is that not the purpose of the panopticon, as devised by Bentham?'

'Ah, I see you have maintained an interest in Bentham. Have you investigated the existence of the supposed Panopticon Society and the cult of the Benthamites?'

'Superintendant Ord does not believe that it exists. He insists that the most eminent figures on the Force and in the Lodge would be aware of it if it did.'

Blacklock smiled. 'Well, the Metropolitan Police and the superintendant's Lodge may think they know a lot, but have they succeeded in progressing at all in the current case?'

I shook my head.

Blacklock looked me straight in the eye.

'Perhaps, Mr Ledbury, the study of the criminal mind is not your greatest strength. I do hope that you have some other plans for your future.'

I thought of Ashbee. Then I thought of Dorothea and Isabella. I couldn't think of anything else so I said: 'I think I would like to help unfortunate people.'

'That is a weighty ambition, but it is probably not as easy as you might think. You will see that in my science rewards are scant and only occasional.'

'But there are some people who believe that the world can be changed.'

'Yes, but who do you have in mind?'

I couldn't think of anyone for a moment, but then two names came into my head.

'Well, there was Jeremy Bentham and now there is Francis Galton.'

'Galton is an idealist. He imagines we can change the world and live in a better place. Others believe that we can only adapt the world around us to be a little more satisfactory for the benefit of ourselves or like-minded people.'

'Do you not think, then, that science can change things for the better? The world is changing so rapidly. Surely we can harness new knowledge to benefit the whole of society rather than just a few rich merchants.'

'Time will tell, Mr Ledbury. But meanwhile each o us must try to control our own destiny. These may be exciting but they are also troubled times. I advise you to consider your own interests. Make your way in the world and tend your garden thoughtfully. With the best knowledge you possess.'

And then he added, to my surprise, 'Perhaps you also have a young lady?'

I didn't know how to answer this but, fortunately, he continued, 'I, myself, live alone. Sometimes, it is necessary to forego any domestic labours in pursuit of a higher cause.'

And, apart from a few perfunctory remarks that was the end of my conversation with Blacklock and I was left wondering if I had learned anything at all.

Chapter Thirteen

SPIDER'S WEB

Like all other arts, the Science of Deduction and Analysis is one which can only be acquired by long and patient study, nor is life long enough to allow any mortal to attain the highest possible perfection in it.

Sir Arthur Conan Doyle,
The Collected Sherlock Holmes

There are times when the law jeopardises those who obey it.

Kathy Acker

That afternoon we gathered again in Ord's office. I related my discussion with Blacklock and the others the result of their investigations into the girls and their families. However, nothing of note seemed to be coming from either line of enquiry. As for Blacklock's evocation of the Panopticon Society, Ord had summarily dismissed it.

'Pash. There is no evidence at all of their existence. And we have already discussed the possible meaning of the symbol. 'We have to look at the case again from the beginning,'

He looked tetchy. I thought it might not be unrelated to the fact that the press had been revisiting the murders and the Daily Advertiser has printed a new pastiche on an older rhyme:

The 'Bobbies' up and down do run,
While murder here is rife,
And who is out there having fun?
The Ripper with his knife.

The 'Bobbies' they do huff and puff,
The villain rubs his hands in glee,
Knowing he can call their bluff,
The fiend called Jeremy.

'There is more to this than simply the exercise of base instincts,' said Ord. 'As may have been the case in the Whitechapel murders.

'And why abduct gentlewomen. There would be a better chance of stealing whores or slavies from the street and going undetected.

'Yet what do these girls have in common. They came from different extremities of the city but they were all in their early twenties, respectable, educated. All were keen readers. All were not unattractive and all had red hair.'

I thought of this.

'And why tease us with these letters and the supposed clues they contain. They are well written and not just mocking. They contain clues or riddles.'

Something struck me.

'Have we actually compared the handwriting of these letters with that of the Ripper? It was often thought that they also contained clues.'

We had not, it seemed. So we send for a facsimile of the Ripper letters.

After a moment, the result was clear, The handwriting on one of the samples was the same! Ord, gave out a long slow groan.

A moment later, however, he seemed to have regained some of his composure again but with a little more effort. For the first time I felt that he was struggling and perhaps showing his age.

'Mr Ledbury, please follow the constable. You will have to give a fuller and more detailed statement regarding the letters you have received in your previous occupation.' The use of the word 'previous' made it clear to me that he was not expecting me to reprise my role as the Doyle correspondent.

'And the rest of you,' he looked around, 'make sure that all your records and paperwork are correct and current.' He banged his fist on the desk.

'Take heed. We may shortly be expecting another visit from the Assistant Commissioner, if not the Commissioner.'

Ord dismissed us, in rather a perfunctory manner. 'I expect you all here again tomorrow, at the same time. Until then, I have to reassess my own thoughts on the matter.'

I was in great demand that day, as Ashbee had also summoned me.

'Thank you for coming at such short notice,' Ashbee said, 'I have another urgent assignment which I hoped you would be able to complete while I am in Belgium on business. Also, I believe that you have something for me.'

I had, in fact, completed one of the tasks he had given me. I showed him the manuscript:

The woman rose early in the morning, long before dawn. The task that was to be undertaken had to be done alone, before even the most junior of the maids arose to set the hearths.

In the kitchen she, methodically, removed all her clothes, not even keeping a scanty pair of drawers for her own modesty. Cleaning the ovens was filthy work and she had to do her own laundry and she would never be able to clean the black off them.

She was a tallish, slightly portly woman in her late thirties, but she was, in a way, attractive. She had large dark eyes, prominent arched eyebrows, black hair like wire and a confident face. In contrast, her flesh was soft and pink and her large breasts hung from her like ripe melons.

Despite the tedium of the work she did, she did not have the demeanour of a drudge. Her eyes gleamed with an inner vitality. This was, perversely, her favourite task. Even though her body tingled with the cold of the morning which gave her goosebumps and made her large and long nipples erect.

She would not stop until the ovens were gleaming. By then,

her aching body would be caked in dirt which would have to be scrubbed from her with lukewarm water and carbolic soap.

Both were luxuries and her favourite part of the working week.

He read it through. 'Excellent, you have a way with words that can conjure up a scene. More of the same would be very welcome. However, I have, rather more urgently, another task.' I have, as I mentioned before, a gentleman who has a letch for women smoking cigarettes. I have a short piece I have commissioned from another writer, but it does not display your capacity for recording a scene and it is, I fear, too loquacious and excessive. I would like you to improve on it using your more direct style.'

He gave me the piece:

I watched her all the night as we sat in the theatre in my private booth. Her lips were broad and rouged. They stretched across her delicious mouth when she smiled as I codded her. But when she relaxed they pouted a little showing their quivering softness.

Her teeth were small, white and in a perfect arc below her lips. When she smoked and drank wine I could glimpse her lovely tainted pink tongue stained red a little at the tip with the claret, and come and go in the milky white smoke. Sliding in and out her mouth and it's little tip caressing the fringes of her lips.

Oh, what a perfection of God is the female mouth. It is the source of all tenderness. It is tight yet all-accommodating. The lips are the most remarkable of instruments that can so gently touch or hold. The teeth that bite so gently. The tongue that can be so soft and yielding yet hard, rolling and cupping. That wonderful thing that would make a man ache to be lost in its liquidity!

"I think you will get the notion,' said Ashbee. 'It is a curious fact that some of my gentlemen become fixed in a certain feature of the human anatomy and a certain course of amatory pleasure.'

I was sorry to realise that I was thinking of Isabella's little mouth with its pretty pink lips and the small kiss she had given me in the carriage and again when she had given me the Bible.

However, I shook myself out of that, took the piece, and left Ashbee, but heavy in thought.

One thing, I thought, was certain, although Ashbee's fictions could be regarded as harmless and only for the pleasure of gentlemen in their own homes, Jeremy and perhaps some others, maybe all the Benthamites, if they existed, were not content simply to exercise their imagination. In the real world, women were sometimes abused and murdered, and for no reason other than to satisfy the sadistic whims of a few evil people.

Of course, I was pleased that Ashbee liked my work, but also concerned. What had started out as only an attempt to earn some money—in order, I suppose, to be able to take Isabella for tea—had taken on its own life. I wasn't sure where these fantasies came from as I certainly hadn't experienced them myself, but they were vivid and lodged in my mind. I knew of course, that the characters were only fictional, but I couldn't help thinking of them as real! I wondered about my anonymous readers who would never be known to me. I suspected that they imagined the protagonists in these little fictions to be real, but they still knew that they were not. There was safety in that, for the pornographic imagination is precisely that, an imagined world unencumbered by the stringencies of the real world: a world in which everything is possible and controlled by the reader, or the writer!

Now I thought, I am really writing these things for my, perhaps also imaginary, readers or for myself!

The boundaries were clouded. Were these really my own secret innermost fantasies?

The strange thing was that, because my characters were female, I couldn't understand the way they thought yet I was striving to understand the way they behaved. And yet, was it really about them? They still seemed subjects of the shadowy men who controlled them, possessed them in a way.

Many questions arose every time I wrote these fictions: did the mistress own the maid? Was she a willing participant in these acts? Was the mistress gaining pleasure from giving her pleasure or giving her pain?

Somehow here there was the crux of the question: what was the difference between pleasure and pain? In pornography the pain, the whippings, the penetrations, always seemed to be portrayed as pleasure of a sort.

Was the mistress a sadist, taking pleasure in someone else's pain; were my readers sadists? Was I? Was Ashbee?

Ashbee said that he had never hurt a woman. Was this true? But even if we did not hurt them physically, was what we were doing not a sort of act of aggression against womankind.

These thoughts buzzed around in my mind, but they came back to one point: who was Jeremy? Blacklock had said that he could be a woman! Was that possible? Was I, in fact, in the little tale of the mistress and maid, imagining the real life exploitation of his victims by Jeremy.

This thought tormented me. My imagination had somehow entered a dangerous territory, yet could I restrain it?

That night, as usual, I lit my little oil lamp and sat at the desk. I took my pen and wrote my diary for the day in one of my notebooks.

This was taking much longer than usual since I became involved in the case of Jeremy and, in fact, the last notebook I had started, the day after I had dreamt of the panopticon, was almost totally devoted to the case.

When I had completed the task, as always, I read a passage from the Bible. I tried to use the miniature Bible that Isabella had given me, but out of the daylight, my eyes strained too much to discern the text so I shut it and placed it back on its little stand.

Then I undressed and put on my nightgown. The linen was cold and I rubbed it against my skin to warm me. It had been outside to air as, almost every night it was soaked in the cold sweats I woke in after my nightmares.

I was not without sin, I told myself. Perhaps that was why I was cursed to have these dreams. But I wished I did not. My idea of luxury was a dreamless sleep, but it was not to be, although some nights were worse than others, all were invaded by some of the extreme imaginings of my mind.

The next morning I was sitting in Lyons tearoom waiting to meet Isabella. She was late and I wondered if her train was delayed. As I waited, my mind wandered and I began to think of my new task for Ashbee. Suddenly, I noticed that, a few tables away from me, two ladies were sitting, deep in conversation. I recognised both of them. One was Mrs Manners. The other I knew as Mistress Ring.

I waited for over half an hour, checking my pocket watch. I then realised that Isabella was not coming. She had told me she had a class at Bedford College at eleven, and I could only guess that, delayed, she had gone straight there.

As I left the tearoom I immediately came across Mrs Manners.

"Why Mr Ledbury, What a pleasant surprise to meet you here.'

I nodded to her.

'Perhaps you would be so kind as to walk with me to the Circus?' she asked.

I made some conversation about the weather and enquired about her accommodation at the hotel.

'The hotel is very fine,' she replied. 'I have determined to stay a little longer, on some business. I have just had a meeting.'

'Lyons is a very convenient place for meeting,' I said.

'Yes, and you perhaps recognised the lady I was meeting?'

I would have denied it, but the expression on my face gave me away.

Mrs Manners stopped walking and looked me straight in the face.

'I will be frank with you. The lady you saw provides a variety of services. I require things when I am in town. Things I cannot get in the country.'

I didn't know what to say.

'It is important that my husband does not know about my meeting today. Do you understand?'

I nodded.

'I know that you are a man of the world,' she said. 'I have heard about your excellent work in the writing of amatory prose. There is a lot of wickedness about. We must be careful and exercise a great deal of discretion.'

How did she know about my secret commissions! Had Mistress Ring told her? Had she been told by Ashbee? I had to think more about this.

'I must leave you, I'm afraid,' I said, 'I have an appointment with Superintendent Ord.'

She leaned closer to me and spoke in my ear. I had a strong sense of perfume.

'Miss Ord is my dear friend but a delicate girl who may not see things the way you and I do! Be careful what you say to her.'

She took my hand and slipped a little card into it.

'This is the card for my hotel,' she said. 'If there is anything more you need to know, discreetly, I will be there.'

I had never met a lady so brazen as Elizabeth Manners. If she was threatening me, she did so very nicely. I was getting involved in a world that I had scarcely imagined before. I was afraid—but part of me was excited as well.

When I arrived at Ord's office, Ord was not yet there. Apparently, he had been summoned to meet the Commissioner.

However, Holdsworth was there and looked excited although a bit apprehensive.

'What have you found?' I asked.

'Well, we took a map of greater London and we plotted the places where the girls were on it found and this was what we got then.'

He unfolded a chart. On it was inscribed the symbol that we had come to know all too well. A circle with four radial lines drawn towards a centre.

'It's the spider's web!' I cried out.

'The four points at the outside of the circle represent the points where they were taken and the points where they were found lead in a line towards the centre.'

'And where is the centre?' asked Ord.

'Not very far from here, in the city

'But,' interjected Ord, 'there have been only three girls taken. Why are there four outer points?'

'We have predicted where the fourth point would be.'

I lifted the map and gazed more closely at it.

'Look', said Holdsworth, here is the fourth point, to the south of the city. In fact, very close to where the Superintendant lives himself.'

At that moment a terrible thought came into my head.

I had abruptly taken my leave of Holdsworth and returned to my lodgings.

I didn't want to ask Holdsworth for the Superintendant's address, and he probably wouldn't have given it to me and it might have raised some unwanted suspicions! Instead, I thought, I was sure that the address was on the little letter that Isabella had first sent to me and that would be on my desk.

I arrived, but as I opened the door, I sensed someone behind me. I turned around. It was a police constable. I quickly opened the door and went inside. The door to the parlour was open and there I saw Mrs Merrilees sitting looking astonished. Either side of her, like two bookends, were two other police constables.

'Ledbury,' one of them said, 'hold your hands out forward. You're coming with us.'

I realised what was afoot. They were going to arrest me! I could only guess that this was something to do with Isabella as my wild thought was that maybe she had been abducted too.

I didn't know what to do but then, fortuitously, Bartholomew came down the stairs with a parcel under his arm. He gawped at the constables then made a turn for the front door and bolted through it with one of the constables following him.

Everyone was distracted for a moment and I took the opportunity to duck between the policemen and run through the kitchen to the back door which I hoped wasn't bolted.

It wasn't.

I was outside for a minute and in the lane behind the terrace. I knew I could run like a hound and that they wouldn't catch me unless they cut me off or I came to some dead end. I was running so fast that it was hard to think but eventually I came to a stop and, looking behind me, couldn't locate any pursuers.

I wandered through the streets of Bloomsbury knowing that most of the Metropolitan Police Force would be looking for me and I had no way of disguising myself. I turned up my collar in a forlorn gesture. I didn't know what to do. If the police truly believed that I was the culprit, they wouldn't be looking for Isabella anywhere else. Perhaps they thought that I was the only hope they had as I was the only one Jeremy might try to contact. But how could he now? I was confused.

Exhausted, I opened a gate to the gardens in Russell Square and found a seat on a bench in the most inconspicuous spot I could find, sheltered by the overhanging branches of an old beech tree which was only just coming to leaf.

Then a terrible and crazed thought struck me. What if, in fact, it were true! What if I was the abductor and murderer of these girls? Isabella had told me that Herr Freud had argued that everyone has a subconscious as well as a conscious mind and that they can lock away deep thoughts there and keep them secret even from themselves. I had had terrible dreams. Could I have lost the distinction between my waking and my sleeping life? But then I thought. Ord had not initially suspected me as he had known my location at the time of the murders. But what I had colluded with another person, for example Bartholomew.

I rose from the bench. I couldn't stand the stillness. I had to walk, even though I didn't know where I was going.

And then, after a few minutes, with my mind still in an unfocused turmoil, unexpectedly, I found myself in Bedford Square— outside the house of Henry Spencer Ashbee.

'Let's examine the evidence,' Ashbee said. I had blurted out a great many things and I wondered if he had followed my argument at all.

'It seems possible that the police are right and that you are the person they seek. Tell me, why should I not just call my butler and ask him to call Scotland Yard. Or perhaps, he looked me straight in the eye, perhaps you will murder me too.'

I realised then that my fancy that I was the murderer was, in fact, just fancy, caused by my despair and anxiety.

'I won't hurt you,' I said. I thought of Dorothea. I've never deliberately hurt anyone. I don't care what happens to me, I just want Isabella to be safe.'

Ashbee poured two brandies from a decanter and gave one to me.

'Some people may think that I am a deluded old man who lives a fantasy life in his secluded library.' He said, 'but I am not stupid enough to be unable to recognise a murderer from an innocent man.'

I drank the brandy.

'Now,' he said, 'you must pull yourself together. Somebody will have seen you. There may not be too much time until they find you here, so we do not have long to solve this mystery'

We went over some of the characteristics of the abductor. 'He beats the girls, but not too strenuously. He also washes them and makes them up. He wants to control them, to completely own them. He blindfolds them so they cannot see him, but he can see them, every part of them. Perhaps he talks to them, we don't know. He doesn't deposit the bodies immediately, so he may keep them for a while after death.'

Something occurred to me. 'The client you asked me to work for, he also wants to have total control over the subject.'

'Yes, but in that case his instincts are to merely look, and he has a preference for sapphic tendencies.'

'In general,' he said. 'My clients want to read about certain things but they do not want to enact them. In fact, it is possible, I believe, that sometimes I am doing a service to society by keeping some of the more bestial of desires in some merely the resource of their imagination so they are not inclined to carry out their tendencies with their wives or their mistresses.'

'But, is it possible that they start by reading about them then, afterwards, want to enact them?'

He grimaced a little. Clearly this was something he did not want to contemplate too much.

'Yes, men and women whip and birch each other for their pleasure. They do it every day at some places in town. But they are agreed on it. Nobody, to my knowledge in these salons is there without their consent. And no-one, in fact, in my fictions, is tortured or murdered in the manner you suggest. I make a point of it!'

'But you can obtain fictions like that elsewhere.'

'Maybe,' but I suspect that gentlemen with such violent fantasies may want to keep them to themselves.'

'But it is possible that Jeremy or his associates, may be among your clients?'

'It is possible,' he reluctantly agreed.

Then it occurred to me, Ashbee was a collector! He categorised and classified every detail of what he did. Surely, he also, somewhere, had kept details of his clients.

He admitted that he did!

'Yes, I have a sort of ledger, but it is hidden, confidential. The gentlemen wouldn't like it if they even knew had I had such details, that I understood their thoughts and wishes so well. Perhaps they are deluded but they probably believe that they are the only ones with their particular peccadilloes.'

He went behind a shelf and, moved some other volumes and came out with a single volume. It was a large book bound in brown buffed calf with a label on the spine.

'I keep lists,' he said, 'classified by the letches that my gentlemen are interested in.'

Going through his list of categories of letches I chose a couple that I thought might reward enquiry.

Then I asked him to go through his book and make a note of

the gentlemen who satisfied some or all of these. He did so and then insisted on first scribbling them down then typing them on a sheet of paper in alphabetical order in a methodical manner.

When he completed the list, he handed it to me. I immediately recognised one name!

Chapter Fourteen

THE SECRET LIBRARY

'And is a library, then, an instrument not for distributing the truth but for delaying its appearance?' I asked, dumbfounded.
  'Not always and not necessarily. In this case it is.'

Umberto Eco, *The Name of the Rose*

A library where the books have melted into each other and the titles have faded away.

Pierre Mabille

The author says that if his story is to resemble the world in any way at all, then it must be formless and without logic, proceeding randomly from one moment to the next. Then, gradually, patterns will emerge which may or may not indicate events, ideas or actions. People will appear who may turn out to be crucially important or else they may banish after a single night, never to be seen again. And then, just when you think everything's got going, it'll all suddenly stop.

Andrew Crumey, *Pitz*

I sat there, dumbstruck, and gazed upon the subsequently empty pages.

' ...Immediately I was struck by one name... '

And that was the end of it! There were more pages in the notebook, but they were blank! The narrative had come to a sudden and unexpected ending. Having let myself be carried away by the story, I had let myself believe that I was reading something like a novel and that, in the best tradition of English literature, there would be a resolution and all the strands of the story would be tied together in a satisfying ending. But this was not a novel, it was a notebook, and it had come to an abrupt end!

The disappointment was devastating! I sat for a long time and brooded over the problem. Was this really to be the end of my investigation. I sat back and closed my eyes. I realised that I was exhausted both physically and mentally. I had to find some way to straighten out my thinking.

I lay on my bed and stretched my legs and arms to the furthest extremities. I couldn't move. I was sinking into a kind of desperate, irretrievable despair.

I suppose I slept for a while. I don't know how long. I had a dream which was not at all clear but in it I seemed to be in a library looking at shelves of books. They all had titles on their spine, but when I moved closer to try to retrieve one, the title faded and the books all looked exactly the same.

When I woke, my limbs were aching, as though they had been

stretched on a rack, but I shook my body awake and sat up and said to myself 'I will not give up'! I evoked some literary parallels: did Christian sink into the Slough of Despond? Did Sir Gawain run from the Green Knight? Would Sherlock Holmes have relinquished a case no matter how many pipes he had to smoke to solve it?.

And then I thought that perhaps that was what I had become, a sort of detective! And detectives, at least those I knew from literature, didn't give up. Just when they seemed to have exhausted all lines of enquiry, something would turn up. Just when the hero was tied to a buoy in a sea of man-eating sharks, or buried in sand to his neck by a nest of venomous ants, something would come along to save them. But that was a literary device, sometimes called a *deus ex machina*, and this, I thought, was real life. Then I began to despair again. In literature everything would be fine, but this was, of course, real life.

Nevertheless, I believed, for no particular reason other than blind optimism, that I could find something if I sat and thought.

But was this just an academic conceit. And to think about what? Well, perhaps I could start at what I was best at—literary criticism. But this approach seemed to lead nowhere at all. According to the stringent theories of structuralism, the text itself was complete. It was absolutely the sum of its parts with its internal rules and devices, dictated by similarities, repetition, opposition. In what way could that be applied to Ledbury's notebook with its incomplete ending.

For a while I wondered if, within the manuscript, the end should somehow reflect the beginning. So I looked closely at the opening section, again and again. And then I thought of Ledbury's strange dreams. Was there a hidden structure to them, something symbolic that hid a some other reference, even a name.

After some time, I realised that I was getting more and more confused. Another literary critic came into my head. Susan Sontag had famously penned an essay called 'Against Interpretation' in which she argued that any interpretation of a text is tainted by the reader's own intellectual prejudices. Did I somehow have to get beyond my own preferences; to look anew at the text through different eyes?

I tried to breathe deeply and keep calm and after thirty seconds or so, I felt more composed and, suddenly, an image of my father came in to my head.

When my father used to play chess with me years ago and I didn't know how to move he'd say 'the hardest move is when you don't seem to have anywhere to go and that is the move that the best players play best.' That was what I heard him say now.

So, I had to make my best move, that was all I could do. Knowing this comforted me a little. But what was my best move?

Go back, I thought. I had to rethink everything again clearly from the beginning and then decide. That was the best I could do. But I wouldn't rush or panic. I needed time. I felt an impulse to get out of Edinburgh. Perhaps not least because of the two unfortunate deaths. So I packed my little suitcase, took the train from Waverley to King's Cross and booked into a small hotel in Bloomsbury.

I sat on the bed after the journey. I was tired but the very motion of travelling had, in its way, induced in me the feeling of some progress. What next? Firstly, I had to make myself physically and mentally more alert and that required, I decided food, drink and some exercise and relaxation.

I washed and shaved and found a clean, if slightly crumpled, white shirt to wear. In a drawer in the hotel room was a folding map of London with some advertisements for bars and restaurants on one side. I noticed one that said: 'Traditional East End Pub— The World Turned Upside Down.'

This was a sudden shock! It had never occurred to me that the subject of Ledbury's dream could be a real place. I checked the address. It was in Southwark, just south of the river. I had no other plans, so it would do well enough.

I took the underground. Paris, New York and Moscow were the only other major cities advanced or foolish enough to have such an transport system like this. I descended, sandwiched among commuters in grey suits, and was catapulted out on to the platform. As more and more people came down the escalator, I was forced closer to the platform edge and gazed onto the rails. The bottom of the line was ingrained with a sort of black dust and a few mice scampered about. There was a smell that was like smoke flavoured with vinegar.

As the crowd descended I thought I could be pushed onto the platform itself, but, just in time, a tube train came along with a rush of sweet-smelling warming wind. The doors opened for a pile of commuters to fall out and the ongoing customers to squeeze in, oblivious to each other.

In some ways, I actually liked London in the rush hour. There was a sense of purpose to it, ranks of office workers released from their servitude hurrying to tube stations sucking cigarettes; businessmen and bankers suitably suited heading to wine bars and pubs.

I passed a fish bar and thought that it would be sensible to eat before I went to the pub. I ordered skate and chips The fish was quite chewy and covered in a crispy batter that had puffed out away from the fillet which had a shiny white surface with the remains of a little skin. The fries were fat and soggy, soaked in vinegar and with a sprinkled covering of salt. I ate it all up with some urgency. I hadn't realized how hungry I was.

As soon as I entered The World Turned Upside Down it struck me that, despite the commonality of the name and the seeming age of the building, there was precious little to be learned here. It was busy and noisy, the setting was modern and functional.

I squeezed up to the bar and asked for a pint of Watney's Red Barrel. I was between two or three men, all of them were muscular with their arms straining at the sleeves of their shirts.

'Oi,' one said. 'You a yank?'

I admitted I was from the United States. 'How did you guess?' I asked, attempting sarcasm that didn't seem to register.

'Cos you ain't speaking the Queen's English like what we does.'

I collected my beer and moved a bit down the bar. 'Oi, mate, no need to get the hump!' I heard him say.

There was an older man standing by the bar. He was dressed in a corduroy jacket and a tight fitting flat cap.

'What you think of the miners, mate?' he asked me.

'I don't know.'

'They say there's not going to be no coal for the electricity stations. Power cuts again. 'Cause of the miners and their bloody strikes!'

'Maybe they are striking because they're being badly treated,' I suggested.

'They ain't been badly done by. They get overtime. They can work when they want. Now, me and me mates. We sell things down the market. Fancy goods and all that. But we don't get no deliveries and we don't sell nothing. Don't know when you get up what you got that day.'

'Bleeding miners!' He shook his head.

Meanwhile, some girls had come into the bar. I could smell the perfume from them. They looked pretty and they were having fun. They gathered around the bar near me and ordered gins and cocktails. They were very animated, laughing and giggling, drinking and smoking cigarettes. For some reason, I found myself looking towards them. Then one of them turned round and said to me, 'Hey, are you that Rick Wright?'

I didn't know how to answer, but she turned away anyway and the others started giggling again.

Another one said. 'She means the keyboard player with Pink Floyd. You would look a bit like him if your hair was longer.'

'I would very much like to be him,; I said, 'but I'm afraid I'm not.'

'Do you like Pink Floyd?' the first girl asked.

I wasn't very sure. 'I think so,' I said.

'I've just got the record: 'The Dark Side of the Moon'. I love that song 'Money'.

In a sort of falsetto voice she sang: 'Get a good job with more pay and you're OK'.

I smiled. Somehow I felt better just being among people, ordinary people not concerned with books, or murder!

'You're my American darling,' she said. 'Hey, we're having a party. Want to come?'

'I have quite a long way to go back to my hotel,' I said.

'Ooh, come along. It could be fun and you could meet some nice people.'

'I'm a bit too tired,'I said, 'to meet a lot of people.'

'It ain't too bad,' she said. 'Just a nice quiet party.'

She added, 'it could be just you and me, sweetheart.'

I removed her arms from around my neck as gently as I could. I made my apologies and left, shaking the pub sweat and bright lights off me in the cold winter air. It wasn't such a bad place, I thought. Not much unlike weekend bars in Pittsburgh or pretty much anywhere else

But I had enjoyed myself well enough. I had needed the escape. To go anywhere that resembled the real world, the real world that I seemed to have left behind on my quest. However, now I had, for reasons that probably no sane person would understand, to get back to that quest

I had determined to start from the beginning so I started with the Ledbury poems. I read them one by one. Many were in the sonnet form. I was struck by the quality. They covered the familiar themes of the late romantic period: love, death, loneliness, but there seemed to be an underlying unity—something I couldn't quite put my finger on.

One poem struck me by its title for some reason, 'The Song of

Silence':

> Though my soul be set in silence,
> Yet I wish my heart to know,
> That my mind is something wanton,
> And my pleasures high and low.

> Do not trust a thought to reason,
> Or your bloom may bolt to waste,
> Never nurture one religion,
> Never savour just one taste.

It was enigmatic and hard to grasp. What was Ledbury trying to say? One more was even more disturbing:

> Out of my bare bone guise grows the age,
> And in this well-worn cage lurks the phantom,
> Only the blade-torn grass knows my age,
> And but a bed-born boy sings my anthem.

It seemed that Ledbury was trying to grasp at the perilous idea of one's own existence. There seemed to be some sign of a disturbed psychopathology. I had perhaps been too close to the first person narrative in the notebook to discount the notion that it might all be a fiction. Was Ledbury quite mad? And were his imaginings the result of a crazed mind?

When I had finished the poems I felt that I knew a little better what sort of man Ledbury was, but I wasn't any closer to finding my own way forward in the mystery.

So I read the notebooks again, carefully trying to detect what was obvious, what, caught up in the story, I might have missed, skimmed over or not realised the significance of. But soon I found that I was not concentrating too hard, just relaxing into the process of reading, hoping that something would, almost magically, jump out at me.

When the answer came, it was blindingly obvious! The list at the end was hidden in one of Ashbee's books. Ashbee had gifted his entire library to the British Museum. Perhaps that was where it was. In the British Library!

The next morning I wandered up through Soho to the British Library. There was a little sun brightening up the dampish air.

The first person I met at the enquiry desk was a slim youngish woman with straight blonde hair. Her prettiness was compromised by an absence of anything resembling a smile, a demeanour I have found perfected by some librarians and archivists, as well as various other professions that serve the public.

'I'm looking for details of a collection donated to the library by Henry Spencer Ashbee.'

'Henry Spencer Ashbee.' She repeated the name as if it came from a foreign planet. 'I don't think I've heard if him. What was his collection a collection of?'

'Spanish literature, Cervantes... and antiquarian amatory literature.'

'Amatory literature?'

'Yes, basically to do with relations between men and women. Sex, if you like!'

She gave me a strange look. 'You will need to speak to one of our special collections librarians. If you take a seat I'll call you when one is available.'

Nearly one hour later, I got to speak to a short bald man with oversized spectacles.

'Arthur Godsman', he introduced himself. 'What can I help you with.'

I explained again that I was interested in Henry Spencer Ashbee.

'We certainly have no designated collection under that name. You say he was a collector of Spanish literature?'

'Yes, notably editions of Don Quixote.'

'Much of our Cervantes collection comes from Spain, donated by Señor Alvarez.'

'But you keep a record surely of the provenance of the books you keep?'

'Yes, but it is not always available to the public. You see, we are a library for scholars, not book collectors.' He emphasised the last two words as if he did not care much for them. 'Our collections are catalogued according to our own classificatory system. We find that best serves our readers.'

I decided to take another tack.

'The books I am most interested in are not Spanish. Ashbee also collected amatory literature from all periods and countries?'

'Amatory literature?'

'I mean books of a sexual nature. Some of them very rare.'

'I'm afraid,' he said, 'that I can't help you in that area.'

'Is there someone who can?'

'Only, perhaps, the head of special collections, Dr Smythe.

If you fill in this form an appointment might be arranged.' He handed me a pink piece of paper. 'It is essential that you include your academic affiliation, your sphere of research and your explicit reasons for requiring access to the library collections.'

This was barely satisfactory, but I took the form and began to complete it.

While I was doing so, a girl with spectacles, curly brown hair and a cute upturned nose said 'excuse me'.

I looked at her.

'Are you a friend of Professor Legman?'

'Who is Professor Legman?' I asked.

'Oh, he's always here. Looking at the same stuff you were asking about.' She looked around her and then, coming a little closer, she almost whispered in my ear, the amatory stuff!'

'Thank you, I said. 'I'm Professor Nowell. What's your name?'

'I'm Jane,' she said, 'Jane Jones. I've only worked here a little while.'

'Professor Legman,' I said, 'do you remember his first name?'

'Gershwin,' she said, I think it's Gershwin.'

It didn't take me too long in an index of scholars to find Gershon Legman. He was an American academic, fortuitously from Scranton, Pennsylvania and, also fortuitously, I found from looking at his latest book, he was living in London.

The tide of my affairs, I thought, following my little period of panic, was perhaps beginning to turn.

That night I spent pleasantly in a small but surprisingly expensive hotel in Bloomsbury, with Jane Jones, a graduate of the University of Wales who was pleased to have been given an internship at the Library before she started her postgraduate course in medieval literature at Imperial College—and also pleased to meet a genuine American professor closer to her own age than most of the crusty old gentlemen she met at work.

In the morning, I had arranged to meet Gershon Legman who, with his distinctive name, had been easy to find in the telephone directory. I had called Al Gilbert, who was lecturing at a liberal arts college in upstate New York, and who, I knew, was something of an authority on American folklore. It turned out that he had met Legman at a conference a couple of years before, so that gave me something by way of an introduction.

I made my way to Bouverie Street in the Temple district of London. As instructed, I opened a small, narrow gate in a nondescript wall. Up a short alley I came to a black door. Legman was expecting me as a piece of paper taped to the door said 'Please Enter'.

Through the door there were a few steps and I descended into what seemed a very old interior with stuccoed walls with niches. There were several bookcases and a desk against one wall with piles of papers. And suddenly Legman was there, appearing from the shadows.

Legman was not a tall man but had a presence, with a big jowly face, deep set but dark and piercing eyes and a mop of tousled hair turning to grey.

'You may be wondering where you are', he said. 'This is a very old part of London and this room is part of the halls of a very old group of people, the Knights Templar.'

He pointed out some features and we had a short conversation about the Knights Templar who had first occupied this part of

London as long ago as the twelfth century. However, I felt that, niceties observed, it was time to approach the subject of my visit.

'A friend speaks very highly of you,' I said. 'I wonder if you could assist me with some research, into amatory literature... ' I knew this would interest him and I could see his eyes light up, ' ... and especially Henry Spencer Ashbee.'

He smiled and beckoned me to be seated.

'I will try to help you,' he said, 'but firstly, you must tell me all that you know about Ashbee. He is a sort of passion of mine!'

I knew that I had no hope of explaining how I had come to know about Ashbee in any simple way, so I simply said that I had come across, through my research, a notebook that told a story that involved Ashbee.

'I don't know what is fact and what is fiction,' I said, 'but I would like your opinion.'

I showed him the document.

He leaved through it.

'I will need a little time to read this,' he said. 'Meanwhile, we will consume a bottle of wine from my cellar.'

He produced a bottle of Chateau Saint Julien Bordeaux. For a while I sat, thinking, and reading. Legman had directed me to some of his books and especially a set of three volumes. 'This is my edited edition of Ashbee's great work, written under the pen name Pisanus Fraxi, *Index Librorum Prohibitum.*'

It was a massive and fascinating work, set in various typefaces and with copious footnotes and bibliographic details of hundreds of books dealing with forbidden topics: prostitution, flagellation, sodomy, etc, etc. Ashbee's interests may have been prurient, but one thing was certain, he was a scholar of immense dedication and knowledge.

Legman read incredibly quickly, his head moving slightly and his eyes darting from side to side still, it took a while, and we had all but finished another bottle of the wine by the time he closed the book, looked up at me and smiled.

'Well, what do think?' I asked.

'Well it is a fine detective story, albeit without an ending.'

'What about the bit about Ashbee?' I asked.

'I think it is all baloney,' he replied. 'If Ashbee had penned all the stuff that this seems to suggest, then surely I would have come across it.'

'But he says it is all distributed in single copies to private gentlemen. They may have destroyed it themselves. At least they are unlikely to have gifted it to a library.'

'Hmm,' he was thinking. 'you must let me have copy of all of this. I can conduct some research.'

I grimaced a little.

He looked at me. 'But that is not what you have in mind?'

I explained my fruitless quest at the British Library and my desire to find the book with the lists.

'Well,' he said, 'the private case at the British Library was founded in 1866. It consists of over sixteen thousand items and, I believe, over one thousand of them were donated by Ashbee.'

'However,' he said, 'it took me some time to get access to the private case. I started filling in forms with my academic resume, then I provided references from universities in the United States and publishers of my books. Then I obtained references from English universities. Nothing seemed to work until I discovered an English lord was both on the advisory board of my English publishers and a trustee of the library. It took me months. It would take you some time too, of course, if, indeed you ever made it!' He laughed a little.

'Unless, of course, you wish to be my assistant!'

As we waited in the Library for some bureaucrat to permit us access to the collection, Legman took out his notebook.

'This is what I have taken from your manuscript about the book with the index: 'large book bound in brown buffed calf with a label on the spine'.'

'It may not look like anything interesting,' I added.

'Then,' said Legman, 'we will a better chance of finding it.'

I gave him an inquiring look.

'I'm afraid,' he said, anticipating my question, 'that a few years ago, the eminent scholars and bibliophiles of the most learned library in the world, in their wisdom, destroyed, for the public good, of course, some of Ashbee's collection.'

'But that was against the specific agreement that he came to with them!'

'Yes, but that held little sway with the puritans in the Museum. It is not ideal to be a collector of erotica. Sir Richard's Burton's manuscripts, years of work, were all burnt shortly after his death, by his own wife!'

He shook his head. 'I will not donate my collection to anyone or anything,' he said. 'It will be sold, but bit by bit at an obscure auction house. That way other scholars can search for the things I once searched for and hopefully have the pleasure of finding it.'

When we got to the inner library, Legman thought of something'

'Ashbee liked puzzles. He gave himself a pseudonym for his own writings, 'Pisanus Fraxi'. 'Fraxi' is, of course, the botanical name for the ash tree.' He scanned down a list of books in the secret catalogue and pointed at one—Anthophila, *Works, &c.*

'Anthophila is the classificatory name for the bee!'

After some cajoling and another two full hours of waiting, we managed to get the book retrieved from the private case. The first few pages and the last few pages were a sort of mock up of a book in dog Latin, but the centre pages of the book contained typed sheets of Ashbee's catalogue with the lists of names inscribed. I soon found the section required.

As I scanned down the list, like Ledbury, I noted the names of some notable and titled people. But, unlike Ledbury, not one but *two* names struck me more forcibly—Knowles, Rbt and Coulthard, Wm!

It was still a cold day—with some sun in the sky but the usual piercing sou-westerly wind when I got to Edinburgh. The only lead I now had led me back to Coulthard and I had to follow it. I was circumspect about approaching the bookshop; wary that, after two recent deaths, there might still be a police presence. But when I got there the doors were open and the exterior was being painted. The name Coulthard had been painted over and a signwriter was in the process of painting 'West Port Books' above the shop. So nearly three-quarters of a century of history were being erased in a few hours.

I entered the shop. Some shelves were only half filled and piles of books were placed in no particular order on the floor. A middle-aged man with silvery hair was ordering some of them.

'We're not open yet,' he said. 'Won't be for another week at least.'

'I knew Mr Coulthard,' I said. 'I just thought I'd pop in to see what had happened after his sudden death.'

'Yes, it was sudden, but he was very old. I bought the shop and some of the books, though most of them are what we call 'dogs'. I can't sell them, so some of them will go to charity.'

'What about the rest?' I asked.

'Oh, Coulthard's private effects and the best of the books are to be auctioned off as stipulated in his will.'

'Where did they go to?' I asked, now concerned that I may never see anything of Coulthard's again.

'Not far,' he said, 'they're at McDowell's auction rooms in Broughton Place. They'll be in their Wednesday sale.'

I walked to the east end of Princes Street, and down the hill to Leith Street. This was the start of the old road to the docks at Leith. In the old days, fisherwives would climb up with creels of fish on their back and merchants would roll barrels of whisky down for export. On my right was the volcanic outcrop of Calton Hill with its strange array of monuments, but I turned left, through Gayfield Square and through to the end of Broughton Place where an old converted church was now the location of William McDowell's auction rooms. A pavement sign said 'viewing today'.

Inside the main part of the church, there were cabinets and shelves and some cases and tables in the centre. A woman was busy arranging some items on a desk in the centre.

'Excuse me,' I said, 'Are these the books from the Coulthard shop?'

'She stopped her organising and gave me a friendly smile. 'Most of them,' she said. 'There are others too, and a collection of maps from the Shillingtree estate.' She had the sort of upper-class accent that all antique auctioneers seemed to possess.

'I'm only interested in the books that came from William Coulthard,' I said. 'I was in correspondence with him about some prospective purchases when he died,' I lied.

'Well, they didn't come to us in any particular order. We've divided them into lots.' She pointed to her left where some boxes and piles of books were stacked against the wall. Scottish topography, art history, biography and correspondence, general eighteenth-century and bindings. And then the best are in small or individual lots. You can find them in the glazed case at the end. I can open it for you.'

She took me to the far end of the room and opened the cabinet with a key. 'There's a catalogue over there,' she said, indicating a booklet pierced by a punch at the corner and fixed to the desk with a string. 'Or you can purchase one for twenty pence.'

I bought a catalogue and started to work my way though the cabinet. There were some quality books: a 1694 edition of *The History of Palmyra* with a fold-out panorama, a first edition of Thomas de Quincey's *Confessions of an English Opium Eater.*

When I opened one volume—it was a volume of Scott's *Lady of the Lake,* I believe, a photograph fell out. It was old and slightly buckled. It was a man, medium height, stocky and clean shaven, with a woman, slight and girlish, with a baby in her arms. Behind them was a seaside scene, but it was not real—it was quite clearly a painted backdrop typical of Victorian photography studios.

It could have been any old photograph, put there and forgotten by whoever had once owned the book, but something about it, for some reason, seemed familiar to me. I looked around. No-one much seemed to be paying any attention to me, so I slipped it into the inside pocket of my coat.

I worked my way through the books, one by one, leafing through each volume to see if there were any enclosures or additions, or even a hollowed-out centre. I found nothing that meant anything to me. I did the same with the general lots, but, some three hours later, I had found nothing. I was beginning to despair yet again.

I approached the lady with the posh accent. 'I know you may not know this, but are these *all* of Coulthard's books?'

'They are all that we have, and I don't think he commissioned any other auction house,' she said.

'There isn't anything else you know about his estate?'

She thought for a moment and shook her head. 'Not really, it was all to be auctioned and the proceeds to go to the Theosophical Society down the road.'

Something clicked! The Theosophical Society. That had been mentioned in Ledbury's manuscript. It was a slender connection, but it was all I have to go on. 'Can you tell me where it is?' I asked

I walked up Broughton Place and crossed Broughton Street, turning right into Albany Street which was a Georgian terrace of solid stone typical of the Edinburgh New Town. The Theosophical Society was plainly indicated.

The entrance hallway was ornate, framed by two stone pillars. There was a small table with a visitor's book and a few leaflets and also a bell with the sign 'ring for attention'.

I looked around at the illustrations on the wall. Some were charts with a series of esoteric symbols. I looked for something resembling the symbol Ledbury had written about but nothing seemed to fit.

After a little while, I heard footsteps, then a door opened that seemed to lead to a staircase down to a lower level. I was confronted with a large woman with a dark complexion and a large lumpish face. She had heavy eyes dark with mascara and a head of dark wiry hair tied back with a ribbon.

'How can I help you?' she asked.

'Are you the president of the society?' I asked.

'Oh no, we don't have a president as such. There are only a few of us. I am the caretaker and I run some classes here. I am Madame St Clair, Constance St Clair.'

'I was hoping to speak to someone who had been here for a while, regarding a member, I think. A member called William Coulthard.'

She nodded slightly and beckoned for me to accompany her into a room on the front left. It had been a drawing room but was now done out like a classroom, with an array of chairs and two plain tables at the front. At her behest, I sat on one of the chairs and she sat opposite me, looking intently in my face.

'How do you know of him, Mr... '

'Nowell,' I said, Professor Robert Nowell. I am doing some research into the books in his private collection. I wondered if he gifted any books to the society?'

'No, I don't think so. We have a small library you are welcome to use, but I don't think Mr Coulthard gave us anything,' she said. 'He hadn't been with us very long. He was an old man. He came to some of my classes. He was interested in a specific thing.'

She looked at me more intensely. Her large dark eyes were disconcerting.

'You are somehow related. I can see it because I have a sense that others do not possess. You are looking for the same thing that he was!'

'What is that?'

'Visiting the past. In dreams perhaps!'

I didn't really understand what she meant. 'Surely it is impossible to visit the past in any way. The past is gone and irretrievable.'

She held her fingers together under her chin almost as if she were praying.

'I teach my students how to employ the hidden powers of their subconscious mind. Some have more success than others. First you have to understand that your subconscious does not exist in limbo, but everywhere. It is a power that does not merely exist in the present, but also in the past; it does not exist here and now but at any place and at any time. It is our gateway into the wisdom of the universe.'

'But isn't it still governed by our conscious, our experiences and our knowledge?'

'That is the convenient perception, but it is not the case. Tell me, have you never dreamt that you were somewhere you had never been in real life, that you have met people you can't recognise. That you are dreaming something that is real but not part of your experience in real life?'

I admitted I had. 'But is that not just the power of the imagination? Do we not just make up fictions of a sort... fictions that come from the elements of what we do experience in real life.'

'I can see that you are aching for knowledge of something,' she said. 'Come down to my kitchen, we will discuss it.'

She rose from her chair in rather an imperious way and led the way through the hall and down the staircase to the basement level. I didn't feel I had any choice but to follow.

The basement was a decently furnished apartment from what I could see. The room to the right of the hall and to the rear of the building was a small kitchen. There was a smell of coffee beans and of something else, like exotic spices.

We sat down around a small table. She offered me tea or coffee. I asked for black coffee. She made herself some tea.

'Can you tell me more about Coulthard?'

'His request was quite simple. He wanted to remember a time in the past—an incident in his life that he had no memory of for some reason. It shouldn't have been too hard, but he was frail, his energy was failing. I don't know if he achieved what he wanted before he died.'

'So you don't know exactly what he was looking for?'

'No, he didn't tell me, but I know it was something very similar to what you wish to know about. I can see it in your eyes. I have the gift. I see that somehow you are one.'

I was puzzled by this.

'But you are much younger. It will be hard for you to go back so far,' she added.

'Can you teach me to do it?'

'Perhaps. Ideally, it would take some time.'

I must have looked disappointed

'But you don't want to take much time, do you?'

'No,' I admitted.

'I am not surprised.' she shrugged. 'You Americans have little patience—unlike my country folk.'

'Where are you from?' I asked.

'Oh, a place called Woking, in Surrey. I am English and I married a Russian army officer, but my parents were from France and Albania. They were Romanies. They understood persecution. That trains you in perseverance and patience.'

'They are very good qualities,' I said, 'As an academic I appreciate them.'

'But you do not have them,' she remarked.

'I don't have time to study much presently,' I said, 'I need to know something, as you said. Something specific that happened seventy-three years ago. Can you really help?'

She finished her tea and gazed deeply into the cup.

'I will give you the best advice I can. I don't know whether it will work, but I am only an instructor. So much depends on the pupil in these matters.'

She went to the kitchen sink and opened a cupboard above it. She took out a jar and, with a little spoon, took two spoonfuls of what looked like tea leaves and put them in a little sachet.

'Infuse these in boiling water, leave to stand for five minutes, drink slowly but regularly. Sit for another five minutes before you begin. The room should be as empty as possible and as dark as possible. You must be naked. Lie flat on your back, distributing your weight evenly. Your mind must be empty of all other things and you must concentrate on what you know of the time you wish to visit.'

Then she thought. 'Do you know the date of the event you want to revisit?' she added.

'Yes, well, within weeks.'

'It will help if you have an item, some token, from that time to keep beside you. Do you have something like that?'

'Yes,' I replied.

She looked at me carefully and a dark mask seemed to come over her face.

'Is anything wrong?' I asked.

'You must be careful,' she said, 'I see something in you, something I also saw in Mr Coulthard.'

What is it?' I asked.

She shook her head.

'I don't know,' she said, it is an image but it is not clear. I just remember that one time he came here and told me he had had strange dreams, not recently, but in the past. Dreams in which he saw things that hadn't come to pass, inventions that hadn't been invented, music he didn't recognise, faces he didn't know, places he had never been to.' She paused and closed her eyes a little, trying to concentrate.

'He asked me if that was possible. I said I did believe it was, but was only experienced very rarely.'

'And is it possible?' I asked.

'I do not now know absolutely,' she said, 'but I do know that quite recently, shortly before he died he told me he had dreamed his own death and he quoted a poem. A few lines have dwelt in my mind: 'Who am I ? And what am I, and where have I come from?''

I went back to my hotel. The blinds did not close well, so I used a spare bed sheet to cover the window. A vase, an alarm clock and a few other things I stowed under the bed. After I had made the brew and drank it, I did the same with the kettle and cups. I stripped off. Finally, before I also put my briefcase and personal things under the bed, I took out a little velvet bag and from it took the silver sixpence dated 1900 that my father had given me. I placed it under the pillow. And then, for some reason, I took the photograph that had dropped from the volume in the auction house and placed it there also.

I lay down and, before I had time to reflect on anything, I slept.

Chapter Fifteen

LE COUCHON
QUI RIT

To find happiness, a man need only live in the moment...
But if he wants meaning—the meaning of his dreams, his
secrets—a man must re-inhabit his past, however dark...

Jed Rubenfeld, The Interpretation of Murder

The whole series of life appeared to me as in a dream. I
sometimes doubted if indeed it were all true, for it presented
itself to my mind with the force of reality

Mary Bysshe Shelley, Frankenstein

I wandered aimlessly but restively up the Rue Chabanais checking my stride which seemed altogether too forced for my purpose. Tonight there was an excited clamour in the street, even the gaslights seemed to be twitching nervously. I thought I heard the occasional muted crash of breaking glass. It was in stark contrast to the dusty and dreary book stalls I had spent the morning with.

The tarts were gathering on street corners and doorways for the night—each emerging, it seemed, from the half light like semi-formed creatures—a torso and Neanderthal brow sometimes lit by a high street lamp, a back or suddenly protruding hip or shoulders. Sudden glimpses of the rouge of their lips and the tight black or scarlet of their short skirts. One or two of whom wore French berets or striped Breton blouses to attract foreigners. As the pastis went to my head I felt stronger. I checked my pace and meandered a little nearer to them. They seemed like wonderful painted creatures and I thought about girls like these—some barely in their teens but with an immeasurably older facade of confidence only occasionally cracked by a sudden fright from a neighing horse or a scuffle in a ruelle. Girls like these, absinthe and cheap perfume had inspired and served Baudelaire, Toulouse Lautrec and countless French intellectuals.

As I moved among the throng, one girl pressed her lips towards me and whispered. I didn't reply but turned aside a little and with a gay little laugh she disappeared over my right shoulder.

I turned to cross the street diagonally towards a caramel seller when suddenly I saw her. At first I wasn't sure what her business was. She sported a fashionable blouson with some delicate lacing down the front that hung attractively over her ample body and full breasts. Her hair was down to her shoulders and very red, So red I suspected that it had been dyed, I guessed, with henna. This was unquestionably Amélie, the barmaid from the Café d'Écosse.

I went over to her and she clearly recognised me as she gave a little gasp—but she regained her composure almost immediately. She smiled with her teeth and her little nose turned upwards. I could almost see a shy smile under the *cracking rouge and mascara.*

'Come along' was all she said and she linked with my arm. I realised that I felt quite excited and almost proud in a way. She took me up a steep cobbled street until eventually we came to a doorway lit with a red lantern. It was clearly ordinary but not the cheapest or sleaziest of the hotels in the vicinity of Montmartre.

The entrance seemed pleasantly clean with polished mahogany, scarlet embossed wallpaper and brocades. There was a doorway to the right that might have been a breakfast room. Le patron hardly looked up but there was a slight nod of recognition towards Amélie—although I realised that that was unlikely to be her name here.

We walked straight ahead—it seemed into a wall, but it was a tiny elevator, coffin-shaped, with slightly stained and worn carpets on three of the walls. As we squeezed together I felt a shudder and as she pulled fast the door I found myself, in this tight space, facing a thin strip mirror covered in streaks—as if champagne, or something worse, had been sprayed in this confined space. I was suddenly shocked to catch an image of myself in the mirror. In the coffin and backed with a small fluttering light, in my dark coat and scarf I looked like some shadow of the night—a creature not yet humanly formed. I then caught in full face my shining dark eyes, my long straight nose and my mouth—intelligent and lightly open, but in wonderment, not in a gawp. My head spinning slightly, I came into communion with myself. At this moment Amélie pulled on my arm until I was bent down towards her and kissed me fully and, I think, passionately, on the mouth. I ran my tongue all around and along her big teeth as if I was forming a smile on her perfumed face and for a moment I felt happy.

The elevator ran upward, jerked up and then down to a halt. With a great push the doors opened to a dimly lit hallway and we walked hand in hand anti-clockwise through corridors until we came to a room.

It was a typical small room for a pension—it had the basic washhand basin, double bed and window overlooking a backyard and fire escape. The window was slightly open and the city air seemed to leak in. I looked out and saw some shadowy shapes against barred windows. I heard the sounds of city life and that distant squawking of voices raised in anger or excitement that goes on all night in this district. Amélie moved behind me and pulled the casement shut. I looked around. The light was dim but adequate—supplied by two converted gas mantles on the wall behind the bed. The room was clean with signs of more than basic acquisitions. There was a vanity case on a chest of drawers opposite the bed and, in a little recess, a dressing table with a range of toiletries and perfumerie. The mirror was tilted slightly forward and seemed to be covered with a sheet of damask.

After we had performed the act, for the first time she addressed me directly. 'I usually need money, you know.'

I didn't see this as a problem. 'I can give you money, what do you need it for?'

'Life.'

For some reason I suddenly became angry. 'What kind of life is this?' I asked. 'Is it whoring?'

She stiffened and she turned away and didn't look at me directly.

'If that's what you call it

'That is what I call it.'

She was angrier now. 'I have my profession and my respect, you know. At least I don't carry a panier.'

I looked at her with such surprise and interest that she suddenly seemed embarrassed Amélie as if she had inadvertently spoken of some deep lost secret.

I was so insistent and so intent that I made her tell me that some low prostitutes and rent boys carried baskets or bags to stand in when they had sex in privies or water closets.

I sat up and envisaged this—hundreds of cheap penetrations standing up in every stinking corner of the city.

I suddenly softened. 'What does it matter. When memory fades you can have a new life. You can't do this forever.'

'Nothing is forever.' She shrugged and laid her head back on the pillow. I perched above her and looked more closely. Despite the short period of months since I had last seen her, some lines had formed radiating from her eyes. Her eyelids looked heavy and almost swollen beneath the mascara. Her eyes were still green—but more distant and the pupils were smaller as if they were floating aimlessly on an opaque sea. There were signs of tears forming in each corner of her eyes

'You can't be one of us,' I said, unsure what I meant.

She looked at me shocked and puzzled. I did feel a small surge of pity but I rose and pulled on my pants. I found two English notes in my pocket and I threw one of them on the bed. Then I turned out my other pocket in which there were a few silver threepennies, a sixpence and some coppers. I gave her those too and then all the little francs and centimes left until my pockets were empty. I could see she was crying now.

I put my arm around her as she sat upright but she stiffened and pulled away.

'There is one thing I have to know before I go. I'm looking for a Madame St Clair. She has certain items I wish to purchase.'

'If I knew I wouldn't tell you.' She turned around, swung her legs from the bed and reached to the bedside where she found a cigarette and lit it. The match created a small glow and a noxious sulphury smell in the room as I pondered what to do.

I thought for some reason of home, then I thought of Paris and of my wavering reflection in the dressing table mirror. I became angry. I grabbed her by the shoulder and the left breast—squeezing her clavicle and her erect nipple hard.

She gasped and then cried out

'You madman, mad, mad, fou, fou!' But she wasn't hysterical. I realised suddenly what I was doing and pulled away. She lay back on the bed, breathing deeply—but I couldn't work out whether she was crying or laughing within the sobbing breaths.

'Please,' I said.

She looked at me keenly, composed now. Smoked for a little while as I sat there feeling fairly helpless. Then she reached down to the drawer of the small bedside cabinet. She took out a card, a little like a carte-de-visite. It was yellowed and looked curiously old, although I couldn't detect any date. It featured an image of a showgirl, dressed in a bodice and suspenders, her foot was on a stool and she was pulling one stocking up to a bare thigh. Her face was turned aside in direct address. The features were stylised and basic but the darkness of the ink and the sudden shock of the probing face made me think it could be Amélie herself.

She might have read my mind. 'It is not mine. Turn it over.'

I turned it over. On the back there was the name 'Le Couchon Qui Rit, Maison de Tolérance,' an address and, in red ink the name 'Camille St Clair.'

What I did next came as a surprise to me. I had come to Paris not just in search for books but for new experiences too. As I looked down on her flushed face for the last time I felt a strange sensation. I knew I could never return.

I left the pension as speedily as I could—galloping clockwise down the staircase to avoid the coffin elevator.

As I took a breath of the misty night air I felt refreshed and suddenly a clear direction seemed to fall in my path. I realised that the search for the books was urgent, but I suddenly realised a deep raw hunger was growing within me. In satiating my sexual appetite I had forsaken all others. In fact, I couldn't remember when I had last eaten. I ran my hands down my sides, my body seemed taut and strong, my legs and arms stretched and satisfied, my stomach flat and ravenous. I stopped a street stall to buy a crêpe. It was small but would suffice until I had completed my final task of the day.

I found Le Couchon Qui Rit. It was barely lit but decorated in a flamboyant rococo style. Madame St Clair did not seem pleased to see me but she softened a little when she heard my English accent and I enquired about books.

'Ah, what you will want is The Man of Pleasure in Paris, *1808 edition. It is popular among the English.'*

I declined the offer.

'Then perhaps you are a gentleman of more cultivated tastes!' She opened a drawer in a demi lune table and took out some papers.

'Here I have the poems of Baudelaire translated into English for the first time for gentlemen of taste and discretion. This is about Paris: 'Fourmillante cite, cite pleine de reves.'

She presented me with the papers. I read the first poem:

I have seen many corpses in my youth:
The salty, saintly, wormy and the plain.
To nightly haunt my dreams they come;
As winged creatures with anonymous names.

When I am alone, flocking to the tumescent candle,
My painted moths speak dumbly with their eyes,
While in the city the harlots track their knotted paths
And the sullen river flames while the breathing city sighs.

And in dreams perhaps my fallen angels snuff the light,
For no-one knew how fugitive their colours would become,

And swift my waking hours fade into the night,
Masking the winged eyes that come from you, the worm.

Teeming city full of dreams, mighty collossus!
Where daylight ghosts accost the passer-by.
In your narrow channels mysteries flow like sap,
And blood seeps through your every secret way.

I did not know if I was a gentlemen of taste and discretion, but some elements of the poem did strike a chord. The description of Paris was excessive but truthful.

However, this was merely a distraction from my primary business purpose. I explained in more rudimentary terms what I really wanted.

'Very well,' she said, 'You will have to come down to the dungeon.'

I was certainly glad to escape from Madame St Clair's dungeon which was designed, I surmised, to satisfy clients with certain special requirements. However, I left *Le Couchon Qui Rit* soon after with two works I was sure would meet the requirements of my collector: La Nymphomanie, ou Traité de La Fureur Utérine, &c *and* Histoire des Flagellans *by the Abbé Boileau.*

I felt good. Today I had obtained these books, some other scarce works in French and German that I had been instructed to return to London. I also had a miniature Bible in English that I thought would please another client. I couldn't return to the Café d'Écosse but I went to the Café de Flore and ordered some supper. I sat back and drank some brandy and thought of my triumphant return to London with the treasures of my bibliographic quest and one new surprising experience.

I drank some tea. It was later than I thought. Lost in the torments of my dream I had slept later than I intended. But I knew what must be done. I dressed as quickly as I could and headed back to the Theosophical Society.

The door was opened not by Madame St Clair but by a small bespectacled man in a grey suit and vest.

'I'm looking for Madame St Clair?' I said.

'Connie. She's finished for now, I'm afraid.'

'I thought that she lived here.'

'Oh no, she lives in a caravan out at Straiton. She does the cleaning here. She needs the money since her husband died.'

'Her husband, he was Russian?'

'He was a scaffolder from Leith. Nice man, but too fond of the cratur!'

I looked puzzled.

'Whisky, it did for him.'

'Doesn't Madame St Clair do classes for you?'

'Sometimes she does tarot readings and things for some of the members, but not officially—that wouldn't be within the remits of the Society.'

'I still need to see her. Can you tell me where she lives?'

'I don't think I can do that, but I can pass on a message. She'll be in first thing tomorrow, we have a workshop on spiritual healing, and then there are sandwiches to make for a trip to Rosslyn.'

'I really need to see her before that. It's about some research I'm doing, important research.'

He looked at me a little impatiently.

'She was very helpful to my research yesterday,' I said. I noticed the donation box. 'And she asked me to give a donation to the Society in return.' I took some notes from my wallet

'I have a class to organise,' he said. 'Look, I suppose you would find her easily enough anyway. Everybody knows her and a lot of people look her out. She has some genuine powers, although they're a bit over-dramatised for my liking.'

He looked at the donation box. 'But thank you for your support,' he said.

'Perhaps,' I added, 'you could put these to the best use yourself, for the Society', I said.

He hesitated for a few moments, then took the notes. 'Straiton caravan park, on the south side. It's the only caravan painted gold.'

The caravan was bright gold on the outside, but the inside was mostly black. There were sofas covered in crimson throws and some ornaments. An old statuette of the Virgin Mary carved out of wood—the paint faded, the nose chipped—a couple of paintings of exotic-looking seaside scenes and a print of a Burne-Jones painting. She saw me looking at it.

'It is called *The Hand Refrains*,' she said. 'Pygmalion has created a statue of the perfect woman, but it is untouchable. He is obsessed by her but he cannot touch her, only observe her.'

'But didn't Aphrodite bring the statue to life?'

'Perhaps, but that is only a myth.' I dismissed this discussion, but the bit in Ledbury's notebook about the girls being made up after death was lingering at the back of my mind. The notion of looking on to something so beautiful that it was beyond life but has it's own perfection somehow stuck with me.

Madame St Clair looked old in the light of the table lamp. A few black hairs on her chin showed through the cake of make-up. She was sitting in her imaginary palace in a caravan painted in tarnished gold on a run-down caravan park in the industrial outskirts of a cold city. I felt a twinge of pity for her.

I sat in front of a small table while Madame St Clair made tea and coffee at the back end of the caravan. I expected there to be a crystal ball. There was not, but there was a set of tarot cards. I inspected them. They looked old and well worn.

'I'm sorry it's a little cramped in here,' she said, 'we had a house out at Penicuik, but the building industry failed, I'm afraid, and my dear husband never received his allowance from the Russian Imperial Army, because of the Cold War.'

She gave me my black coffee in a little Goss crested china cup and saucer.

'The tarot cards are very ornate, I said.

'They are very old,' she said. 'They were given to my grandmother by the man who designed them. He was a great mystic but a wicked man. Crowley was his name.'

This was another coincidence. Crowley was one of the characters recalled by Ledbury.

'So', she said, 'you have had a dream, a very vivid dream. And you think that there may be within it a memory that is not your own?'

I nodded.

'Some of what you have dreamed will have seeped in from your conscious memory. What we must do is recognise that and then identity what your subconscious has picked up.'

I thought about this. And my mind strayed to my own memories of France and the French. To my own little trip to Paris as a young lecturer and my book-buying adventures. To Nancy and her French books, to Amelia and her dissertation on French literature.

'The dream started in Paris, on the banks of the Seine, where I have been, on a study trip, but then it moved to a part of Paris that I have never visited.'

'OK, we will concentrate on that part of the dream. Did the places, the streets, seem real?'

'Yes. But the way I saw them was different. I wasn't afraid. I wasn't tired. I was looking at them as if I was somehow above it all, as if I could control everything.'

'That is a common feature of lucid dreaming. But did you feel the scene was familiar. As if you had been there before?'

'Yes.'

'Then it is possible that you had been there before, in an earlier life or in the memory of another person.'

'How can that be?'

'Our memories don't just remain with us. They are passed on somehow, through generations, through some sort of communal thought process.' She paused, examining my face thoughtfully.

'So, who did you meet in your dreams?' she continued.

'There were some girls.'

'Did you know them from the real world?'

'Well yes… No. I mean they seemed similar to people I knew from the real world, but they weren't the same.'

'Well' let's ignore that. Part of your mind is trying to make something strange more familiar to you so it is easier to understand. Now tell me what happened.'

'I hesitated. 'Some of it is a bit racy.'

She didn't seem put off by this at all.

After I had recounted the whole tale, judiciously excluding some not so pertinent facts such as the similarity to her own name and the unfortunate new experience my dreaming self had had, she said, 'There are several things that we must glean from your dream.

Firstly, it is set in a place you yourself do not know, so we can only presume that you are seeing it through the eyes of someone else—someone who knows the location.'

For some reason I didn't want to reveal to her suspicions about the identity of the 'someone else'.

'But aren't they just imaginary locations?' I asked, although I already knew the answer.. 'Locations that I've made up in my head from books or movies?'

She nodded slightly and slowly.

'I know Paris. My mother lived there as a child, many, many years ago and she would tell me stories. The two places you name...'

'Le Couchon Qui Rit and La Maison de Tolérance'

'Yes, they are, or were, real. I have heard of them. But I believe they date to the Paris of *last* century. Have you a notion of why you were there in the dream?'

I did not reveal any more at this time. 'No, but I need to know more. I haven't yet found what I was seeking.'

'There is nothing more that I or any earthly power can do to enable that. Your dreams will reveal to you what you need to know when it is time.'

Madam St Clair looked tired. It was time to let her rest. I was tired too, but I was now beginning to understand what had been revealed to me.

I took the overnight train back to London. I didn't get a sleeping car so I sat in a darkened carriage thinking and only occasionally dosing off.

I slept but then, in my dream, I woke. Slowly, a scene developed in front of me. It was a wall of books lit in a shimmering lantern light. In front of me was a desk with a pad and a pen and what looked like a ledger and some other books.

To the right there were more bookcases only dimly lit. A sort of consciousness came over me, but not a full consciousness, as if a fog still hovered between my mind and my senses.

I looked to the left. There there was a mirror on the wall and as I focused on it I awoke a little more.

Was I Ledbury? Was I looking through the eyes of someone else in some other time. No, I was not Ledbury. I knew who I was as soon as I looked in the mirror. And then the face in the mirror and my own melted and merged and I was, again, lost in a dream...

Chapter Sixteen

DISCIPLINE
AND PUNISH

Nothing is of higher importance to us, as men and as
Christians, than to form a proper estimation of human life
without either loading it with imaginary evils, or expecting
from it greater advantages than it is able to yield

Hugh Blair, *Sermons*

Human beings are the only animals that kill for ideas.

Laurens van der Post

I recognised the door. It was night, but the gas lamps lit a street sign. It said Seething Lane. Turning back to the frontage of the shop I read the sign. It said 'Coulthard & Knowles: booksellers'!

I could see clearly, but who was I? I thought that I was Robert Nowell, but the eyes I saw through, the body I inhabited, was that of Bob Knowles!

In the bookshop was a central desk, a variety of bookcases and piles of books. And also in the centre was Mrs Berkeley's famous horse with the Ord girl strapped to it. Her hands tied and a mask muffling her face. Facing the desk was a chair and Ledbury sat there, his hands tied to the back. I remembered that I, or rather Knowles, had ambushed him as he tried the door. Somehow he had deduced the centre of the spider's web and found his way here. Or was he led here.

'You cannot keep us here,' Ledbury said. 'I have telephoned the Yard. Superintendant Ord will be here any minute.'

'I'm afraid that is not the case. Scotland Yard are looking for you, and I doubt that you have had the opportunity to lead them here in the absence of your friend Ord,' He glanced at the girl, 'this young lady's father.'

The girl managed to mumble through her gag, 'My father *will* find me.'

'No, I'm afraid he won't,' said Blacklock. 'Thanks to a little note that I have sent to the Commissioner recently, he thinks that you and your father and Mr Ledbury are all involved in some way with Jeremy and the other girls. I suspect your father is being interrogated now.'

'They'll believe him and he will assure them that we had nothing to do with it,' said Ledbury.

'There may be some difficulty with that,' said Blacklock, 'especially since I have sent them the sample of your handwriting that looks very much like Jeremy's, or Jack's, or, indeed, mine!'

Ledbury looked surprised.

'Oh yes, I got it from between the leaves of this volume here.' He pointed to some books on the desk.

Ledbury looked surprised.

'Yes, I have these, and your lachrymose poetry and your little excursions into other forms of writing that, I suspect, Miss Ord knows nothing about.'

Ledbury looked furious and strained to pull at the knots that tied him.

'Please, Mr Knowles, ensure that those binds are secure.'

I did as he said and fiddled for a moment with the ropes that tied Ledbury to the chair.

Blacklock addressed Ledbury again.

'My late assistant, Bartholomew, brought them to me. So, you see, your life is as open to me as are your books. Bartholomew was a great assistance to me. As well as monitoring your affairs, he controlled your imaginings! You have been mine for some time,' Mr Ledbury. 'I have even controlled your dreams.'

Ledbury gave him a strange look.

'Ah, You wish to know how I do that!'

He shrugged. 'It is not very difficult. A mere bit of chemical trickery. A sprinkling of powder added to the bowl of your paraffin lamp at night. You are too trusting and forgetful and careless with the locking of your bedroom door.'

He laughed.

'I'm afraid it may have caused you some vivid if not very pleasant dreams.'

'It is time for something of a lecture. Admittedly you are a smaller group than I usually address at the College. But, while you are sitting comfortably, Mr Ledbury, and you are comfortable enough for now, Miss Ord, I shall begin. Mr Knowles, of course, knows the greater part of it, having been my assistant for some time, but I will have some sport for him soon.'

I stood stock still. I did not know what he was referring to.

'To start at the beginning, the first serious experiments I conducted into human behaviour became infamous. All the perpetrators were my patients at the asylum. I had discovered that, with the appropriate stimulus and a regime of punishment and reward, I could control them absolutely.

'The first subject was a harrower who had gone insane when his four children had died in turn of peri-natal tetanus. The victim was a young whore I had previously chastised for laughing at me in compromising situations. Situations such as, I have now determined, I have no need for.

'The second was conducted by a hatter who had consumed an excess of mercury. The third was a cutpurse and ne-er do well. The fourth was a gentleman of sorts, except that he had squandered the family fortune on gaming and whoring and came to me with an advanced case of the kissing disease.

'They all came back to me, of course, like doves to a dovecot, because I fed them—not their bodies but their minds. I took the appropriate steps to ensure that they did not reveal any details of their excursions to anyone else.'

Ledbury looked aghast, but sat still. It was clear that Blacklock was referring to the infamous Whitechapel murders.

Blacklock continued.

'Because I had determined certain similar characteristics to the activities, the police and the press assumed that they were the work of one man. This was another discovery for me. By judiciously sending some veiled messages, I created a legend. Jack, I called him after the knave who inhabits playing cards

'So,' Ledbury interrupted, 'you flogged one innocent girl and because she might have told someone, you murdered her and another three innocent girls!'

'Hardly innocent, Mr Ledbury, they were all whores. I did not 'murder' them. They simply died as part of an essential experiment. However, if you insist in using that term then surely you can see that what I have done is elevate 'murder' to an art of sorts. Why do men murder? Usually it through one emotion or the other: fear, envy, anger, desire… I have surpassed all those.'

'Whether they were whores or not, they deserved to live!'

'Pah, hypocrisy. Like all gentlemen you live by the edict that the natural role of women is to serve their masters and to procreate. Yet day by day now we see women transgressing: suffrage, attending colleges. Trying to usurp the true role of men.

'All the women I have chosen were of this unnatural type. All sought books that were unsuitable for their consumption, so I chose them as an example, to teach them the rightful path of subservience to man. Since I could fulfil all the functions required myself, I enlisted a willing servant in the enterprise.'

I realised he was referring to me. I also realised that he was quite mad and, in his hatred of those he regarded as inferior to himself, fuelled by his own impotence.

'Five.' Ledbury suddenly found myself saying. 'You said four. There were five Whitechapel murders.'

'The fifth came as a surprise to me,' he replied. 'I was already content with my experiment when it occurred. It was not one of my patients at the time, but he came into my hands shortly afterwards, through the services of an eminent person who knew some of my methods. The gentleman was a physician, who, sated with his desire to save lives, decided to destroy one. He was so inflamed with the other acts that he committed an atrocity in imitation of them. It is a phenomena I have since observed. I call it copy-catting. Needless to say, for spoiling the symmetry of my project, I had to punish him very severely.'

'And', said Ledbury, 'you had as little concern for that poor victim as you had for any of the others, or any woman or man whose life you determine to destroy!'

'You still do not see,' said Blacklock. I have become a creature of pure will. I am beholding neither to God or to Satan. If I wish to cause women pain or pleasure I can. If I wish to cause you pain or pleasure I can. Shortly, I may allow Mr Knowles to show you other ways a man can treat a woman. I am sure he is enjoying our encounter as much as I am.'

There was a pause as if we all were overwhelmed by the intensity of Blacklock's self-obsession.

'Now,' Blacklock addressed Ledbury, 'you many wish to know why you are here.

'I admit that I have a certain vanity. I could probably attain my ends more easily, but I have the instincts of a playwright. I like to step my little scenarios with a certain precision.

'When Bartholomew informed me about the idiotic device that set you up as the amanuensis to a certain imaginary Sherlock Holmes, I couldn't resist involving you. Bartholomew soon told me everything about you, including your obsession with your dear departed Dorothea. How he found out, I don't know. Bartholomew was ostensibly a clerk in a shipping office, but he was really the rare breed of person, a professional snoop, trading information with anyone who needed to know what was going on. The Americans train them very well, I believe, although it was a Scotsman who started them off.

'After this, my efforts will have the following results: the public will live in fear of the second coming of the Ripper, the detective forces will be completely discredited and, a little extra, thanks to your part in the drama, Mr Ledbury, that patriotic oaf Doyle and his ridiculous alter ego will be shown to be a pointless fiction.'

'What satisfaction will you get from killing me?'

'Ah, Mr Ledbury, you do not quite see. I do not intend to kill you although I fully expect you to die—presently with a rope around your neck. I believe that you are aware of that process from your visit to the recent execution of the poor Evans, another of my experiments.'

The girl began to murmur.

'Consider the profile of the killer,' Blackwood continued. 'Someone who had suffered a traumatic event in the past. Someone who is creative but thwarted in his ambitions. Someone who spends a lot of time alone. Someone who harbours dangerous fantasies—your work for Mr Ashbee will testify for that!'

Ledbury looked shocked.

'Of course, that was also arranged. You don't think that those sentimental little magazine pieces about country life enticed Ashbee to give you the job, do you? Mr Knowles supplied him with more suitably salacious material on your behalf.'

The girl made more sounds so, instinctively if not willingly, I disciplined her again. This caught Ledbury's attention and distracted him from Blacklock for a moment, but the Professor continued.

'You auditioned perfectly for the part when you took the counterfeiting job for Doyle. Don't you see. You were chosen. You *are* Jeremy. The new spring-heeled Jack. You will be a great sensation. The toast of the popular press. You will be talked about for years to come.'

'Why?' asked Ledbury, almost plaintively, but still with a little note of defiance.

'Why? Because a few years ago I created a character to live in the popular imagination forever. But I couldn't deliver a genuine fiend to the public. Now I have achieved that. I am the creator of Jeremy, and he has come to life in you!'

At this point I couldn't help but think of Frankenstein and his monster and the invention of insanity!'

'Two men,' Ledbury suddenly said. 'There were two men, the third girl said so!'

Blacklock nodded. 'Yes, you had an accomplice. The unfortunate Mr Bartholomew. I say unfortunate because you murdered him earlier today. Your landlady will be quite shocked to find that she has been harbouring two notorious murderers.'

'I will tell the police all about you!'

'No-one will believe you.'

'Superintendant Ord will believe me!'

'A foolish old man. He couldn't even protect his own daughter. His day is done. The police will believe that a madman will contrive any story to protect himself and that I am the object of your ire for helping to identify you.

'My drama is perfectly contrived. As tight as a drum. Each piece fits exactly into the whole. When I have finished this particular part of the experiment you will be surfeit to my requirements. You will be found in the street near the vicinity of another murder ranting and half unconscious which I will ensure with a little more of my elixir. Thereafter, I expect the slow grinding wheels of justice will eventually do their work.'

Hearing this and thinking on the mention of the 'late' Mr Bartholomew, I wondered if I would be surfeit to requirements too. Knowles may not have realised it, being completely in thrall to Blacklock, but I did. I was captured in the body of a madman who, on turn, was in thrall to another madman.

Blacklock turned to address the girl. 'I have known you for some time, Miss Ord, since you went to school by the woods whereby I walked to work at the asylum.'

He came towards her and I thought he intended to touch her, but instead he just ran his hands around her profile about twelve inches away from her body, as if somehow gauging her size and shape.

'As has my assistant,' he said, indicating me. 'Remove her mask, Mr Knowles.

'Of course, he has instincts that I do not.' He looked towards the desk with its part-written papers. My records and my library are my collection and my passion. I do not indulge in venial desires.'

'Perhaps it's because you cannot satisfy a woman that you hate them so much and wish to destroy them!' The girl spoke up! I wished that she had not.

Blacklock nodded to me. I adjusted the horse so that it leant forward, also bending her body forward and exposing her rear parts. I had a rod hanging from my waist. I unfastened it and applied it to her buttocks. Perhaps anticipating this, she had clenched her teeth and made hardly a sound. Then I wondered why I had done so. Was I Knowles, or was I Nowell?

'Stop, stop,' Ledbury shouted. 'Why are you so sick? Why do you hate women so much?'

'Oh no, Mr Ledbury. It is not about hatred, it is more like a kind of love, but love that reveals itself as knowledge. Once I know every intimate part of the subject, the nooks and crannies of their bodies, the deepest desires of their minds, then I fully possess them. Then that knowledge gives me the power to do as I like with their fragile lives.

'We are creatures of intellect. There are very few of us but we are the puppet masters Why should we not exalt in our superiority? We have been given the gift to control and rule over others. Galton has so far elucidated only a part of our great project. To categorise and control the people so that they can be used, manipulated as to our will.'

'You think you are God.' The girl struggled to speak, choking a little. 'But you are really just as petty as those you despise.'

'Yes,' added Ledbury, 'You are not doing this for any greater good, only through your own cruelty and bloodlust. It controls you as much as you control anyone else.'

'Your pretty words don't matter a jot to me,' Blacklock said,.'You are like a moth pinned on a board or a maggot wriggling on a hook. You are mine. As I will, I can open up any part of your body and any part of your mind.'

'You can't own me,' the girl said.

'Apply the rod,' Blacklock said.

I did. It made a swish and then the sound of the impact. I suddenly felt my own, or rather Knowles's, excitement rise in my loins. Who was I? If I was Nowell, I felt that my mind was still mine, but I did not yet feel that I could fully control the feelings and actions of the body I inhabited.

This time the girl did not remain silent. She made a squeal and her whole body tensed as if she were struggling to escape her shackles. Then it relaxed again.

Then she began to sob.

'Can I give her some water?' I asked.

Blacklock nodded.

On one of the bookshelves there was a jug and a little glass. I poured some water and held it so that the girl could sup it. She seemed a little more composed.

'You can see, Mr Ledbury,' said Blacklock, 'what a considerate lover Mr Knowles is. He is a romantic like yourself. He is part of me now too. I regard him with some affection.'

Blacklock turned to directly address Ledbury. 'Mr Ledbury, you are very fortunate that you came here today. I am going to demonstrate to you that, with the right application of reason and discipline that, not only can I persuade Miss Ord that my arguments are correct but I will be able to get her to say that four and one equals six—and to believe it.'

'Wait,' said Ledbury, 'this cannot just be an experiment, you must want something more of us?'

'No,' said Blacklock, 'I have chosen both of you to aid me in an experiment in control. You, like the other three girls, are incidental to my main purpose which is to demonstrate my complete dominance over my chief subject.'

'Perhaps, in fact, it's only because you're getting older and more impotent that you want to return to torturing and murdering women again!'

Blacklock nodded to me. I applied the rod again, this time, I decided, harder, and below the two red streaks I had already caused and closer to the exposed coney where the undergarments had been removed.

The cheeks of the buttocks seemed to melt and then quiver, like jelly or butter. The girl shrieked and then began to gasp for air as if she were drowning.

The girl wasn't bearing up as well as the others. The last one found it hard too. That is why I didn't kill her despite what Blacklock ordered. She hadn't seen either of us face to face so I thought it would be possible.

I pulled myself together and shook myself a little. I felt like slapping myself on the face. I was slipping. I was beginning to think and act more like Knowles. But I wasn't Knowles, and I was still in my dream, was I not.

Then something struck me, and I couldn't stop myself from addressing him, but whether I did so as Nowell or as Knowles wasn't clear to me.

'Professor Blacklock,' I asked, 'who is your chief subject?'

He smiled slightly. 'Why, you are, of course,' he replied.

'Before… ' Ledbury interrupted, 'before you continue to experiment with us, then tell me what is your answer to the profile I have drawn up of you. The profile that will enable Superintendant Ord to discover you and bring you to justice!'

'Nonsense,' said Blacklock, 'you have done nothing that can lead them to me.'

'You have clearly not read the last page of my notebook, then.'

Blacklock looked down at the books on his desk and Ledbury suddenly rose. The knots that had I tied carelessly behind his back broken. He pushed back the chair and hurtled himself at Blacklock. But Blacklock saw him coming and he threw a punch, glancing off Ledbury's jaw and knocking him backwards.

'Grab him, you fool!' Blacklock shouted at me.

I looked at Ledbury and at Blacklock and at the girl all trussed up.

And then I launched forward—not at Ledbury but at Blacklock and, catching him by surprise, knocked him to the floor, knocking over his papers and pen and ink and the lamp on the desk.

I had one hand round Blacklock's neck holding him down as his hands stretched up, clawing at my face and eyes. The papers caught light and the oil from the lamp mixed with ink and created a black pool of flame. I looked back at Ledbury

'Get the girl!' I said.

But this moment of distraction allowed Blacklock to push me over and half rise to his feet. He grappled and he pushed me backwards into one of the bookcases against the wall.

The bookcase collapsed, sending books and papers scattering into the pool of flame and they too caught light.

I looked across through the flickering flame and smoke towards where Ledbury and the girl had been, but they were no longer there.

Blacklock and I were still locked in combat but struggling, we fell over. Then I realised someone else was there beside us. But it was not a living thing. It was the dead body of Bartholomew which must have been hidden behind the bookcase. I realised now. Bartholomew was Blacklock's agent in the shipping industry and the one who delivered the letters to Ledbury and had, as requested, delivered Ledbury's notebooks to Blacklock. He was, in fact, just as much a stooge of Blacklock's as I was myself. And now he was dead! Presumably another victim of Blacklock—or of Knowles!

Then suddenly all three of us were falling and I landed on top of Blacklock, knocking him unconscious!

What had happened is that the weight of the bookcase had caused the trap door into the cellar to collapse. And there we lay in the rubble. Above us all I could see was a wall of flame as all the books and papers in the book shop burned. I thought of Blacklock's own library and, for some reason, wondered what would happen to it now.

Beside me, unharmed, were the Ledbury books and, for reason, I clutched at these and shoved them in my jacket pocket.

Blacklock, Bartholomew and I were set to be entombed here but suddenly I saw the only means of escape, a hint of dusky light from the door to the coal chute that fed the cellar. Still clutching the books, I scrambled and clawed my way towards it.

Then I awoke.

Chapter Seventeen

STONE COLD LIGHT

That stranger youth and I approached each other in silence,
and slowly, with our eyes fixed on each other's eyes. We
approached till not more than a yard intervened between us,
and then stood still and gazed, measuring each other from
head to foot. What was my astonishment, on perceiving
that he was the same being as myself!

James Hogg, *The Private Memoirs and
Confessions of a Justified Sinner*

…but hurry, time meets us, and we are destroyed.

Federico Garcia Lorca

My father was right. Bad blood.

That was why my father had to die. And that was, probably, why my grandfather had to die.

Madam St Clair was right too. What I did to discover a secret from long ago did not bring me joy, but only the truth. And it brought me close to death. So close that there could—can—be no return. It was like flying into the face of a bony wind, like a cold stony mirror, like the hand on your shoulder that you have always feared but have known would come. When I first saw through the eyes of Bob Knowles I became part of him and perhaps he became part of me. Whatever it was, it was then I *knew*. Not everything but enough to put things into place, and enough to lead me to this place.

Bob Knowles was, of course, my grandfather. Madam St Clair had told me that the best way to travel back in time was through a family connection and that was how I managed it, with the aid of the silver sixpence my grandfather had given my father. That he was my grandfather I knew, I believe, as soon as I began to inhabit his body—blood recognises blood. Who he was to become, I recognised as soon as I saw his or my face in the mirror in the vestry.

So I can piece together his story as best I can as follows. Knowles realises that he is regarded as dead, lost in the fire in the vestry. But even if he is not, yet, known as a murderer, he cannot return home in his real identity. What happened to poor Coulthard, I do not know, but he had to be disposed of in some way. Having lost his partner, it could be understood that he decided to relocate his business—and where better than the burgeoning capital of north Britain. The proper machinations to wind up the bookselling business could be undertaken at a distance and consequently the shop was re-opened in Edinburgh—where, I presume, and I am only really guessing here, my grandfather, with his mild Scottish twang, hailed from—by him now in the guise of William Coulthard.

As a conceit, however, he keeps the name of Knowles as part of the business title supposedly in memory of his deceased partner. A little later, presumably, he meets someone in Edinburgh and my father is born, his mother dying in childbirth. At first I was confused as to why his name is changed slightly I can really only guess; perhaps he too was christened Robert Knowles, but when he is given up for adoption, his new parents for some reason—perhaps because they couldn't spell very well or, I thought, because they intuitively found something disturbing in the name—change his name to Nowell. But, of course, the name inscribed on the works of Burns is 'Robert Nowell' and, maybe more likely, when my father is a little older, he takes his name from the inscription. And, more perplexingly, if my grandfather himself had changed the name for the inscription, why? Did he feel a little ashamed of his own name? Or was he leaving a conundrum to be solved by someone in the future—myself, for example?

But then, of course, I realised. It was obvious! My father had taken his name from the inscription in the book given to him by his father. 'Nowell'—a new birth—yet with vestiges of his own past. At this moment, perhaps, my grandfather held some hope for the future, perhaps he felt some remorse for the past. I don't know and the only opportunity I had to ask him slipped away.

So, if I had any hard evidence to lay before the police or the public, I could tell a fine story. Knowles, having lived in disguise for most of his lifetime, nearing death, suddenly finds his murderous urges re-kindled, perhaps excited by the full red head of Amelia, or by her dance in the Western Bar. He kills her, but the very same night, exhausted by his endeavours or fraught with guilt, he succumbs to death himself. Yes, that would be an excellent story, but it is, of course, not true.

The Sinking Spring church in Abingdon is empty on this grey wintery day. The snow outside has turned a little to slush. Where else should I return to on the final step of my journey? The only place where, perhaps, for a while, I might have felt I truly belonged. This place was grey and damp and probably indistinguishable from many other such places, but it was full of a sort of heavy silence that seems to slow down time.

How much happiness are we allowed in life? I have no idea, but I have come to think that I haven't experienced true happiness, maybe the absence of pain, but that is not the same thing. Maybe, strangely, I am privileged to be as I am? I used to think that. But, since I encountered John Ledbury, I have realised that that is not the case.

I have come here, to the place where perhaps I was happiest in some way—in the innocence of youth. When my calculating brain lost its grip on the real world and I could, almost unknowingly, swing between past and present, I began to try to seek some sanctuary in place or time. Perhaps this is it.

I had flown back here from an equally dark and gloomy London, but before I did so, I had had to make two more journeys: First, to South Norwood metropolitan burial ground

The graveyard should have been silent but was not, there was life here—cooing and puffing pigeons lived in the boundary mausoleums under their peaked tops. Dark, flattened gravestones were criss-crossed by glistening trails of slime from slugs or other creatures.

It took me some time searching, but at last I found what I was looking for on one cold stone gravestone fringed with some new snow:

Here lie the remains of John Ledbury
1871–1917
Killed in the Great War
Until the day break and the shadow fall away

And added in a slightly different script below.

And also of his widow
Isabella Ledbury
1877–1949
At rest at last
God Treasure Her

And then, recently added, it seemed, in another script.

In remembrance of John Ledbury
1902–1973
Interred in Edinburgh
God Preserve Him

There were a few flowers scattered around, some dying or blown in the wind, a couple quite fresh. I felt guilty that I had not brought some token of my own remembrance, but I turned and left, knowing I would never return.

My next stop had been at the British Library, in search of Professor Hezekiah Blacklock. I read through hundreds of obituaries for the year 1900 but, surprisingly, nothing came to hand. I scrutinised several biographical dictionaries with the same result. Was Blacklock a creature of Ledbury's imagination, or a pseudonym for someone else? Of course, I could have searched further. To look for some resemblances in medical records. I could have searched through police files or registrars' records. I could have tried to piece together the whole story of John Ledbury as a fragment of some sort of real life. But I knew that that would be futile and irrelevant.

My instinct as an academic had been to seek closure. However, although I have outlined the end of the story as I can now imagine it, there are still nagging questions and the greatest of those lies in the sequence of dreams that Ledbury described. What do they actually mean? Were they, in some way, premonitions? They seem to be clues to the nature of the crime, with His Nibs really Blacklock revealing himself as the archetype of the fictional Moriarty—manipulating all those around him for the pure pleasure of control or a sort of omnipotence. Or were they, in fact, intended to describe supernatural interventions leading to the identity of the murderer?

Whichever way we look at it, however, they seem less and less real and more and more of a fictional device. So the final question is this? Was Ledbury, the aspiring, struggling, and sometimes brilliant young writer really penning a work of fiction—a novel to rival the great Conan Doyle, perhaps to be serialised by Clement Shorter in the *Sphere*. If so, that was clearly never to be. The notebook was lost that night in the fire, we presume, to resurface years later and fall into my hands.

Perhaps then, the final irony is that an invention—a work of fiction—had led me down this pretty path. And the fact is that, now it has become a sort of reality itself. Night after night, the characters and places from Ledbury's dreams return, but now they appear in my own waking dreams.

John Ledbury may now rest in peace and his notebooks and all their secrets will now go to the grave with me. I reflect on the last poem in Ledbury's collection:

A tree that cannot flower,
A bird that cannot fly,
A pendulum that keeps no time,
A question with no why.

Tell me Father Greybeard,
You that have travelled so long,
Who am I? And what am I?
And where have I come from?

The final questions echoed in my head. Who, in fact, was I? The fact was, I did not know what was true or false anymore. Reality was receding from me and all I had left were my dreams, or were they *my* dreams. Whatever they were I couldn't endure them now.

I reflect on this as I sit, alone in the church pew. Ledbury's notebooks, of course, vividly outline two of the three or more murders committed by my grandfather.

To my knowledge, my father only committed one murder, but also of a fiendish nature. Poisoners, according to Henry XIII, were the worst of felons and he ordered them to be boiled alive. My father, like his father before him, was obsessed with control of his victim. In retaliation for the numerous jibes and stifling inhibitions visited upon him by my mother, he watched her die slowly, poisoned by an extraction from the antifreeze used for his precious lawnmowers. How he discovered its effects I do not know, but he was confident that the hick doctor my mother insisted on wouldn't detect it.

I knew that he had done it the night he quoted scripture at me on the staircase. It puzzled me for a while why my father had so determinedly spouted 'bad blood' to me. Was it that he saw in my own face that brought that to him? However, the answer seemed clear to me on reflection. The way I had personally been able to visit the past was aided by a traumatic event and the company of something old, something to connect me to the past, something with a *family* connection. In his last days, my father had the book that his father had gifted to him beside him and, after the death of my mother, and for reasons that were more than immediately clear, he had experienced such an event. So, I believe, my father also had the experience of visiting my grandfather's murderous mind.

Of course, I did not know this at that time. However, thanks to the concordance that my mother had kept, it took me only a moment to check the source of my father's last words. Proverbs 23:31, 'Look not upon the wine when it giveth its colour in the cup, for it *poisons* like a serpent... '

And that is what started me on my own murderous career. I knew what he had done and I suspected that he wanted to die. I won't say that it did not also occur to me that my inheritance from the lawnmower business and the sale of the family home would allow me to escape from Abingdon and pursue my intended career in law.

I simply trebled the dose of his sedative that night when I took it up to his bedroom. Barely ten minutes later a wet cloth from the bathroom placed judiciously over his face and it was over quickly. I intended to consider in due course how to dispose of the business but fortune favoured me with the ensuing fire.

Each man will favour his own method of disposal. I am not a sadist and I have never had any desire to cause my victims undue pain or distress. Therefore, I developed the technique of smothering them. It has the advantage that, if applying firmly and professionally, it will barely leave a mark. The subject may even be left with a calm and contented demeanour—as if in a long sleep. Invariably, I would spend some minutes watching them, dead but quite innocent. I suppose that, like my father and my grandfather before me, I enjoyed this form of control, of knowing that, even in death, they were in abeyance to me.

I had also really had enough of Brigid. After the long diatribe I had suffered I sat on the porch for a while with the chipmunks and lightning bugs for company. Then I went up to her bedroom. She was reading a book and was about to start her raving again, but I put a finger to my lips to silence her. Perhaps she thought I was looking for some kind of reconciliation. She was young and fit, so I had to apply all my body weight on top of her and the pillow.

Amelia, on the other hand, was much easier. She was in a drunken stupor from the whisky and was snoring with her mouth open. In fact, regarding Amelia, my original intention had been to return the shop keys to her handbag. However, I changed my mind. Perhaps I thought it was just too risky or perhaps I just wanted her to be at peace. Either way, it was over in seconds.

With the old man, however, I had little choice. He had discovered me in the act of illicitly entering his premises. He screamed and threw an old brass paperweight from the desk at me. He was frail, but I still had to use all my strength to hold the back of his head and my hand over his mouth and nose while his ramshackle limbs fluttered and waved like a string puppet. And then I had to arrange him, speedily before he grew stiff, like a mannequin in a tableaux at his desk. Of course, I did not know at that time that he was my grandfather.

Madame St Clair truly had psychic powers that were beyond my ken. When she looked in my eyes on that final, fateful day, I knew she could see things about me. So I dispatched her to the spirit world that she so keenly wished to inhabit. She was right, it needed a deep-felt emotion to allow me to begin my voyage. Providently, disposing of her provided that impetus.

Sometimes, things turn full circle, just as the cursed silver sixpence, now lost in time, returned itself to my grandfather and, indirectly, delivered to him the death that he deserved and for which he had to wait so long.

As for my part in the whole story? It would be vain and inappropriate for me to seek any amelioration of my own sins. In essence they were of the same ilk as those of my father and grandfather. They came from a desire for total control.

I am every bit, and maybe more, the monster that my grandfather was. Only God has the ultimate power over life and death. As I sit here now, in the semi-dark, and see a little wintery light leak through the stained glass window on to the little cross at the altar, I understand that. I understand the nature of sin. However, I can still feel no remorse.

There is no future for me. I cannot face another sleep. The nightmares, the past revisiting me; it is beyond endurance. So today will be the last day of my life. Here I sit. The Ledbury notebooks have been disposed of, my own manuscript will be deposited where it may never be found. I only have the little book entitled *Fugitive Poems, &c*

Flicking through it, I come to a poem, chosen at random, and, as I read, I almost feel that I can rekindle a little of the pleasure I once felt on discovering new literary texts, the struggle to understand them, to place them somehow in the schema of the wide world. But the experience is dull and lifeless now and, after I read a little, the volume falls from my hands and the pages flutter for a moment as some dead and drying leaves from the graveyard blow over it. I grab one page before it is lost among the leaves. It is all of Ledbury's I have left now. A short poem titled 'The Voyage.'

What voyage is this I enter upon?
A sackful of hopes is all I bear,

What country is it that I seek?
What foolish fruit will grow there?

How many lives have I to weigh?
Through my stubborn will to bend.
When will the tree its burden drop?
Where will the fruitless journey end?

POSTSCRIPT

We had no photographs or anecdotes. Even our memories were uncertain. Testimony without corroboration is invention. There were no facts left. I looked in my suitcase; not a single one. Our bags that had been so heavy weighed nothing now. The world had seeped out of them.

Jeanette Winterson, *Adventure of a Lifetime*

As I sit here writing this, everything has already happened. The past and the future no longer exist. Either for me or for you. Nothing remains but the words.

Ryan O'Connor, *The Voids*

It is with great regret that I read the last few words of my father's epic detective fantasy which is published here for the first time.

Regret for the fact that my father clearly died without knowing that he had a son and regret for the fact that I never grew to know my father or even meet him before his unfortunate and premature death.

I should, first, reveal that I have transcribed the two manuscripts that make up this narrative as accurately as possible from the two hand-written copies of different periods (although there is some question as to their respective dates and provenance). They have been ordered, I believe, as my father wished, as was clear from his marginal notes and postscript. My intention is simply to present a not unaccomplished work of fiction to the public and I have no intention of over-burdening the reader with scholarly annotations. Therefore, what I have written below is no more than a gloss. My intention has been to highlight my father's work. However, perhaps as a little conceit, I have allowed myself to append the introductory quotes to each section which, I hope, will lead the reader from the salacious contents of part of the work towards pertinent issues on the nature of crime and punishment and the peculiar rationality of both the nineteenth-century and the 1970s.

The circumstances through which I discovered the identity of my father were quixotic. My mother, unfortunately suffered shortly after my premature birth from post-natal depression.

Also, I was somewhat a sickly child and I was largely raised by her parents, my grandparents, and, as a child, never thought it odd that, unlike my peers, I had neither a father nor a mother present. However, eventually that was to change.

I will briefly relate how I came about the manuscripts. When my mother removed to Raleigh after the brief scandal concerning my father in 1968, she slowly recovered, enrolled at school and set about improving her lot. She had no compunction about settling her child more permanently with her parents. Later, she became an elementary school teacher in Morrisville where she still lives, although she is now retired. Although I saw her fairly regularly, she never encouraged me to enquire about my father. Despite the short time they had been together, I think that she had a genuine and deep-rooted fear of him.

However, when I had graduated and begun to follow an academic career myself I began to feel more curious about my father. I knew my mother would say nothing so I had to conduct my own enquiries. After some time checking local archives and clippings from the local press (which proved illuminating), eventually I was led to the University of Pittsburgh.

However, when I met the chair of the English Department at the University I was initially disappointed. Yes, there was a brief record of my father's employment for a few years in the seventies but there was no-one remaining at the University from that period and no substantive record of his career there.

I thought of the only named connection with the University in the manuscript and mentioned him by name: Norman Levy.

After some telephone calls I at last had a positive response. Yes, a colleague remembered Emeritus Professor Norman Levy and believed that he was still enrolled with the University library.

So, eventually, the library obtained for me an address for Levy and, a few days later, I had contacted him and agreed to meet in the Original Oyster House near the Andy Warhol Museum.

Levy seemed old, dispirited and strangely anxious about something. He admitted that he had known my father and that he remembered him leaving the University rather suddenly; although he wouldn't be drawn on any reason for that.

He didn't seem keen to prolong our conversation and suddenly took a package from the inside breast pocket of his coat.

'I think this is what you will want. It was posted to me at the University post-marked from an office in Virginia.'

'I haven't really read anything in it', he hastened to add. I felt, however, that he was lying.

That concluded our meeting. However, as we now know, Levy was to die suddenly and tragically that very weekend. So it is no longer possible to question him further regarding the provenance of the two manuscripts.

The package consisted to two manuscripts: one was the purported diaries of John Ledbury, the other the text of the extended novel now put before you.

For various reasons, it has not been thought judicious or possible to bring the rather shocking and salacious contents of these manuscripts to public attention until now.

Firstly, initially, I wanted the manuscript and notebook simply in order to have something of my father's to keep close to me and I did not believe that they were of any value other than personal to me.

Secondly, current times are more fastidious regarding some

issues, notably sexual violence towards women, than the 1970s. When I decided that publication was possible I thought that was desirable, in the best tradition of textual editing, to make every attempt to present the book following my father's intentions as far as possible. However, certain sections have been excised and I am grateful to the publishers, their sensitivity reader and their legal representatives for advising on this.

So, then, what of the text? It goes without saying, of course, that the events of the narrative are totally fictitious. My father since boyhood, had been a voracious reader and I have no doubt that, despite the early successes of his academic career, he had always harboured a desire to write a novel. It is surprising that he chose the subject of murder perhaps, but we must remember that his particular speciality at the University had been the Gothic novel.

However, it is also clear that many of the characters in Ledbury's notebooks were, in fact, real.

Henry Spencer Ashbee did exist, as did Annie Besant, Francis Galton and others. Others are fictitious. Notably, no record can be found of Superintendant Robert Ord and of Professor Hezekiah Blacklock, as my father suggests himself in the last section of his novel.

In the more recent part of the novel account, the subsidiary characters, with the exception of members of my father's family, are fictitious as far as I can gather with one exception. Gershon Legman, the folklorist and cultural critic did exist and died as recently as 1999.

Now to the more perplexing subject of the existence or otherwise of John Ledbury, the central character in this novel.

In the United Kingdom census of 1871, only one John Ledbury is recorded, who lived to the age of 89 and died in 1970. The gravestone memorial to Ledbury in South Norwood Metropolitan

Cemetery recorded by my father in the book simply does not exist.

Predominantly, the Ledbury family in England are found in Worcester near to the small market town of Ledbury in the Malvern Hills. Despite its size, Ledbury has a long poetic pedigree having been home to William Langland, John Masefield and Elizabeth Barrett Browning. What better name for an aspiring poet? However, since no published poetry exists, to my knowledge, under this name, I can only come to the conclusion that John Ledbury is purely a fictional character.

It is, however, true that copies of *Fugitive Poems, &c* do exist in the British National, Scottish National and Mitchell libraries. All are catalogued as 'Anon (the City Voice)' and there are no catalogue amendments or inscriptions relating to any named author. Therefore, I have to question whether my father ever had such a volume in his possession. Norman Levy, in fact, *could not recall* the incident in which my father claimed he presented him with the book. Also, the poems my father quotes in his manuscript simply *do not exist* in the volume in question, which consists of amateurish pieces about popular events! So, once again, I have to presume that my father was intent on exercising his literary imagination in a form of a pastiche of Victorian literature.

Also, the notion of the 'counterfeit detective' who answers the letters addressed to Sherlock Holmes is an urban fiction and there is no evidence for this occurring in real life at all, although it seems to have been a popular myth and is used as a device in a more recent collection of essays.

Of course, the consequence of addressing the fact of John Ledbury's existence is clear. What is the origin of the manuscript that my father has employed for his novel. Naturally, I contend that it, too, is a work of fiction that could, in fact, have been written by anyone, at almost any time: even by, or most probably by, my father himself! In fact, it would only take a more objective reader a moment to realise, on reading the Ledbury 'notebooks' that they are not notebooks at all. They read, in fact, like a novel

Regarding places mentioned in the text, many are real, and some do still exist. The Sinking Spring church in Abington did, and does, exist. The World Turned Upside Down public house did exist in 1970s London, but, although it is a common name for inns or public houses, I cannot find any evidence for a place with that name in 1900. A bookshop fitting the description of Coulthard's bookshop in Edinburgh exists, but it is called West Port Books and has been for many years.

I could continue, but the matter is evident, the contents of this volume are a mixture of fact and fantasy and must be regarded as a pure fiction with a smattering of verisimilitude created by the use of historically genuine characters.

Finally, but importantly, the details my father gives regarding his own family are largely accurate gainsay the fact that there is absolutely no evidence that my grandfather killed my grandmother or that my father killed his father. This, I believe, is simply a fantasy of my father's excessively Gothic imaginings.

Also, regarding my father's claim that he committed four murders in the winter of 1973—one in Pittsburgh and three in

Edinburgh—I can categorically state that I am not aware of any evidence of this and that there is no record of anyone with any of the precise names he mentions being recorded as the victim of a criminal act at the times suggested. On the advice of the legal representatives of the publishers, I can comment no further regarding this matter.

Professor Duncan Goodlad
University of North Carolina
Haight-Ashbury

10th October 2022

AUTHOR'S NOTE

This is a work of fiction as is cogently explained in the Postscript which, of course, is also a work of fiction itself.

However, many of the people and places mentioned did, and sometimes do, exist and, for anyone interested, I have appended the following notes.

ABINGDON, VIRGINIA is the county seat of Washington County. The population in 1960 was around 5,000.

THE ALHAMBRA was a grand music hall and theatre in the Moorish style originally opened in 1854 as the Royal Panopticon of Science and Arts. Early moving pictures were shown there at the beginning of the century. It was demolished in 1939.

ARTHUR'S SEAT is a volcanic plug in the city of Edinburgh consisted of a rocky summit and a series of rocks known as Salisbury Crags.

THE ARTHUR'S SEAT COFFINS consisted of seventeen miniature coffins containing figures which were discovered on Arthur's Seat in 1836. Eight survived and were donated to the National Museum of Scotland were they can still be seen. Their origin is uncertain but some have linked the figures with the victims of Burke and Hare murdered in or around the West Port in 1828.

HENRY SPENCER ASHBEE was a prolific collector of erotic literature and the works of Cervantes. He was the author of three works of erotic bibliography and almost certainly the author of *Walter: My Secret Life*, a detailed collection of tales of Victorian sexual adventure as first suggested by Gershon Legman in *The Horn Book* and fully investigated in a biography – Ian Simpson, *The Erotomaniac*. There is, however, no evidence that he wrote any other forms of erotic literature, to order or for personal pleasure.

JEREMY BENTHAM was a philosopher, teacher and social reformed regarded as the founder of utilitarianism. He advocated the abolition of slavery, equal rights for women and the decriminalising of homosexual acts. On his death in 1832, Bentham left instructions for his body to be first dissected, and then to be permanently preserved as an "auto-icon" (or self-image), which would be his memorial. This was done, and it is now on public display in the entrance of the Student Centre at University College London

ANNIE BESANT was a leading member of the Theosophical Society, a feminist and political activist, and a proponent of Irish and Indian home rule. She joined the Society in 1889 and was a friend of its co-founder, Madame Blavatsky. Besant became President of the Theosophical Society and was also a member of the Fabian Society.

THE BOSTON REDSOX are a noted baseball team founded in 1901 who play home games at Fenway Park, Boston.

BURKE AND HARE (William Burke and William Hare) were guilty of sixteen murders in Edinburgh in 1828. The bodies of the victims were supplied as cadavers for dissection to the medical school.

EDINBURGH BOOKSHOPS called Thin's and Blackwood's

did exist in the 1970s.

ROBERTO CLEMENTE was a Puerto Rican professional baseball player who played eighteen seasons for the Pittsburgh Pirates as a right fielder. After his sudden death in a plane crash in 1972 he was posthumously inducted into the National Baseball Hall of Fame, becoming both the first Caribbean and the first Latin-American player to be enshrined.

SIR ARTHUR CONAN DOYLE, famously, was the originator of Sherlock Holmes and one of the founding fathers of the detective novel. In 1900 he did serve as a doctor in the Boer War. This period is sometimes known as the Great Hiatus (1893-1902) during which he did not write about Sherlock Holmes after he had 'killed him off' at the Reichenbach Falls in a story. The idea of the 'counterfeit detective' who answers letters addressed to Sherlock Holmes is pinched from an essay in a book by Elizabeth Wilson, *Hallucinations*.

ALEISTER CROWLEY was an English occultist and member of the Hermetic Order of the Golden Dawn. His non-conformist views and behaviour have engendered various views of him, from an enlightened libertarian to a proponent of Satanism known as 'the great beast'.

JAMES HOGG was a Scottish poet and novelist whose *Confessions of a Justified Sinner* is now regarded as a progenitor of the Gothic psychological thriller.

THOMAS DE QUINCEY, best known for his *Confessions of an English Opium-Eater*, was an English essay writer who spend the latter days of his life living in the West End of Edinburgh. He is buried there in St Cuthbert's Kirkyard. He penned the essay 'Murder as a Fine Art'.

GODALMING is a market town in the borough of Waverley in Surrey. Mary Toft, the rabbit woman of Godalming famously tricked doctors in the eighteenth century into believing that she had given birth to rabbits.

THE LONDON DOCKER'S STRIKE generally refers to the strike of 1889. The main claim was for a minimum wage of sixpence an hour. The strike resulted in the formation of the Dock, Wharf, Riverside and General Labourers' Union. However, further strikes were to follow, including one in 1900.

HENRY HAVELOCK ELLIS was an English doctor and sexologist and one of the first proponents of the pseudo-science of eugenics.

SIR FRANCIS GALTON was a polymath and the scientist who coined the term eugenics, perceiving it as a moral philosophy that aimed to improve the stock of human beings through selective breeding.

THE LABOUR PARTY was effectively founded in 1900 from the trade union movement and Fabian and other societies. A meeting of these parties at the Congregational Memorial Hall on Farringdon Street, London on 26 and 27 in February 1900 passed Keir Hardie's motion to establish 'a distinct Labour group in Parliament'. In the 1900 election, however, only Hardie and one other member were elected to parliament.

GERSHON LEGMAN was an important scholar of erotica and folklore, whose *Rationale of the Dirty Joke* is a work of immense scholarship. He has been attributed by some as the inventor of the vibrator and as coining the term 'make love, not war'. Be that as it may, he is an erudite and engaging writer whose work is always worth dipping into. He also contributed to the study of folk song and the works of Robert Burns and paved the way for the study of sexual material when it was still problematic to gain access to it at all. Legman was born in Pennsylvania but he spent a great part of his later life, in fact, in a residence of the Knights Templar in the south of France. I have moved it to London for convenience.

CESARE LOMBROSO was an Italian criminologist who believed that criminality was genetically inherited. It was said that he 'studies madness with a yard measure'.

THE LONDON METROPOLITAN POLICE was founded in 1829 and by 1900 consisted of nearly 16,000 officers, organised into 21 divisions, responsible for law enforcement within an area of nearly 700 square miles. Nevertheless, detection methods were quite crude and the Force was much criticised for its failure to discover Jack the Ripper.

ROBERT LOWELL was an influential American writer who twice won the Pulitzer Prize for Poetry. Born into a wealthy New England family, he taught intermittently at Harvard University but, due to mental illness, was treated in the psychiatric hospital, McLean Hospital, in Belmont, Massachusetts. He was jailed as a conscientious objector during World War Two.

LYON'S CORNER HOUSE in the West End of London was

one of a chain of tea shops founded in 1894.

WILLIAM MCDOWELL, more than a century ago, was a noted Edinburgh antiquarian, bookseller and auctioneer. I should know him well enough, as I lived a few years ago in the house that he occupied, in the West End of Edinburgh! He did not have an auction house in Broughton Place, however, although the auctioneers Lyon and Turnbull do now have their premises in the location mentioned.

MILNE'S BAR still exists and has expanded into Rose Street by taking over another pub. It has no longer any particular connection with literature and many of the portraits of poets that once adorned its walls have been removed. However, a painting featuring many of the poets of the period including Sidney Goodsir Smith and Hugh MacDiarmid still features over a fireplace.

THE NATIONALITY CLASSROOMS can be found in the University of Pittsburgh's Cathedral of Learning, a neo-Gothic skyscraper built in opened in 1931 and the second tallest university building in the world. There are 29 in all and they have been designed to reflect the culture of various ethnic groups that settled in Allegheny County and Pennsylvania in general. The University of Pittsburgh originally dates back to the eighteenth century.

THE ORIGINAL OYSTER HOUSE is Pittsburgh's oldest bar and restaurant which, since 1970, has been run by the Grippo family. It has been designated a historic landmark by the Pittsburgh History and Landmarks Foundations and is often used as a setting for movies filmed in Pittsburgh.

SINKING SPRING PRESBYTERIAN CHURCH was first founded in 1772 and still exists in East Main Street, Abington, Virginia.

THE THEOSOPHICAL SOCIETY was founded in 1875 by Helena Blavatsky and two others. Its stated aims were (and are):

1) To minimise the sum of misery in the world;
2) To forget self in working for others;
3) To eliminate selfishness and substitute love as the rule of the world; and
4) To live to the highest that is within us.

Their Edinburgh office still exists although it has moved location to the Arthur Conan Doyle Centre in Palmerston Place.

ARTHUR EDWARD WAITE was a New Yorker who became a poet and mystic and wrote extensively on the history of the occult.

THE WESTERN BAR still exists as one of three pubs on opposing corners sometimes known as the pubic triangle. Dancers still perform daily although that practice is much less common than it was in the seventies—when it was common throughout Edinburgh—and today has a sleazier reputation than it did then.

THE WEST PORT BOOKSHOP, ably managed by Bob Barrett, did indeed exist, and still does, although under a different name and owner.

THE WHITE HART dates to the seventeenth century and remains a popular public house in Edinburgh's Grassmarket.

The title derives from the tradition that David I was hunting near Salisbury crags went he encountered a white stag which appeared whose head appeared surmounted by a large cross. Because of this mystic encounter, it has been suggested, Holyrood Abbey was founded.

THE HERMETIC ORDER OF THE GOLDEN DAWN was a society founded in the late nineteenth century devoted to the study of the occult, magic and spiritual development. It resembled the Masonic Order in its hierarchy and elaborate initiation rituals. Aleister Crowley joined the Order in 1898.

CHARLES MACKAY was a Scottish journalist and poet best known for *Extraordinary Popular Delusions and the Madness of Crowds*.

CLEMENT SHORTER was the editor of the *London Illustrated News* and editor and founder of *The Sphere*. He was an authority on the works of the Brontë sisters. He was married to Dora Sigerson, a poet in the Irish Revival.

THE SOUTH AFRICAN WARS, now more commonly known as the Boer Wars, were two wars fought between the British and Dutch settlers in southern Africa. The latter, between 1899 and 1902, is referred to here.

EUGENE SOLOMON TALBOT was the author of *Degneracy: its Causes, Signs and Results*.

THE WORLD TURNED UPSIDE DOWN was once a not uncommon pub name in the United Kingdom. The expression has been taken equally to refer to a state of chaos or revolution and traditional customs such as the Festival of Fools and the Lords of Misrule. In London, the best known was in Old Kent Road and operated for around two centuries until closure in 2009.

ALSO BY SIMPSON GREARS FROM RYMOUR BOOKS

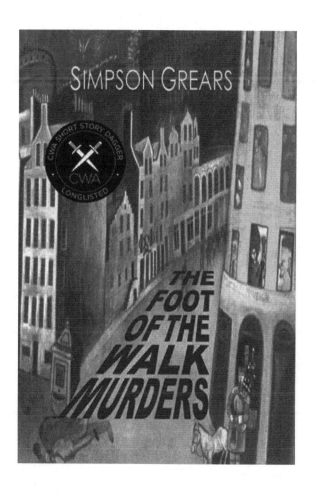

RYMOUR BOOKS

poetry · history · debate